BLOOD

OF THE PACK

D1283610

Praise for Jenny Frame

Soul of the Pack

"I enjoy the way Jenny Frame writes. Her characters are perfectly suited to one another, never the same, and the stories are always fun and unique...there is something special about her urban fantasy worlds. She maximises the butch/femme dynamic and creates pack dynamics which work so well with those."—*The Lesbian Review*

Heart of the Pack

"A really well written love story that incidentally involves changers as well as humans."—*Inked Rainbow Reads*

Wooing the Farmer

"This book, like all of Jenny Frame's, is just one major swoon."
—*Les Rêveur*

"This is the book we Axedale fanatics have been waiting for...Jenny Frame writes the most amazing characters and this whole series is a masterpiece. But where she excels is in writing butch lesbians. Every time I read a Jenny Frame book I think it's the best ever, but time and again she surprises me. She has surpassed herself with *Wooing the Farmer*."—*Kitty Kat's Book Review Blog*

Royal Court

"The author creates two very relatable characters...Quincy's quietude and mental torture are offset by Holly's openness and lust for life. Holly's determination and tenacity in trying to reach Quincy are total wish-fulfilment of a person like that. The chemistry and attraction is excellently built."—*Best Lesbian Erotica*

"[A] butch/femme romance that packs a punch."—*Les Rêveur*

Royal Court "was a fun, light-hearted book with a very endearing romance."—*Leanne Chew, Librarian, Parnell Library (Auckland, NZ)*

"There were unbelievably hot sex scenes as I have come to expect and look forward to in Jenny Frame's books. Passions slowly rise until you feel the characters may burst!…Royal Court is wonderful and I highly recommend it."—*Kitty Kat's Book Review Blog*

Hunger for You

Byron and Amelia "are guaranteed to get the reader all hot and bothered. Jenny Frame writes brilliant love scenes in all of her books and makes me believe the characters crave each other."
—*Kitty Kat's Book Review Blog*

"I loved this book. Paranormal stuff like vampires and werewolves are my go-to sins. This book had literally everything I needed: chemistry between the leads, hot love scenes (phew), drama, angst, romance (oh my, the romance) and strong supporting characters."
—*The Reading Doc*

Charming the Vicar

"Chances are, you've never read or become captivated by a romance like *Charming the Vicar*. While books featuring people of the cloth aren't unusual, Bridget is no ordinary vicar—a lesbian with a history of kink…Surrounded by mostly supportive villagers, Bridget and Finn balance love and faith in a story that affirms both can exist for anyone, regardless of sexual identity."—*RT Book Reviews*

"The sex scenes were some of the sexiest, most intimate and quite frankly, sensual I have read in a while. Jenny Frame had me hooked and I reread a few scenes because I felt like I needed to experience the intense intimacy between Finn and Bridget again. The devotion they showed to one another during these sex scenes but also in the intimate moments was gripping and for lack of a better word, carnal."—*Les Rêveur*

"The sexual chemistry between [Finn and Bridge] is unbelievably hot. It is sexy, lustful and with more than a hint of kink. The scenes between them are highly erotic—and not just the sex scenes. The tension is ramped up so well that I felt the characters would explode if they did not get relief!...An excellent book set in the most wonderful village—a place I hope to return to very soon!"—*Kitty Kat's Book Reviews*

"This is Frame's best character work to date. They are layered and flawed and yet relatable. Frame really pushed herself with *Charming The Vicar* and it totally paid off...I also appreciate that even though she regularly writes butch/femme characters, no two pairings are the same."—*The Lesbian Review*

Unexpected

Jenny Frame "has this beautiful way of writing a phenomenally hot scene while incorporating the love and tenderness between the couple."—*Les Rêveur*

"If you enjoy contemporary romances, *Unexpected* is a great choice. The character work is excellent, the plotting and pacing are well done, and it's a just a sweet, warm read...Definitely pick this book up when you're looking for your next comfort read, because it's sure to put a smile on your face by the time you get to that happy ending."—*Curve*

"*Unexpected* by Jenny Frame is a charming butch/femme romance that is perfect for anyone who wants to feel the magic of overcoming adversity and finding true love. I love the way Jenny Frame writes. I have yet to discover an author who writes like her. Her voice is strong and unique and gives a freshness to the lesbian fiction sector."—*The Lesbian Review*

Royal Rebel

"Frame's stories are easy to follow and really engaging. She stands head and shoulders above a number of the romance authors and it's easy to see why she is quickly making a name for herself in lesfic romance."—*The Lesbian Review*

Courting the Countess

"I love Frame's romances. They are well paced, filled with beautiful character moments and a wonderful set of side characters who ultimately end up winning your heart...I love Jenny Frame's butch/femme dynamic; she gets it so right for a romance."
—*The Lesbian Review*

"I loved, loved, loved this book. I didn't expect to get so involved in the story but I couldn't help but fall in love with Annie and Harry... The love scenes were beautifully written and very sexy. I found the whole book romantic and ultimately joyful and I had a lump in my throat on more than one occasion. A wonderful book that certainly stirred my emotions."—*Kitty Kat's Book Reviews*

"*Courting The Countess* has an historical feel in a present day world, a thought provoking tale filled with raw emotions throughout. [Frame] has a magical way of pulling you in, making you feel every emotion her characters experience."—*Lunar Rainbow Reviewz*

"I didn't want to put the book down and I didn't. Harry and Annie are two amazingly written characters that bring life to the pages as they find love and adventures in Harry's home. This is a great read, and you will enjoy it immensely if you give it a try!"
—*Fantastic Book Reviews*

A Royal Romance

"*A Royal Romance* was a guilty pleasure read for me. It was just fun to see the relationship develop between George and Bea, to see George's life as queen and Bea's as a commoner. It was also refreshing to see that both of their families were encouraging, even when Bea doubted that things could work between them because of their class differences...*A Royal Romance* left me wanting a sequel, and romances don't usually do that to me."
—*Leeanna.ME Mostly a Book Blog*

Visit us at www.boldstrokesbooks.com

BLOOD
OF THE PACK

by

Jenny Frame

2019

BLOOD OF THE PACK

ISBN 13: 978-1-63555-431-1

This Trade Paperback Original Is Published By
Bold Strokes Books, Inc.
P.O. Box 249
Valley Falls, NY 12185

First Edition: August 2019

Credits
Editor: Ruth Sternglantz
Production Design: Stacia Seaman
Cover Design by Melody Pond

Acknowledgments

Thank you to Rad, Sandy, and all the BSB staff for their tireless hard work. A huge thank you to Ruth for her guidance, patience, and advice. I'm deeply grateful to have you help me make my books the best that they can be.

Thanks to my family for their support and encouragement.

Finally, thanks, hugs, and howls to my very own little Frame pack, Lou and Barney. Your love, support, and unwavering loyalty means the world to me. I'm such a lucky girl.

For Lou and Barney Boy—The Alpha and second of our little Frame pack.xx

Chapter One

Humans were so predictable. They had an innate distrust of the different, anyone that didn't conform to their norms. Even after eight hours in an airplane, Kenrick Wulver was still getting *looks* and what the other passengers surely thought were subtle glances.

By now, Kenrick was used to stares whenever she went outside her pack lands of Wulver Forest in Scotland. She did admit her appearance was perhaps striking to humans. As a dominant werewolf she was tall, well built, and strong. But more than anything, her hair was probably what people stared at the most. Kenrick had a thick mane—as her mother described it—of dreadlocked hair, held by a leather band in a ponytail that hung to the nape of her neck. The sides were undercut, as was the fashion of her generation of wolves, with the Celtic wolf symbol shaved into one side.

The humans' attention was distracted from her by the sound of the drinks trolley coming down the aisle. Kenrick looked at her watch and let out a sigh. Two hours had passed since she boarded at Glasgow Airport, and she had at least another seven ahead of her, with a change at Jackson to connect to Utah and her destination of Wolfgang County.

She drummed her fingers on the armrest. Kenrick was not used to being idle for this length of time, and her wolf was getting restless. At least she was in first class and had some room to move. She fiddled with the twisted leather bracelets on her wrist, each one significant, each being awarded for a stage in her development and her rank in the Scottish Wulver pack.

The drinks trolley arrived at her side, and one of the female cabin crew bent over and said, "Can I get you something?"

The blond woman was beautiful and had been flirting with her the whole flight. That was the other side effect of how she looked. A portion of the human female population seemed to find her attractive. Kenrick didn't understand it herself—she was just an ordinary wolf. Maybe it was the wild they could see in her, the wild primal energy of the forest.

"Aye, just some water, please," Kenrick said.

"Still or sparkling?"

"Still." Kenrick looked at her name tag and added in her lilting Highland tones, "Thanks, Lucinda."

"You're welcome. I love your accent by the way." Lucinda handed her a cup and opened a small bottle of Wulver Spring mineral water.

Kenrick felt heat flare in her cheeks.

As Lucinda poured the water into the cup she said, "I hope you don't mind me asking, but I saw your name on the passenger list. Are you a Wulver of Wulver Springs and Wulver Single Malt whisky?"

Kenrick was immensely proud to see the lovingly made Wulver products whenever she went out in the world. It was her pack's livelihood and essential to their way of being, but Kenrick herself did not like to take the limelight.

"Yes, it's my father's company." For the next month anyway, Kendrick's mind reminded her, and the thought made her stomach twist with tension.

This information seemed to inflame Lucinda's interest. She leaned in and whispered in her ear, "You know, if there's anything I can do to make your flight go a little more quickly, come and see me at the back of the aisle, by the restroom."

Kenrick gulped. Despite giving the appearance of being a confident dominant wolf, Kenrick was old-fashioned. Perhaps it was the romantic in her, but she had long ago made a promise to herself to wait for the wolf the Great Mother had planned for her, but it had been a long, long wait.

The other wolves in her age group had found their mates long ago, and as the only child of the Wulver Alpha, having a mate was essential.

How could she get out of this proposition without offending? A white lie wouldn't hurt. "Thanks, Lucinda. But I'm spoken for."

Lucinda's smile faltered. "Pity. She's a lucky woman to have such a loyal partner."

Kenrick just smiled and Lucinda moved away.

Lucky, and nothing more than a fantasy.

Kenrick slammed the back of her head against the headrest. The leadership of the pack was about to pass to her in a month's time, and not only did she feel unworthy, she couldn't provide her pack with a Mater—the heart of any pack.

She rubbed her temples as the pressure she felt inside grew with each passing day.

❖

"Zaria? Have you got everything you wanted?"

In the kitchen of the small-town diner where she worked as a server, Zaria Lupa quickly filled her bag with the day's leftovers—some bread, soup, and a half an apple pie.

"Just a second, Chrissy," Zaria shouted.

When you earned part-time minimum wage, leftovers and out of date stock became your staples. She hurried out to where her manager was waiting to close up.

"Come on, honey. Let's get out of here," Chrissy said.

Of all the jobs Zaria'd had, and she'd had a lot, Chrissy was the nicest boss, always looking out for her, trying to give a little extra. It was a shame she would have to move on soon, as she always had to.

Chrissy locked the door and said, "You sure you don't want a ride home?"

Zaria felt badly refusing her, but anyone who knew where she lived was a risk to her, and to themselves.

Zaria smiled. "It's okay. I like the walk. See you tomorrow."

"Goodnight, honey."

Zaria walked away quickly and pulled up the collar of her jacket, not because she was cold, but to hide her face. It was a twenty minute walk to her studio apartment, and everyone she passed on the sidewalk was a potential threat.

Zaria looked behind her quickly. She had the dreaded feeling that she was being watched, but she saw no one. Her heart started to pound and she hastened her speed. This was the first time since she'd come to Knoxton two months ago that she'd felt that familiar fear of being watched, being found out.

This was a lot longer than she usually stayed in one place. She'd moved from town to town in Rutherford County since she was sixteen, but never out of the county. She had to be near Wolfgang County.

Finally she arrived at her rental complex and ran up to her room. It was a squalid apartment building with people hanging around the hallways, drug dealers plying their trade, and all the subjugation of women that went along with it.

Zaria had managed to keep out of everyone's way so far, of course she could look after herself if she had to, but that would mean giving up her secret.

She unlocked her door, got in, and locked it quickly. She let out a breath of relief. Was it just her own paranoid thinking she was being watched, or was she really being tracked again?

Zaria took her bag over to her small table where she had an old hotplate. After a day in good company at the diner, coming back to this dump was depressing. It was grimy, the wallpaper was peeling off the walls, and she was often kept company by bugs who made their home there. It wasn't much of a life, and her wolf longed for the company and safety of a pack, but the alternative was too terrifying to contemplate.

She quickly heated her soup and took it over to her bed. Zaria swept her long dark hair into a ponytail and set her tablet up on the bedside table. This tablet and the internet connection were where all her money went, and why she slept in this dump and ate leftovers. She had to be connected to the Wolfgang Pack.

Most packs in the world had websites you could log into if you were a member. This kept pack members connected and updated with all their news. Zaria found a computer geek a few years ago who helped her hack into the Wolfgang site. She logged in now, and the Wolfgang website popped up. She took a sip of soup and clicked on the Wolfgang Academy page. She smiled when she saw a picture of the high school football team posing with a trophy. They had just won the championship, and all had happy smiling faces.

It was worth it. All her sacrifice, it was worth it.

Zaria was interrupted by a banging of the door. "Zaria! Your rent's two weeks late."

Her stomach twisted with tension. How was she going to get out of this one? She had spent everything paying her internet bill. Zaria hurried over to the door and said, "I just need some more time, Mr. Raymond."

"Open the door now, Zaria, or I'll use my key," Mr. Raymond said.

Zaria reluctantly opened the door, and the large, sleazy guy pushed his way in and shut the door behind him.

"Where's my money?" he said.

Zaria was disgusted. She always felt him watching her and mentally undressing her, and there was nothing she feared more. She had felt those looks before, and they'd frightened the life out of her.

"Can you wait till Friday, Mr. Raymond? I get paid then," Zaria said.

"Friday is too late. Pay now or you're out."

Zaria zeroed in on the beads of sweat on his top lip and they made her stomach growl. She had to get him out.

"Please, Mr. Raymond. I need this room. I can pay you extra on Friday. Please?"

The greasy looking man gave her a cruel smile and started to back her against the wall. Zaria's wolf started to scratch and demand she do something, but she knew if she did, her cover was blown. She had to calm this down.

"Mr. Raymond—"

He grasped her lightly by the throat. "If you're nice to me, you can stay. Can you make Ray feel good?"

Zaria's wolf raged at the touch of his sweaty hand. "Step back or I will hurt you," Zaria warned.

He just laughed and squeezed her throat. "I've wanted you since you first came here, little girl, and it's time to pay."

Zaria saw the fear in his eyes as he saw her start to shift. He screamed as she growled, snapped the arm he held her with, and pushed him across the room so hard, he hit the other wall and was knocked out cold.

Zaria panted heavily and wiped the blood off her partially shifted mouth. She had to get out of here—he would wake up soon, and she would be found out. Zaria couldn't kill, it wasn't in her nature, so running was her only option.

She gathered up her things quickly and leapt out of the window to the street below. Zaria was running again, but running away would always be her life.

❖

Dante Wolfgang grabbed her suit jacket and ran downstairs to the basement of their house. She thought she would find her daughter down there. The basement of the Alpha's den housed her war room, a place where Dante and her elite wolves met to discuss pack business and security.

As her oldest child and the strongest of her age group, Dion was the future Alpha of the Wolfgang pack. Such a task was a heavy burden to carry when you were young, as Dante knew from her own childhood. At fifteen and going through the rush, the werewolf equivalent of puberty, knowing you had such a big future ahead of you, and such great responsibility, didn't make growing up any easier.

Dante found Dion coming down here more and more and sitting and thinking at the large oak table, contemplating her future, no doubt, and full of self-doubt as Dante had been. She had started to invite Dion to some of the more mundane meetings just to give her the flavour of the job, and Dion loved it.

She stopped at the bottom of the stairs and watched her daughter gazing at the coat of arms hung on one wall. Dion was almost Dante's double, and sometimes she could burst with the pride in her heart, not only for Dion but her whole family—Meghan, a few years younger, and then Conan, her one-year-old son.

But for the last few months her pride was tinged with guilt. The Lupa pack, led by their Alpha Leroux, had attacked the heart of their pack, her mate, Eden, and they had lost the cub she was carrying. Dante felt like a failure for not finding Leroux and making her pay, but there had been no leads—the Lupas had disappeared. None of her wolves who had been sent out on reconnaissance, or humans she had offered money to, knew of the Lupas whereabouts. But they couldn't hide forever.

Dion looked around and smiled. "Hi, Pater."

Dante walked over and stood beside her daughter. "Ricky called. She finally got her delayed connecting flight, so we need to leave for the airport, if you still want to come."

"Yeah, I can't wait to see Ricky. She's so cool."

Dante chuckled. Her cousin Kenrick was five years younger than her. With the different style of the Wulvers and younger dress sense, Kenrick was the peak of dominant wolf cool for Dion.

Kenrick's father was a first cousin of her own father, and they grew up sharing summers together. Sometimes Dante would visit the Wulvers, and other times Kenrick and her brother would visit them here in Wolfgang County. They had such fun together, but this visit was about more than pleasure. Kenrick's life was about to change, and Dante was going to help her.

Dante ran her hand reverently over the wood and steel coat of arms. In the centre was a wolf's head in the middle of a Celtic cross. Around it were arranged the symbols of all the ancient British and Irish packs of which the Wolfgangs descended.

All the cubs of the Wolfgang pack were brought up with the stories of the Wolfgangs' ancient beginnings, but Dante wanted Dion to grasp how important it was to them.

"Tell me our story, Dion."

Dion reached out and touched the wolf in the centre. "When the first wolf pack arrived in Britain millennia ago, they formed four packs in ancient Britain and Ireland, so that our kind could colonize every part of the land. There were the Wulvers,"—Dion touched the symbol of the silver sword, then moved her hand to the ancient Irish axe—"the Irish Filtiaran pack, the English Ranwulfs represented by their shield, and the Welsh Blaidds." She finished by touching the Welsh symbol of a spear.

"And what happened then?" Dante asked.

"War came to our paranormal world, between vampires, witches, fae, and shapeshifters, and then humans hunted us through fear. The packs had a grand council between them and they asked for volunteers to build packs in the New World, so our bloodline, our ancient beginnings, would survive."

Dante put her arm around Dion and gave her a squeeze. "No wonder you got an A in history. That's right, and we are one of the North American packs descended from those gallant pioneers. Luckily the ancient packs in Britain survived and grew, keeping our wider family of werewolves strong. That's why I and all the Alphas before me have had this coat of arms on our wall. It's to remind us where we came from, to remind us we are from something greater than ourselves. We share our blood with these packs, and we draw from their traditions."

Dante turned around and put both hands on Dion's shoulders. "But the most important thing to remember is that because we share blood, the Wolfgangs are never alone in this world. The blood of our pack bonds us together in a way that cannot be defeated. That thought always gave me comfort when I was awed at the thought of leading the pack. Remember that, Dion. You will never be alone."

Dion smiled and seemed a lot less tense at that thought. "Thanks, Pater. I understand and I won't ever forget."

"Let's go and get Ricky then."

As they walked upstairs, Dante thought of the Lupas. Some pack historians believed if you went back far enough, all werewolves shared ancestry, but that was a long time ago. The Lupas arrived in America from an Eastern European pack and had immediately begun to fight for the Wolfgangs' bountiful territory. They seemed to have jealousy and destruction in their bones.

I will find you, Leroux, Dante vowed.

CHAPTER TWO

Zaria had hidden as best she could on the edge of town for most of the night. To any passer-by she just looked like another rough sleeper, not a werewolf hiding from the police. She hadn't slept a wink worrying about what-ifs, hoping she hadn't killed Mr. Raymond. Even though what he had planned for her was abhorrent, Zaria despised violence and knew only too well what it had cost her and her family.

She hid behind a building across the street from the diner, waiting for Chrissy to arrive and open up. Zaria had to get her wages and get out of Knoxton as soon as possible. She grasped the haematite stone pendent she wore around her neck and closed her eyes. The pendent had been passed down the submissive line of her family for generations, and in her darkest moments it gave her courage, strength, and hope, as the stone was meant to.

Zaria saw Chrissy pull up in the parking lot at last. She waited until Chrissy got in and hurried across the road. When she entered the diner, Chrissy jumped.

"Jesus, Zaria. You nearly gave me a heart attack. You're not due in for another hour."

Zaria walked to the diner counter but kept glancing outside nervously. "I need to leave town, Chrissy. I'm sorry to let you down, but something really important has come up."

Chrissy looked her up and down, obviously seeing her dishevelled appearance. "Is everything all right, honey? Are you in trouble?"

"No, no. I just need to leave. I'm sorry to leave you in the lurch— you've been so kind to me. Could I have my pay?"

Chrissy pulled her into a hug. "Sure. It's been nice working with you. Just take care of yourself, okay?"

"I'll try," Zaria said.

"Give me a second and I'll get the cash out of the safe."

While Chrissy went into the office, Zaria opened up the local newspaper she had brought in. Her stomach dropped when she saw the front page.

Local businessman Eric Raymond was attacked last night and left for dead. Witness heard screams and growls, and doctors say his injuries were consistent with an animal attack.

"Terrible, isn't it?" Chrissy's voice made her jump.

"Terrible," Zaria replied.

"Makes you wonder who or what got into his apartment building."

"Yeah." Zaria caught sight of a black car with blacked-out windows pulling into the lot, and her instinct told her she was in danger.

"Can I have the money? I have to go," Zaria said.

Chrissy frowned, seeing Zaria nervousness. "You are in trouble, aren't you?"

Zaria looked back outside and saw two big dominant wolves get out of the car, one male and one female.

"I'm sorry, Chrissy. I need to go out the back." Zaria grabbed the wages envelope and ran through the kitchen to the back door. It was locked and Chrissy had the keys, so she used her strength and shouldered the door out.

Zaria stepped outside and scented werewolf coming from behind. She started to run but was grabbed around the waist and pulled to the ground.

She fought and tried to break the male wolf's hold but he was too strong. He pinned her down and smiled at her.

"We've been looking for you for a long, long time, little wolf. You'll make a perfect prize for my Alpha and pack second."

She spat in his face. "Over my dead body."

His face and claws partially shifted, and he clawed down the side of her face. "That could be arranged."

The female wolf came around the corner and said, "Stop playing with her, and let's get her in the car and get out of here."

They carried her kicking and screaming around to the front of the diner. Zaria saw Chrissy with her phone to her ear, probably phoning the police.

"Run, Chrissy, run," Zaria shouted in vain.

The female wolf opened up the trunk of the car and she was thrown in there. "Maybe this will shut you up, bitch," the male wolf snarled.

He put silver manacles around her wrists, so she couldn't use her strength to burst open the trunk.

"No!" She screamed but was soon engulfed in darkness in a confined space. There was nothing she hated more than a confined space. Wolves needed wide-open space to feel calm, and the burning silver leeching the strength from her body made her situation worse.

This was hell, but she felt even worse when she heard one of them say, "Get ready to go, I'll go and get rid of the human."

Zaria hit the trunk lid, but her arms and legs felt like lead weights. "Don't hurt her!"

❖

Kenrick finally got through immigration. Apparently she looked suspicious, but when they realized she was a Wulver of the Wulver beverage dynasty, it was decided she wasn't a threat. She'd had to keep tight control of her wolf. After a prolonged journey, she was frustrated enough as it was, but to be kept waiting in an interview room answering stupid questions was nearly enough for her wolf to bite the immigration guy's head off.

Kenrick slung on her rucksack and pushed her bags on the luggage trolley through to the airport entrance. She couldn't wait to see her American family. The Wulvers shared family bonds with all the Western European wolves, but she'd always felt a special kinship with the Wolfgangs, and especially Dante and Caden.

She saw Dante and Dion waving from the other side of the entrance area. She smiled and waved back. Kenrick loved cubs, and Dante and Eden's were amazing to be around and play with. As she walked over to Dante, that ever-present knot of stress returned to her stomach. Dante in her professional looking designer suit looked every inch the Alpha of the Wolfgang pack, and then she looked at herself. Ripped jeans, black

T-shirt with skulls and gothic designs, and heavy black boots—how could she ever be like Dante?

But that was why she was here. In a month her father was stepping down as Alpha of the Wulver pack, no longer the strongest and most dominant wolf in the pack. That was now Kenrick, and the pack and business would be handed over to her. Doubts had been plaguing her since her father made the announcement that it was time to enjoy his retirement.

Since leaving school, she had worked in the hands-on, physical labour side of the business, maintaining the forest and the fish stock in Wulver Loch, and working on site at the Wulver bottling and distillery plant.

Kenrick enjoyed her life, but now she had to step into the office and run the business side and take leadership of the pack. Dante had made the same transition when her father died, and Kenrick's father thought spending time with Dante and shadowing her in business would give her confidence in her abilities.

Dion ran the last few yards to her and hugged her. "Hi, Ricky."

"Hi, Wolf, you get bigger every time I see you," Kenrick said.

"Your T-shirt is totally cool," Dion gushed.

Kenrick pointed to Dion's which had a rock bands album cover on it. "Cheers. Yours is too. I love that band."

Dante walked over and joked, "They give me a headache."

She opened her arms to Kenrick, but Kenrick thumped her chest in salute first in respect, then hugged her cousin.

Dante said, "You don't have to do that. We're equals now."

"Not for another month," Kenrick said trying to put some distance to her new life that awaited.

"It's great to see you, Ricky. You're looking good. Dion? Push the luggage trolley for Ricky."

"Sure, Pater." Dion walked a few steps ahead of them.

"It's good of you and Eden to have me, Dante," Kenrick said.

"We're glad to have you. You're always welcome."

Kenrick felt she had to say something but didn't want to upset Dante. She lowered her voice so Dion wouldn't hear her. "How is Eden? Mum, Pater, and I were so sad to hear about your cub."

Dante looked at her, and Kenrick was sure she saw Dante's eyes fill up, but she quickly gulped the emotion away.

"She's doing much better. The body heals but the mind and heart take longer," Dante said.

Kenrick shook her head. "The Lupas have never been happy with peace, but to come into your land and attack submissive wolves is the height of cowardice." Kenrick stopped Dante and put a hand on her shoulder. "You know the Wulvers stand with you always. If you need anything, any wolves or help, it's yours."

Dante smiled and clasped the back of Kenrick's neck. "I always know that. Thank you."

When they broke away from their clinch, they laughed when the humans passing them by stared.

Dante said with amusement, "Humans aren't accustomed to close contact are they?"

Wolves needed contact with each other, both dominants and submissives. That's how they were brought up, and there was no awkwardness.

They continued walking and got to the door of the airport. "How're Caden and Lena? Is Caden coping with having a pregnant mate?"

Dante laughed. "She's a bag of nerves and is driving Lena crazy, so I hear. The cub's due any day now."

"It must be nice," Kenrick said wistfully.

They reached the parking lot and began the drive to Wolfgang County. Kenrick shifted uncomfortably in the front seat of Dante's Jeep Cherokee. It seemed like years since she had let her wolf run free.

"Your wolf restless?" Dante said with a smile.

"Aye, just a bit."

"Well, we'll be back at the house in about an hour, and then Dion will take you out to the forest. You can run a bit of that teenage energy off her."

Kenrick laughed. She remembered how crazy the rush made her feel at that age. When Kenrick was going through it, she didn't have a girlfriend to test out those early feelings with. It made her even more restless.

Dion sat forward and popped her head between the two front seats. "Yeah, come with me, Ricky. I'll show you all my favourite places."

"I'd love to. How's school going, Dion?" Kenrick asked.

"Great, we just won the football championship," Dion replied.

Kenrick gave her a high five. "Fantastic, although we'll have to have a game of proper football while I'm here."

Dante rolled her eyes. "Don't listen to her, Dion. I've had to listen to this since we were cubs. Soccer is for submissives."

Kenrick was just about to reply with a witty retort when she saw something in the road up ahead. "Dante, look."

Dante slowed as they got nearer. "It looks like someone's lying in the road." She pulled over. "Dion, stay in the car."

"But Pater—"

"No buts. Stay here," Dante said firmly.

Kenrick got out of the car quickly and hurried over. A woman was lying there, and from her scent, a wolf. She dropped to her knees and saw silver manacles around her wrists and a silver bolt sticking out of her leg. The woman had the most beautiful long dark hair and dark olive skin. Kenrick lifted her hand to take her pulse, and she ran her nose along the woman's hand, inhaling.

She was hit with a dazzling array of scents that made her heart thud loudly. Initially she scented the top layers of fear, terror, and loneliness, but Kenrick closed her eyes and allowed her wolf to take those apart and see what was underneath. She saw lush forest, blue sky, the deepest bluest loch—it was home.

Kenrick's eyes sprang open. How could she scent Wulver Forest on this probably American werewolf?

"How is she?" She was shaken from her thoughts by Dante's voice.

"Do you have bolt cutters in the Jeep for these manacles?" Kenrick said.

"Yes, give me a second." Dante ran off.

Kenrick scanned the mysterious woman's body again. As well as the bolt sticking out of her leg, there was blood spattered on her forehead from a head injury, and cuts and bruises over her body. There was a large hill bordering the road, and Kenrick guessed she fell or was pushed down it.

She traced her fingers down the woman's grazed cheek and said softly, "What has happened to you, lassie?"

Dante and Dion arrived back with a bolt cutter and a first aid kit. "Stand back, Dion," Dante said.

Kenrick held up the woman's wrist to give Dante a better angle to cut the restraints. "We need to get her to hospital before that silver bolt kills her."

Dante snapped the cuffs and threw them to the side. Suddenly the woman gasped, and her eyes snapped open. They were the deepest shade of brown, like the forest trees in autumn. Kenrick was entranced, but then she saw the terror in them, and that made her angry at whoever had frightened her so much.

Almost as soon as she opened her eyes, the woman went unconscious again.

"Let's get her back to Wolfgang County quickly. Dion, go and open the door," Dante said. Kenrick put her arms under the woman and lifted her with ease. Dante stopped her and said, "Wait a minute."

"What is it?" Kenrick asked.

Dante pulled a stone necklace from beneath her T-shirt. "This is hematite stone. The stone of the Lupa pack."

Kenrick's stomach fell. "She's a Lupa?"

Kenrick held the injured woman in her arms with gentleness and reverence in the back seat of the Jeep. Dante drove fast and made phone calls to her elite wolves as they drove. She could feel Dante's stress and couldn't blame her. The Lupas attacked her mate and killed her cub, not yet born. But Kenrick could feel no malevolence from this submissive wolf. On the contrary, she sensed the fear and anxiety seeping out of her pores, and looking down at her injured and helpless, all Kenrick wanted to do was protect her.

They pulled up outside the hospital, and Kenrick saw the Blaze the sheriff, Flash, and Xander—all people she had spent endless summers with—were waiting with guards and looking decidedly serious and ready to battle.

Kenrick held the injured woman tighter. "Dante, is there any need for this? She's a submissive wolf, unconscious and dying if we don't get her help."

Dante leaned over from the front seat, looking deadly serious. "Because of the Lupas, my mate was attacked, Caden's mate was attacked, we lost a cub, and two brave wolves died protecting them. She will get help, but we need to know her story. It's very necessary."

Kenrick nodded. She couldn't argue with that.

The back door was opened by one of the elite wolves she didn't know, and a trolley was brought forward by hospital staff. Kenrick lifted the unconscious woman out and shrugged off the attempts to take her.

"I can do it," Kenrick said with a growl. She placed her on the hospital trolley gently and was loath to let her go.

One of the nurses said, "Dr. Jaycen is waiting for her in surgery."

Kenrick nodded and felt her heart tighten as she was wheeled away. Dante joined her and said to one of the guards, "Drive my daughter home."

The guard saluted and got into the Jeep. Blaze, Flash, and Xander all greeted Kenrick.

Dante indicated two faces Kenrick didn't know and said, "Kenrick, this is Ripp and this is Joel—two new members of my elite wolves."

"Good to meet you." Sensing Kenrick's dominance, they both inclined their heads in respect.

"Where is Caden, Ripp?" Dante asked.

"I called her but she hasn't turned up yet. I'm sure she won't be long," Ripp said.

She nodded and said to Blaze, "Did you send wolves to our dens in case this woman is a distraction?"

"Yes, Alpha. Our mates are safe," Blaze replied.

"Let's get inside then and see who and why this woman is here," Dante said.

Whoever that woman was, she was frightened, and Lupa or no Lupa, Kenrick was going to make sure she was safe.

CHAPTER THREE

Leroux sat in the dining room of the mansion they had acquired in Knoxton—*acquired* by disposing of the resident owners. She scanned the tablet she had been handed and navigated to the website browsing history.

"This was found in Zaria's room," Ovid said. "She attacked her landlord and put him in hospital."

"Zaria is very interested in the Wolfgangs." Leroux put down the tablet and tapped her claws on the table. "I wonder why?"

Ovid gave a sly smile. "We've finally found where she is, and that's all that matters. I sent two of our best wolves out to find her."

"Then I will happily dispose of her. My mate and cub wouldn't be dead if it wasn't for her. No one runs from Leroux."

Ovid slammed her hand down on the table. "You promised she'd be mine."

Leroux shot up and bared her teeth in an instant. "You challenge me, Second."

Ovid lowered her face, eyes to the side in submission. "Forgive me, Alpha. I have been waiting a long time for her."

Leroux calmed her wolf. "After all this time you still want her? I know I promised if we found her she was yours, but that was a long time ago."

"Yes, Alpha, I chose her, and I want her. We have unfinished business," Ovid said.

Leroux thought for a few moments. Maybe watching Zaria suffer would give her some kind of satisfaction, and suffer she would if Ovid had her.

"Very well, she's yours, but keep her subdued and under control. That wolf has caused a lot of problems in our pack."

"I promise, Alpha. I will control her," Ovid said with a hint of glee in her voice.

Leroux heard the front door open and she sensed two of her pack mates coming into the house.

"Your wish might be about to be granted."

Two wolves, a male and a female, walked in and she could smell their fear. Something had gone wrong.

"Did you find her?" Ovid asked.

"Yes, Second," Cero, the female wolf, answered.

"Well? Where is she?" Leroux said. She could feel Ovid's anger and frustration building. These wolves better have a good explanation.

Cero replied, "We had her and put her in the trunk of our car. Somehow she got out. We chased her and shot her with a silver bolt but—"

"But what?" Ovid snarled.

Artem continued, "She rolled down a steep embankment, but when we got down there she was gone. I'm sorry, Alpha."

Ovid launched herself at Artem and ripped his throat out, a wolf's weak spot. He dropped down dead with a look of shock still on his face. Then Ovid grabbed Cero by the neck and lifted her off the ground.

Leroux had to step in—she could not afford to lose too many wolves. "Second, put her down."

Ovid hesitated.

"Now, Second," Leroux growled.

Ovid did, and Cero gasped for air. Leroux grabbed her shirt and pulled her up to her feet. "Do not fail us again, Cero. Or you will suffer the same fate as him." Leroux pointed to the bleeding body beside her.

"Yes, Alpha. I promise," Cero replied.

"Get him out of here," Leroux ordered.

Once Cero dragged the body out, Ovid turned to her, looking furious, blood dripping down her face. "You should have let me kill her. This was the closest we've gotten to her in years."

"We have limited resources. Your obsession with her may be your undoing, Second."

"She was promised to me, and I want her one way or another, Alpha."

Leroux had always wanted to find Zaria and kill her, but their top priority was the Wolfgangs. Killing Dante would change their lives and fortunes. She was worried this would become a distraction, especially sensing the Ovid's anger, hunger, and obsession.

"We will get another chance to find her," Leroux said. "I have a plan. We need to make a journey."

❖

Dante sat with the rest of her senior elite wolves in the hospital waiting room. The only ones on their feet were her wolves guarding the entrances and exits, and Kenrick, who paced up and down nervously.

She showed a protectiveness for the young wolf they had found even after they learned she was a Lupa. It was good to show concern for a fellow wolf, and especially a submissive, but that kind of compassion could be exactly what Leroux wanted, and Dante was not going to give Leroux what she wanted.

Blaze walked through the doors to the waiting room.

"Blaze, did you find anything?"

"Not much. But we ran the name on the bank card, Zaria Spero, and it seems she never stays in one place for long. Moves from job to job every month or so. At first glance she doesn't appear to be running with the Lupa pack."

"Appearances can be deceptive," Dante said.

Flash nodded and added, "She doesn't go by the name Lupa then. Interesting."

Kenrick walked over to where Dante, Flash, and Xander were sitting. "Spero? That rings a bell. It's Latin, I think. Give me a sec."

Kenrick pulled her phone from her pocket and typed the name in her search engine. It popped up instantly. "Hope. It means hope."

Blaze took off his hat and said, "There's one more thing. There was a reported animal attack on a human male in the apartment building where Zaria Spero lived."

"She could be dangerous then," Dante said.

Kenrick couldn't explain why, but that assessment of this woman made anger simmer in her stomach. "Zaria is terrified, Dante. Fear, terror, helplessness, and loneliness were what I scented from her. She's not dangerous."

Dante looked at her silently. Kenrick had probably said too much. This was not her business, not her pack, but someone had to speak up for Zaria.

Before Dante could reply, Dr. Jaycen came out to speak to them. Dante stood and the others followed. "How is she, Doctor?"

"I've removed the silver bolt and she is responding well. You must have gotten to her soon after she was shot because the silver hadn't yet progressed too far. She needs some recovery before she can shift and heal. Maybe a few days."

Kenrick let out a breath in relief. "Is she awake, Doctor?"

"No, I gave her a sedative to make her sleep," Jaycen said.

Before anyone could say anything, Caden burst through the doors holding Lena.

"Doctor, the cub's coming, but Lena's bleeding," Caden said.

Dr. Jaycen and the nurses jumped into action and ushered them down the corridor. Kenrick could feel the fear in her old friend Caden. She had always craved love but loving someone also made you fear you could lose them.

The younger elite wolf, Ripp, said, "Alpha, I need to go with Caden."

"Of course, I'll follow you in a second."

Ripp hurried after them, and Dante called over Blaze, Flash, and Xander. "I have to go and support Caden. Make sure there are guards on Zaria Spero's door and one in the hospital room."

Kenrick said, "Could I sit with her, Dante? If she wakes up, I'd like to be there."

Dante hesitated for a few seconds, then said, "Okay, and if she wakes up, try and get her to talk."

"I will. Give my best to Caden and Lena," Kenrick said.

She prayed to the Great Mother to look after Lena and the cub, because she doubted Caden could live on without her mate. Caden had waited so long to find her mate, and she couldn't lose her now. When Kenrick's parents passed on the news about Caden finding her mate, she had been so happy for Caden—but the news also gave her hope that the Great Mother would send everyone their mate, even if they'd nearly given up hope.

Her thoughts turned to Zaria, the woman she didn't know but felt the need to protect.

"I'll go and sit with Zaria now, Blaze."

"Let us know if there's any change," Blaze replied.

"Aye, I will do."

Zaria walked out of the large wooden hut that was used to school the submissives. She laughed with her friends over something one of them said. Zaria loved school—it was the only place she got to feel light-hearted and relaxed. The den that she shared with her sister was chaotic, and they both lived in fear.

Her light-heartedness ended when she felt eyes on her. She looked up and her throat and stomach tightened with fear. The pack Second, Ovid, was standing outside the school gate.

She had been brought up around Ovid, but the last year or more, Zaria had felt her eyes on her whenever she went. It made her feel so uncomfortable. Ovid was ten years older than her, and Zaria knew instinctively those kinds of looks were creepy and wrong.

Zaria hadn't told her sister, because she had too many of her own problems to worry about.

Her friends must have noticed because one of them said, "Just keep close to us, Zari."

When they got to the gates, Ovid walked over, and they all bowed their heads.

Ovid smiled. "I've come to walk you home, Zaria."

Zaria took a step closer to her friends and said, "We were going to get milkshakes at the cafe, for my birthday. I'm sixteen today."

Ovid's smile didn't falter. "Yes, I know it's your birthday, and I think it's best if you come with me."

Fear seeped through her bones. You didn't say no to the pack Second. She reluctantly walked away from her friends. "See you tomorrow."

After a few paces Ovid took her hand and held it possessively.

"I thought we'd go on a walk through the forest on your way home," Ovid said.

Zaria was terrified. She looked at all the wolves that they passed in the street with a pleading look, but they just averted their gaze. They weren't going to intervene when the pack Second was involved. Leroux and Ovid ran the Lupa pack with an iron fist, and that bred fear.

❖

Dante watched Caden lean her head against the hospital wall and her partially shifted claws dug into the plaster.

"Caden, try and control your wolf."

"My mate is in there bleeding, our cub is in danger. I should be in there with her," Caden roared.

Dante knew not to touch a wolf in this kind of distress. "Dr. Jaycen just wants to look over her without you growling at his every move. He won't take long."

Caden took a breath and got her wolf under control. "I'm scared, Dante. She's a human and maybe giving birth to a werewolf is too much for her."

"Lena is much stronger than you give her credit for. She helped defend Eden against dominant werewolves. She's an amazing human. Just give her some time."

Ripp, who had been hanging back behind Dante, came to Caden's side. "If there's anything you need me to do, just say, Cade."

Caden patted her on the shoulder. "Being here helps. Thanks, Ripp."

Dante knew Caden was so proud of the progress Ripp had made since joining the pack. She'd taken all of Caden's teaching to heart and made her transition from human to werewolf using Caden's blood. It went perfectly, and soon Ripp had made herself an irreplaceable part of the pack.

When two wolves retired from her elite wolves because of age, Dante had to choose the two most dominant wolves of the next generation, and those were clearly Ripp and her best friend Joel.

"Who is this Lupa wolf you brought in?" Caden said.

"We're making inquiries. Don't you worry about her just now. She's well guarded, and Kenrick is sitting in with her."

"I forgot that you were picking up Ricky. Is she okay?" Caden said.

Dante thought of the tender, protective way Kenrick held Zaria. It was something she would have to keep an eye. She couldn't afford any wolf in her lands to be taken in by someone who could be a danger to her wolves.

"She's good. Once your cub is born healthy and happy, we can all run together," Dante said.

A nurse came out of the hospital room. "Second, you can come in now. Your mate is about to deliver."

Caden gulped and Dante was sure she saw Caden's hand shake. She remembered that feeling only too well.

"Good luck, Cade," Ripp said.

Caden nodded and walked into the hospital room.

Ripp growled, "I wish there was something I could do. I feel helpless."

Dante pulled her close. "Don't worry—they will be okay." She could see tears in Ripp's eyes and feel her anger.

Ripp explained, "Cade and Lena have been so good to me, like the mother and pater I never had. I can't lose Lena."

"You won't. Caden and Lena and their new cub will be at your mating ceremony in a few weeks." The pack had been preparing for Ripp and Kyra's mating for weeks, and Caden and the elite wolves had been helping Ripp build their den.

Dante needed to distract the young wolf. She needed an occupation.

"Ripp, I need you to do something for me," Dante said.

Ripp immediately dried her eyes and stood to attention. "Anything, Alpha."

"Lena would feel better if the Mater and your mate Kyra were here with her, but I don't want them traveling here alone, not while we have a Lupa mystery on our hands. I need you to go and pick the Mater up and bring her here with Kyra. I think Stella was with the Mater, so she will watch our cubs, I'm sure."

"I'll go right away—you can count on me, Alpha." Ripp thumped her chest in salute.

Dante smiled. Since Ripp was newly transformed to a were, she had all the insecurities and struggles of controlling her wolf that a teenage wolf like Dion did, but in an adult body. She looked in the direction of the Lupa wolf's room and thought about how much they had to protect now. She wouldn't let anyone come in the way of that.

❖

Kenrick paced the hospital room, barely able to contain her worry. Zaria was hooked up to all sorts of machines and IVs were giving her fluids.

It was not usual to see a wolf in this condition. Any injuries they could shift and cure, but not when they had silver in their system. She ran her hand over her dreadlocked hair, then scratched her shaved scalp above her ears. She couldn't imagine any dominant shooting a submissive with silver or attacking them in the first place. It was the height of cowardice.

For the last ten minutes Zaria had been murmuring in her sleep, and Kenrick could scent her fear and stress. She wanted to wrap her arms around her and make her feel safe, but that wasn't her place. She didn't even know this wolf, or if she had good intentions, but her intuition told her Zaria was not a threat.

Zaria suddenly started to throw her arms out, as if struggling with an imaginary foe, threatening to pull out the wires and drips she was attached to. Kenrick just reacted without thinking. She hurried over and grasped her hands, trying to keep her lines from coming out. She saw the welts on Zaria's wrists from the silver shackles and her anger burned deep inside.

Zaria cried out, "Don't, don't touch me. No, no!"

Whoever was frightening Zaria in her dreams, Kenrick wanted to scare them away. She put her hand on Zaria's cheek and whispered, "You're safe, Zaria. No one will hurt you. You're safe, I promise."

After repeating this a few times, Zaria's body started to calm. Then Zaria's eyes fluttered open. She looked at Kenrick for a few seconds, then scrambled off the other side of the bed.

"No, don't, you'll hurt yourself," Kenrick said.

Zaria huddled in the corner of the room and shouted, "Stay back. Don't touch me."

Kenrick stayed where she was, not wanting to seem like a threat. "Zaria, you're safe. You're in Wolfgang County Hospital. We just want to help you."

Zaria, shaking and panic-stricken, started to pull out her IV lines roughly, and blood ran down her arms.

Kenrick said, "No, you need those. You have silver in your system."

The wolves guarding the door burst into the room, apparently hearing the commotion. Zaria looked like she was trying to shift to protect herself from this new threat, but the doctor had said she wasn't strong enough to shift yet. It could be dangerous.

Kenrick had to get control of the situation. She pointed to the guards. "You two—out now. I will deal with this."

They hesitated, and she gave them a hard stare. "Go now."

Yielding to her dominance, they nodded and walked out. Kenrick turned back to Zaria, who was still trying to shift. "You can't shift, Zaria. You've had silver in your body. It's too dangerous."

Zaria just growled.

Kenrick tried to think how she could quickly show Zaria she wasn't a threat. Then she had it. She would approach her like any wounded animal.

She walked around the bed, and Zaria walked further into the corner. "Get back."

Kenrick dropped to one knee, put her head down, and held out her hands. "I'm not going to hurt you, Zaria. We found you injured on the road and brought you back to Wolfgang County. You're safe now, but you need to rest and you can't shift. The silver is still in your system."

Zaria's struggle to shift seemed hard and futile. She growled in frustration, then through her fear she saw the wolf who had been guarding her, on her knee, in apparent submission. This shocked her to her core, and her breathing started to calm. The wolf was big, very dominant, and powerful, yet she had her head bowed in apparent submission to her.

Never in her life had she seen a dominant wolf give a submissive posture to a submissive. In the Lupa pack no dominant would ever lower themselves to do that. Could she trust this wolf, or was it a trick? She didn't sound like a Wolfgang. She had a lilting Scottish accent.

Zaria tried to calm her breathing and asked, "Who are you?"

The wolf slowly inched her head up from the submissive position, and Zaria saw those dazzling blue eyes that had caught her breath when she woke up.

"I'm Kenrick of the Scottish Wulver pack. I'm here visiting my cousin, the Alpha. We found you on the road when the Alpha was picking me up from the airport. You are safe—I give you my word."

Zaria found herself captivated by Kenrick's gentleness, despite her size and her obvious strength. But if this wolf meant her no harm, then why was she under guard?

It was then that she felt the pain from ripping out the IVs. She looked down at the blood dripping down her arms. She was a mess. How had her life been turned upside down in twenty-four hours?

"If I am safe, then why am I under guard?" Zaria asked.

"I'm sorry about that. It's just a precaution. We guessed you were from the Lupa pack, going by your pendent, and the Wolfgangs were recently attacked by the Lupas."

Zaria gulped and closed her eyes. She knew only too well what had happened and felt shame that she had failed in her promise to her sister—to protect the one thing that was precious to them both.

Kenrick moved forward a few steps and held up her hand to Zaria. "Take my scent. You'll see I am no threat to you."

Zaria was frightened to bend her head in case it was a trap. Dominants had never showed her gentleness and she didn't trust them.

Kenrick lowered her head again and put her other arm around her back. Why was this wolf trying so hard to convey she was not a threat? It was strange. But maybe if she could make an alliance with this wolf, she could get out of here, and then she could make contact with the wolf who meant more to her than anything.

She lowered her head and gasped when she inhaled Kenrick's scent. It conveyed strength, power, but gentleness, and underneath that the fresh scent of a lush forest after a rainfall. It was beautiful.

Kenrick raised her head and Zaria looked in her eyes, and her heart fluttered. No wolf had ever done that. She found herself reaching out to touch the mane of soft dreadlocked hair Kenrick had on her head and felt an urge to scratch her claws along the shaved sides, but she pulled her hand back at the last second. What was she doing?

"I'm going to stand up slowly, okay?" Kenrick said softly.

Zaria watched Kenrick raise to her full height. She was taller and stronger than any Lupa dominant she had encountered, but in contrast to her strength and power, Kenrick held herself so openly and gently. Zaria was quite disarmed.

"Will you get back into bed and let the nurses put your IVs back in? All we want is to make you feel better," Kenrick said.

Zaria took a moment and trusted her instincts about Kenrick. Besides, she had to get better to get out of here and seek out her reason for living on the run since she was sixteen years old.

"Yes, I will."

CHAPTER FOUR

K enrick woke up suddenly and was unsure of her surroundings. Then she saw the young woman sleeping in the hospital bed in front of her and it all came rushing back. She stretched her arms, rubbed her face, then looked at the clock. It was five o'clock in the morning. She must have fallen asleep in the chair.

Once Zaria had let the nurses hook up her IV lines again, Kenrick had watched her drift off to sleep. Surprisingly, Kenrick's wolf was being extremely understanding, considering she hadn't run since leaving Scotland. Somehow she understood this was where she was meant to be.

Kenrick watched Zaria sleep, and even in sleep she could see the strain and tension in the play of her muscles. Last night's events proved Zaria was a creature used to fear, used to having to protect herself. Her mate, if she had one, should be helping her with that. She felt a strange sensation in her chest, so much so that she rubbed her breastbone with her fist. It was urging her, pulling her towards Zaria. Maybe the Great Mother was asking her to protect Zaria?

Kenrick got up and walked the few steps over to Zaria. She wouldn't presume to touch her without permission, but she felt compelled to be closer. Her eyes surveyed Zaria, taking in every inch of her face. She felt Zaria's beauty in the deepest part of her soul. Her olive-coloured skin was punctuated by the cutest little freckles. She had deep brown eyes that Kenrick could lose herself in, and dark wavy hair that she had the urge to run her fingers through.

"What a bonnie lassie you are, and I don't think anyone has ever shown you that." Kenrick caught herself reaching out to touch Zaria's cheek and quickly pulled her hand away. "What is wrong with you?" she asked herself.

She hadn't felt the urges or the tightening in her chest with any wolf before. It was crazy—she didn't even know this woman but felt like she did. Last night when Kenrick had talked Zaria down and calmed her, she felt like they were connected somehow in some way she didn't understand.

Her thoughts were interrupted by one of the guards knocking at the door and popping his head around. He was smiling broadly.

"Kenrick, Lena has delivered the cub. Both she and the cub are healthy."

Kenrick felt joy in her heart for her old friend. There was no one more deserving of love and family than Caden.

"Wonderful news," Kenrick said.

The guard nodded and said, "The Second has asked if you would join them."

"I'd be honoured. Will you keep an eye on Zaria? Don't be aggressive or show your dominance—she doesn't react well to it."

The guard bowed his head. "Yes, Kenrick."

Kenrick walked along the deserted hospital corridor and knocked at the hospital room door.

"Come in," she heard a voice say.

She walked in and was greeted by Eden first. "Ricky, I'm so glad to see you."

She inclined her head in respect. She would never dare touch another's mate, especially the Alpha's, even though she had known Eden since they were children.

Dante had her arm around Eden's waist, and beside them Ripp stood with a young blond woman who she recognized, but she couldn't remember her name. Kenrick assumed this was Ripp's mate, going by the way she was possessively wrapped around her.

"Hi, I'm Kyra."

"Kyra." Kenrick thought carefully. "Ava's wee sister, aye?"

"Yeah. That's right." Kyra smiled.

"Ricky? Come and meet my mate and my new baby cub," Caden said.

Kenrick could have sworn Caden was five inches taller. She was a proud wolf with a smile that went ear to ear. She had her arm around her mate, who was cradling the new cub.

"Hi, Ricky, Cade has told me so much about you."

"Pleased to me you, Lena. Congratulations on the wee bairn."

Lena looked blank, but then Caden said to her, "Bairn means baby in Scottish. She says things like that sometimes."

Lena giggled. "Well thank you, Ricky. Come closer and see him."

Kenrick leaned over and saw a chubby little baby face and thick dark hair. "He's a handsome wee cub."

"We think so." Lena reached up and stroked Caden's cheek. Kenrick's heart ached at the tenderness of the act. Then she looked around the room and suddenly felt so alone. Everyone had smiles on their faces and hands on their mates, even young Ripp, who had been half human but had found her wolf. She had no one and that made her sad.

"Have you come up with a name?" Dante asked.

Lena smiled at Caden, then said to her friends, "Yes, this little boy cub is named after Caden's pater. Say hello to Chase."

Zaria's eyes fluttered open and she had a few seconds of panic before remembering where she was. She grasped her pendent and took a deep breath to calm herself. *I could be dead just now, or worse, at the hands of the Lupas.* At least she was safe with the Wolfgangs and closer to her goal.

She turned around and saw the time was ten o'clock at night. She'd been sleeping a long time. She needed to shift, her wolf was demanding it, but it was in her interest to follow the Wolfgang pack's rules—for now.

Zaria noticed a handwritten note on the bedside table. She picked it up and read:

Dear Zaria,
    I had to go but I will be back to sit with you first thing tomorrow. Have a good night's sleep.
    Your friend,
    Kenrick

Zaria felt a smile creep up on her face. What a strange wolf this Kenrick was, unlike any she had ever known. Zaria was always suspicious of anyone she met, but her wolf told her that she could trust Kenrick.

She remembered last night and the strange approach Kenrick had to making Zaria trust her. "She kneeled to me. Why would she do that?" Zaria wondered out loud.

Kenrick had told her she was from the Wulver pack in Scotland, one of the old UK packs. As a Lupa, Zaria was brought up and taught to harbour a distrust and dislike of the Western European packs, especially the Celtic and British ones.

The Lupas and the Volk, American wolf packs, drew their ancestry from Eastern European wolf families, and over the centuries, hatred and distrust grew between them. Zaria never quite believed the propaganda, and neither did her sister, and that was why when they ran, they ran to the Wolfgangs.

As much as she was frightened last night, she knew she was safe for the moment. The Wolfgangs were taking care of her even though she was a Lupa, and every nurse that came in with medication or food had a kind smile for her.

She allowed herself to imagine what it would have been like growing up in the Wolfgang pack. She felt warmth, laughter, friendship, and happiness. How wonderful it would have been compared to her own experience of terror, fear, and isolation in the Lupa pack.

That was what made her mission and her promise to her sister so important, and she would die before breaking that promise.

There was a knock at the door and the doctor came in. He smiled at her and said, "Good morning, Zaria. How do you feel today?"

"Why are you being so friendly to me. I'm a Lupa—you all know that."

Dr. Jaycen walked over to the monitors and checked all her readings. "I believe in giving everyone the benefit of the doubt, and my wolf tells me you are not a threat. You will have a harder job to convince the Alpha. The Lupas have cost our Alpha and Mater a lot. She'll be in later to talk to you."

"To *question* me," Zaria corrected him.

Dr. Jaycen shook his head and smiled. "Talk to you. *We* are not a threat to you. The Alpha just needs to understand why you're here."

Zaria let out a breath, feeling her wolf get more and more restless. "When can I shift?"

Dr. Jaycen lifted her chart and studied her vitals. "Hmm. Maybe this morning."

"Can I run?" Zaria asked hopefully.

"That's up to the Alpha. You can ask her when she's in later."

Zaria had to get out of here, and if she had to play along, she would.

❖

Kenrick felt exhilaration as she ran through the Wolfgang forest. After a good night's sleep, she was desperate to run and was only too happy to take the Alpha and Mater's cubs out, giving them a Saturday morning to themselves for a change.

Along the way they had picked up some of Dion and Meghan's friends. The more the merrier as far as she was concerned. Kenrick loved cubs and always did this with her own friends' cubs back in Scotland.

She looked back at the cubs following and laughed inside at Dion, who was determined to catch up with her. Kenrick remembered being Dion's age. Everything was a competition, everything was a test, and that's what built strong dominant wolves.

Kenrick decided to veer off in a different direction and catch the cubs by surprise. She leapt over a fallen tree and scrambled up an embankment out of the forest. It was now open grass fields till they got back to the Alpha's den. Kenrick enjoyed running in the Wolfgang forest, but it was different from her home. The Wolfgang forest scent was green, warm, and dry, while Wulver Forest was wet, lush, and green, and there was nothing Kenrick liked more than a drizzly day in Wulver Forest.

She checked back to make sure the cubs had made it up the bank okay. When they did she deliberately slowed her pace so that Dion could catch her. Dion pounced on her back.

I got you, Ricky, Dion said telepathically.

Aye?

Kenrick flipped Dion and wrestled her to the ground. They were soon joined by the rest of the cubs, and they all piled on top of her, laughing.

Okay, okay. You got me. Let's get back for breakfast.

Yeah! they all replied.

Kenrick led them back to the Alpha's den and into the mudroom at the back of the house, where there were showers and changes of clothes. Once they were cleaned up and Kenrick was dressing, the cubs surrounded her excitedly.

"Can I come running with you again?" Marco asked. He was Flash and Vance's son. "It was so much fun."

The dark haired boy was dominant, but a lot less confident than his dominant friends Dion and Nix. She pulled him into a hug and said, "Aye, why don't we make it a regular thing while I'm here?"

"Yes, that would be so cool," Tia said.

Dion had her hand around Tia's middle, and Nix was standing close to Meghan, with an adoring look on her face, although Meghan seemed to be unaware. This group of friends had its very own pack dynamics already, and it appeared Marco was the odd wolf out. Kenrick knew how that felt.

"Marco, why don't you lead us tomorrow and take us to your favourite place?" Kenrick said.

"Me?" Marco looked to Dion nervously.

Dion behaved like the great Alpha Kenrick knew she was going to become, lifting others when they needed some confidence. Dion smiled at him and said, "Yeah, Marco, that would be fun. You lead us."

Marco was all smiles. "Yeah? Okay."

Kenrick got a kick out of helping teach the cubs. Pack dynamics were a tricky thing, and these small groups of friends were a good way to test out the rules. She pulled on her leather bracelets, and the cubs said a collective *whoa.*

"You like them? I've brought some with me. You can each get one tomorrow." Kenrick was engulfed by hugs.

Eden walked out from the kitchen door and said, "You look like you had a good time. Marco, Tia, Nix, let's call your parents and ask if you can stay for breakfast." When the cubs ran in, Eden said, "Dante's downstairs in the war room. She'd like a chat."

"Aye, I'll just be a minute." Kenrick tied her mane of hair back with her leather hairband and made her way into the house.

Conan came toddling over to her and said, "Up, up!"

Kenrick swept the two-year-old up in her arms. "Up? How high?"

She lifted him above her head and swooped him around like an airplane. "Is this high enough?"

Conan giggled, and she brought him down into a big hug. She heard Eden laugh.

"You're like the Pied Piper of cubs, Ricky. You need to make a whole gaggle of your own."

Kenrick cleared her throat bashfully and handed Conan over to Eden. "Aye, well, I need to find a mate first."

"She's out there, Ricky. The Great Mother won't let you down," Eden said.

❖

Dante leaned against the large wooden conference table in the war room. On the large screen in front of her was an image of the Lupa wolf Zaria, attached to a report by Blaze, the sheriff. She heard footsteps and turned to see Kenrick walking down the stairs.

"Good morning run?" Dante said.

"Aye," Kenrick said with a smile, "those cubs of yours have some amount of energy."

Dante rolled her eyes. "Don't I know it. Sit."

She watched Kenrick gaze up to the monitor.

"What have you found out about Zaria?" Kenrick said.

Dante sensed her interest in their guest, her protectiveness, even if Kenrick hadn't, and that was one of the reasons she wanted to talk to her.

"The human police don't know what to make of it. The property manager we assume Zaria attacked is telling police that Zaria turned into an animal before attacking him. Luckily he is a known drug dealer and user, so they're taking that testimony with a pinch of salt."

"But?" Kenrick said.

Dante used her small remote to click on to a picture of an older woman. "This is Christine Patrick. She was the manager at the diner where Zaria worked. The morning after Zaria attacked the property manager, Ms. Patrick was found mauled to death by an animal. Police don't know what to think of it."

Kenrick tapped her fingers on the table nervously. "But that doesn't mean it was Zaria. We found her with silver manacles on. That means there was someone or something else on the scene, probably wolves." She could not imagine the scared young woman at the hospital could attack a human for no reason.

Dante was silent for a few seconds then said, "Possibly. I just wanted you to have all the facts and remind you that we have no idea of her intentions. She is a Lupa after all."

"You don't have to remind me, Dante. I know what havoc and pain the Lupas have caused, but Zaria is a terrified, scared submissive wolf. I told you what happened last night."

"I know. I'm not saying she is a threat. I'm just asking you to be cautious. I can see you have a natural protectiveness towards her."

"Just as I would to any submissive wolf in fear." Kenrick knew the feelings she experienced while looking into Zaria's eyes and taking in her scent were more, but she pushed those thoughts aside.

"Good," Dante said. "Now on to happier matters. The working part of your stay."

Kenrick sighed. "The whip-Ricky-into-the-perfect-CEO-and-Alpha part of the trip?"

Dante shook her head. "You are already everything an Alpha should be, you know that. Your father just wanted you to work with me and get a feel for what it will be like to go into the management side of the business. I had to do it, and I know it's not easy."

Kenrick got up and walked over to the British wolf coats of arms. "You took to it like a duck to water, Dante. I've spent my life maintaining the forest, the fish in Wulver Loch, the distillery, the bottling plant. I've never sat in the office nine-to-five like my father."

Dante got up and joined her. "Remember, I was the same. I spent my time out on the pasture with Caden, looking after the cattle. My father was taken too early, and I was forced into the role. I had to learn and make mistakes on my own. You have your father to give advice and counsel. I know that's not the real reason why you're doubting yourself, Ricky."

Kenrick touched the sword on the coat of arms representing the Wulvers. "Maybe it should have been Donell. He was popular, good with other wolves, always laughing and joking. Maybe he was the natural Alpha."

Dante put a hand on her shoulder. "I can't imagine the pain of losing a brother. Donell was all those things you mentioned, but an

Alpha has to be calm, authoritative, not everyone's friend, and you always had to look after him. We both know that."

Kenrick felt her usual despair and self loathing when thinking about her twin brother. "I couldn't look after him well enough, could I?"

"Stop that. You know his death wasn't your fault," Dante said.

Kenrick didn't reply. She couldn't answer that question honestly. She looked down to the side where a bar area displayed bottles of Wulver whisky, including the special reserve that Kenrick brought with her. Next to it was a fridge with Wulver Spring water in it.

"Do your customers still enjoy a taste of Wulver whisky?"

Dante laughed. "Oh yes, I always offer it to my human business contacts and customers. I only wish I could drink it too."

Kenrick chuckled. Only the Scottish and Irish wolves had a tolerance for whisky. It was in their blood, a tolerance built up over generations, but the American packs had lost that over time. Now even a sip would make them lose control of their wolves and become sick. "Remember the summer we snuck some from your pater's stock? You were ill for a week."

"I'll never forget it, believe me. I've told Dion that story many times to try and warn her off doing the same."

"Aye, you're better sticking to the clear loch water of Wulver Spring," Kenrick joked.

Dante folded her arms. "How are things in Britain?"

"The packs are doing well, but there's been a bit of tension in our paranormal world with the vampires."

"I couldn't believe my ears when I heard Byron Debrek had become bonded by blood. She's never been the one mate type," Dante said.

"I know. It was a shock to us all. Her mate is a human too," Kenrick told her.

"Really?" Dante said.

"You've met Byron, haven't you?" Kenrick asked.

Dante nodded. "Our businesses have crossed paths. She is very intense, but above all, honourable. I've always admired the way the Debrek clan is run."

Kenrick always had a distaste for vampires. Although the Debreks had never done anything to interfere in the Wulver pack, the Dreds were hated by them, and that hatred would never die.

"You know the leader of the BaoBhan Sith?"

"Yes, the vampire fae? They live in the Debrek castle, right on the tip of Scotland," Dante said.

"Aye, well Hilda told us the Debreks and the Dreds are in open conflict. The paranormal world is changing. Exactly the wrong time to be changing the leadership of the Wulver pack."

Dante shook her head. "No, it's exactly the right time. Your father is wise, but he is not strong enough any more. He recognizes that, and that for whatever lies ahead, the Wulvers will need your strength. The Wolfgangs will always have your back, you know that."

Kenrick smiled. "We know that. Thanks. I thought I'd go and sit with Zaria today, with your permission."

"Of course. I'll be there in the afternoon to talk to her."

Kenrick's heart fluttered at the thought of seeing Zaria again. She just prayed that Zaria wasn't what they feared.

❖

Leroux's car drove through a part of New York City the paranormal community called New Hibernia. Long ago paranormal immigrants from the British Isles came to this bustling city and carved out a section of it for themselves. Every wolf, vampire, fae, and shapeshifter didn't live in New Hibernia, but they knew they could come home to be with others like themselves.

Leroux's driver pulled down a side street and stopped by a nondescript door to an old building.

Leroux had been granted an audience with a very special witch and was told to meet her here at the Hibernia Club. Madam Anka was a woman of immense power and one shrouded in mystery. She rarely communicated with others in the paranormal community and was surrounded by dedicated followers who protected her and her privacy. Because of this people feared her, and although Leroux would never admit it, she did too, and would never have wanted this meeting if she wasn't desperate.

Leroux had put all her resources into defeating Dante. The Lupas had little, and less hope of creating a better future. If Leroux couldn't take the Wolfgang lands and riches, then the Lupa pack would continue to die a slow death.

Leroux had to make this work. Since their last fight with the Wolfgangs, the Lupas had spent their time gathering money from unsuspecting humans. Madam Anka always demanded money for her help.

Ovid opened the car door for her and Leroux stepped out. "It's a long time since I've been here, Ovid."

"The scents of vampire and witch turn my stomach." Ovid spat as a passing witch glared at her.

"I know, but we need the help of a witch. So let's hold our tongues to get what we want," Leroux said.

"Yes, Alpha."

They arrived at the door just as a witch was walking in. The doorman said, "I haven't seen you or your wolves here before. Name?"

"Leroux, Alpha of the Lupa pack. I'm here to see Madam Anka."

The man—Leroux scented he was fae—looked her up and down and gave her a sly grin. "On you go."

A knot of disquiet started to twist in her stomach. Was this really a bad idea?

In the end it didn't matter. She hated Dante so much that she would see every last Lupa wolf die in an effort to destroy her.

They were led by a tall male witch to a booth on the other side of the room. As they approached, Leroux scented witches surrounding the area at the other tables. Madam Anka was well protected.

Madam Anka was an attractive black woman with an afro tinged with brown at the tips. She was beautiful in a extremely sensual way, dressed in tight black leather trousers and an open flowing blouse, showing off her full breasts in a low cut top and strings of black beads.

There were a lot of myths about Anka. No one knew her real age, and no one knew where she came from, but Anka appeared to enjoy the layers of mystery and enjoyed creating them.

Leroux stood by the side of the booth and waited for Anka to address her. Anka was busy stroking a black cat which sat on the table. Weres hated cats, but then, Anka knew that.

"Leroux, welcome. Please sit," Anka said.

Anka had a voice like honey, and every movement she made was seductive. Leroux hated herself, but she was aroused and hungered by Anka and the way she silently gazed at Leroux across the table.

Finally, Anka lifted her cat down onto the seat. "Do excuse Sybil. She doesn't like canines. No offence."

Leroux said nothing but despised the fact that she had to crawl on her belly to this woman, rather than take what she wanted.

"Drink? Oh, of course you can't." Anka turned to her attendant and said, "Bring some ice water for our new friend."

Leroux felt like a dog being given a bowl of water. Anka sipped her whisky, then lifted the bottle to pour more. "Ah, Wulver whisky is my opiate. You can't get any better."

Leroux felt yet another jibe. The Wulvers, like the Wolfgangs, were weak wolves who sold their wares to humans like dogs. When the water arrived, it was Wulver Spring water, and Leroux bit her lip, trying not to show her anger. The water was left unopened.

"So, Leroux—you want to defeat the Wolfgang Alpha?"

"Yes, that is my goal. A contact told me you could help with that," Leroux said.

Anka smiled. "I could, for a price," Anka said. She was almost insulted to be asked to help or consort with such a pitiful wolf. The mere fact that she could feel this wolf's arousal made her quite ill. The Wolfgangs were strong for a reason. Dante was an extremely powerful wolf, and Anka could use that to her advantage.

"Of course. How much?" Leroux asked.

Leroux reminded Anka of a dog bringing her an empty bowl and pleading with its mistress for scraps. "The price I will tell you shortly—first, you have to listen," Anka said.

She pulled off one of her rings. It was gold with a purple stone, a relatively new possession.

"If you wear this when you fight Dante, it will drain her power. Every powerful blow she gives will enter the ring and make her weaker. You will gain her strength and power as long as you are wearing it."

"Sounds perfect." Leroux made a grab for it, but Anka pulled it away.

"There is a price," Anka said.

"Name it."

Anka could already see the glee and hunger for the ring. What a weak pathetic soul Leroux was. "All I ask is that you bring back the ring to me afterwards," Anka said.

"That's all? You don't want money?" Leroux said.

Anka smiled. "I have enough, wolf. Do you agree to my terms?"

"You have a deal, Madam Anka," Leroux said.

She could already see plans forming in Leroux's head, about what she could do with this ring. Leroux had no intention of bringing it back. But it would come back to her.

Anka handed over the ring and Leroux immediately out it on. "Thank you, Madam Anka. Good hunting."

"The same to you, wolf." Anka nodded and watched Leroux and her associates walk away.

Asha, one of her most trusted followers, came closer and said in a low voice, "Why are you helping werewolves, Madam?"

She took Asha's hand and rubbed her thumb over the back. "I have no interest in werewolf politics, but I have my own agenda. Things have changed in our world. The so-called greatest witch in the world, the Debrek matriarch, has finally died, and change brings opportunities. I'm planning for those opportunities. Follow her, and make sure I get that ring back after she uses it."

Asha bowed her head. "Yes, Madam."

Chapter Five

Zaria was finally feeling like herself again. The doctor had allowed her to shift at last, as long as she promised to shift back to human form immediately. Now she was feeling like a caged rat. She needed to run, needed to get out of here and keep her promise to her sister.

There was a knock at the door and she heard a Scottish voice say, "Can I come in, Zaria?"

It was Kenrick. Zaria's heart sped up and she ran her hands through her dark hair quickly. *What am I doing? She's one of my captors.* No, that was unkind. Kenrick was considerate to her yesterday. "Yeah, come in."

Zaria gulped hard when Kenrick walked in. She was wearing ripped jeans and a distressed sleeveless black T-shirt with a skull and crossbones on it. Zaria was transfixed by Kenrick's muscular arms, so much so that she ran her tongue along her teeth like she was assessing a prime piece of beef.

Kenrick sat down and said something, but Zaria was so distracted she didn't pick up on it. Zaria mentally slapped herself. She wasn't used to lusting after another wolf—in fact, she never had. Dominants had always scared her, not aroused her.

"Sorry, what did you say?"

"You look better today," Kenrick said.

Zaria cleared her throat and shook off the strange feelings that Kenrick was inducing in her. It must be all the drugs she had been on yesterday.

"Yeah, the doctor let me shift, but I need to run. My wolf is clawing to get out," Zaria said.

"They will. Dante—the Alpha—will be coming in the afternoon to talk to you. I'm sure you'll get to run after that."

"In the meantime you've been sent in to question me?" Zaria said accusingly.

"No, don't be daft." Kenrick looked offended. "I asked the Alpha if I could visit you. I didn't want to think of you sitting here all alone. It's not good for a wolf to be alone."

I've been alone most of my life. "Sorry," Zaria said.

Kenrick's frown was soon replaced with a big smile. "That's okay. As long as you're feeling better."

The combination of that smile along with Kenrick's accent was quite disarming. What Zaria couldn't work out was why a dominant was being so kind and gentle. In the Lupa pack dominants were called dominants for a very good reason, and gentleness was a sign of weakness.

But then, everything was different here. If the Lupas had found her, she wouldn't be in a hospital being cared for. She'd be in a cell, threatened with violence and assault.

Kenrick rummaged in the bag she brought with her. "I almost forgot. I asked the Mater to make you up a breakfast sandwich. I know what hospital food can be like."

She brought out a foil-wrapped package, but Zaria could smell it already, and her mouth started to water. Zaria was starving. After not eating for a few days, the hospital breakfast just wasn't enough, but she was hesitant to take it when Kenrick held it out.

"Did you tell the Mater it was for you, or for me?" Zaria knew what the Lupas had done to the Mater—attacked her and caused her to lose a cub.

"Aye, don't worry. The Mater is really kind and always gives people the benefit of the doubt. Take it."

Kenrick put the package right next to Zaria's hands. She wanted Zaria to trust her and felt the need to take care of her. A few seconds passed. Then Zaria took the package and unwrapped it quickly.

"Thank you, Kenrick."

Kenrick smiled. "Call me Ricky—all my friends do."

Zaria looked at her silently, then tucked into the sandwich with gusto, making humming noises as she ate. Kenrick couldn't take her eyes off the sandwich. Her mouth watered and her gums ached as she watched Zaria. She gulped hard. She shouldn't be thinking thoughts like that about Zaria. She was alone and vulnerable. Kenrick had a duty of care to Zaria, and that didn't include lusting after her.

But, by the Great Mother, she had never seen such a beautiful wolf in her life.

Stop it.

Kenrick went back into her bag and brought out two bottles of Wulver Spring. "I brought you some water too."

"Thanks." Zaria put down her sandwich and opened up one of the bottles. She took a long gulp. "That's beautiful. So fresh and clean tasting. The Wulvers bottle water and make whisky?" Zaria asked.

"Aye, that water come from Wulver Loch," Kenrick said.

"Loch?"

"Sorry, it's Scottish for lake. The water is the best you could find anywhere."

"It tastes like it. I've never been able to afford bottled water."

That comment told Kenrick a lot. Zaria must have been on her own for a long time. She was certain Zaria wasn't a card-carrying Lupa wolf. There was a story behind her and probably a sad story. The thought of a scared and hungry Zaria living in that horrible apartment building Dante had shown her made Kenrick incredibly sad.

"I'm not a Lupa here to cause trouble," Zaria said out of the blue.

Kenrick moved her seat closer. "I already knew that."

"How did you?" Zaria asked.

Kenrick gazed into her dark brown eyes and said simply, "My wolf told me."

There was a silence as they gazed at each other. Eventually Zaria closed her eyes and breathed deeply. "Have you been out running? I can smell the forest air on you."

Kenrick smiled. "Yeah, I took the Alpha's kids and their friends out."

"Oh? What are their names?" Zaria asked.

Kenrick hesitated. Even though she trusted Zaria, they didn't know her story yet and she didn't want to give too much away about the Alpha's family until they knew more. They had lost too much already.

Zaria must have understood her silence because she said, "It's okay. You need me to prove myself to the Alpha first."

"Forgive me, but the Alpha and Mater have lost so much to the Lupas," Kenrick said.

Zaria continued to eat her sandwich in silence, but Kenrick wanted to know more. A lone wolf wasn't unheard of—some didn't fit in with the pack and needed space—but it was unusual, especially for a submissive.

Kenrick cleared her throat. "Do you have a mate somewhere, Zaria?"

"No," Zaria snapped, "and I never will. Mating is the subjection of the submissives."

Kenrick was taken aback at that response. "How could you ever think that? Mating is a sacred partnership, brought about by the Great Mother."

Zaria looked at her with haunted eyes. "Not where I come from."

Kenrick decided to let the subject go. Obviously Zaria had a troubled past with dominants, going by her reactions since she got here. She wasn't going to push it.

After Zaria finished her food she asked Kenrick, "What is that symbol shaved into your hair?"

Kenrick touched her hair. "This? It's the Celtic symbol for the wolf."

"I've seen some pictures of your pack land on the Wulver website. It looks beautiful," Zaria said.

"Thank you, aye, we think so." Kenrick was delighted and surprised that Zaria had checked them out.

"Can I ask you something?" Zaria asked.

"Aye, what is it?"

"Why have you been so kind and gentle to me?"

Kenrick leaned forward in her seat. "It's who I am. Who we all are, the Wolfgangs and the Wulvers."

"But you're a dominant, aren't you?" Zaria said.

Zaria obviously had a warped view of how a dominant behaved. "Why can't a dominant be kind and gentle?"

Kenrick saw Zaria touch her neck briefly but didn't answer. Zaria had a lot of scars on the inside, and she wanted to find out what they were and what caused them.

❖

Dante pulled up in front of Caden's den. They had made plans to go over to the hospital and talk to their Lupa visitor. Dante could have just beeped her horn, but she wanted a quick visit with baby Chase if he was awake. She was so pleased for her friend. Caden had waited a long time for a family of her own. Growing up without her parents had a big impact on Caden.

She opened her car door and sighed as she got out. There was also a part of Dante that was still mourning the loss of her own cub. She had failed in her charge to protect her mate and that was never going to happen again, which was why this Lupa wolf turning up troubled her.

Dante walked up to the door and knocked. Caden answered the door holding Chase resting on a towel draped over her shoulder.

"Ah, Lena's got you well trained already, Second. That's what I like to see."

Caden smiled and ushered her friend in. "Lena doesn't have to persuade me to look after my baby cub—in fact, we have wrestling matches over who gets to hold him."

Dante stroked the baby's head with her fingers. "Good morning, beautiful boy." Chase grabbed for Dante's finger and she laughed. "Definitely a dominant wolf. Trying to challenge his Alpha already."

"Sure is," Caden said proudly, rubbing his back. "I'll just be five minutes, Dante. I said I'd take Chase so Lena could have a shower. She won't be long."

"No rush. You seem to have gotten over your fear of holding him," Dante said.

Caden chuckled. "Yeah, I was so frightened when I brought him home. He was so fragile."

Lena joined them a few minutes later. "My heart melts when I see you like that, Cade."

Caden's cheeks flushed. "Yeah, well. I love my baby cub."

"Morning, Lena. You're looking well," Dante said.

"Thanks, Dante. Caden's been terrific." Lena came over to them and put her arm around Caden's waist.

"Eden said she would come over today to help you," Dante said.

"That's great. I don't know where I would be without Eden and the girls." Lena reached out her arms and Caden handed over baby Chase.

Dante knew Lena had been sad that she had no family to help her. Caden said Lena had contacted her mom and dad to say they had a grandchild, and her mother hung up on her. It made the rest of the pack more determined to make Lena feel supported.

"How's the girl you found?" Lena asked while she rocked Chase.

"Dr. Jaycen called to say she shifted and is doing well and following our rules," Dante said.

"Poor girl. What she must have gone through," Lena said.

Caden pulled Lena close. "She's a Lupa, Lena."

"Give her a chance, Cade. Going by the way the Alpha found her, she's been really badly treated."

Dante cut in, "We will give her a fair chance, if she's honest with us. Don't worry."

"But if she's here to cause trouble—" Caden started to say.

"We will handle it appropriately, Second."

Zaria paced up and down the hospital room, while Kenrick leaned nonchalantly against the window. "Calm down, Zaria. Everything will be fine and dandy," Kenrick said.

Fine was the last thing Zaria felt. Her nerves were making her jumpy and her wolf was telling her to run. She hugged herself. "How can I be? The Wolfgang Alpha and her elite wolves are on their way to question me. I need to get out of here."

"You don't need to be frightened. No one will hurt you."

Zaria eyed the window but she was trapped. As long as Kenrick was there, she wasn't going anywhere. "Dominant wolves are dangerous, selfish. They take what they want and leave submissives broken—a dangerous law unto themselves."

Kenrick shook her head and walked over to Zaria. "Where did you get this warped view of dominant wolves? I'm a dominant wolf and I haven't tried to harm you, have I?"

That was the strange thing. Zaria didn't feel scared or nervous in Kenrick's presence. Kenrick was unlike any dominant she'd ever known. It wasn't that she was weak, far from it. She was bigger and stronger than any Lupa wolf, but somehow her strength was tempered by gentleness.

"You're different," Zaria said.

"I'm not. Any Wulver or Wolfgang dominant that hurt a submissive wolf would be disgraced and driven from the pack. Just because we have different strengths, doesn't mean that one has superiority over another," Kenrick said firmly.

There was a knock at the door and Zaria shot to the window. Kenrick stopped her and held her arms gently. She felt a tremor of fear in Zaria's arms and her eyes were like a rabbit caught in headlights.

"Zaria, don't. We need to get this cleared up to get you out of here. Give me a second. Just sit on the bed. I promise you're safe."

Kenrick went to the door and slipped into the corridor. Dante, Caden, Blaze, Flash, and Xander were ready to come in.

"Everything all right?" Dante asked.

"Dante, Zaria has a fear of dominant wolves. It would be better if just you and Caden came in, if you want to get her to talk."

Dante was silent but Caden said, "Maybe it's fear of getting caught?"

Kenrick ran her hand over her dreadlocks and sighed. She could understand Caden being so distrustful. Zaria was a Lupa and Caden had a new cub. New parents were very defensive and careful.

"Please, Dante. She's scared, and I have the feeling that the Lupa dominants have done that to her. I'm trying to show her we are different."

Dante nodded. "Blaze, Flash, Xander, stay out here. Ricky, lead us in."

"Thank you, cousin," Kenrick said.

Kenrick walked back in and Zaria was sitting up against the back of the bed, looking terrified.

"It's okay, Zaria. I promise. Dante just wants to talk." Kenrick stood by her side while Dante sat in the chair beside the bed.

To her credit, Kenrick saw Dante soften her body language. Caden, though, was standing defensively behind Dante with her arms crossed. Kenrick caught her attention and indicated with her head to uncross. Caden did it with a sigh, but she did it.

Dante sat back and crossed her legs. "Zaria, how are you feeling? Have you had enough to eat? Has everyone been looking after you?"

Zaria looked from Dante to Kenrick quizzically. Clearly she wasn't expecting those kind of caring inquires.

"Um…yes. Everyone has been kind," Zaria said nervously.

"And have you recovered from the silver infection?" Dante asked.

"Yes, the doctor seems to think so, but my wolf is anxious to run."

Dante gave her a soft smile. "We'll get to that, but we have to ask you some questions. I hope you understand. We recently came under attack from the Lupas, and finding a Lupa wolf in need, on our doorstep, could be seen as a trap."

"I am only a Lupa wolf by birth." Zaria grasped her necklace. "I only wear this Lupa symbol because it was handed down from my grandmother."

Kenrick could feel and scent Zaria's stress, and her wolf was desperate to wrap itself around her, to protect her, even from her own cousin. It was crazy. She didn't want to touch Zaria without permission. Kenrick sensed Zaria feared a dominant's touch, so she took a step closer and held her hand loosely next to Zaria. If she wanted comfort, it was offered freely.

Dante leaned forward and clasped her hands. "We will help you and you will be safe here, if you tell us the truth."

Zaria looked up at Kenrick and she nodded. "It's okay. Tell us. You're safe. I promise." She watched Zaria close her eyes as if summoning up the strength to tell her story.

"I left the Lupa pack on the night of my sixteenth birthday. My older sister and I took what we could and ran."

"Why?" Caden asked sternly.

Kenrick found herself growling slightly at her friend, warning her to be careful with Zaria.

"My sister—" Zaria's voice broke as tears started to spill from her eyes, and Kenrick felt Zaria take her hand.

Kenrick didn't need to be asked twice. She kneeled and took Zaria's smaller hand between hers. "You're safe. No one will hurt you."

Zaria looked from Kenrick to Dante and said, "My sister was the Lupa Mater. She was Leroux's mate."

"This is a trick, Alpha," Caden said. "Leroux has sent one of her family into the heart of our pack."

Kenrick grasped Zaria's hand tighter and growled at Caden. "You don't know that."

Zaria was surprised at Kenrick's reaction. Was a dominant wolf actually defending her?

The Wolfgang Alpha intervened and said, "Caden, let her finish. Zaria, please continue."

Zaria's heart was pounding with anxiety, but she felt…different. She looked down at her hand in Kenrick's, and for the first time since her sister died, she didn't feel alone. Another wolf was in her corner prepared to growl for her. It was a strange sensation.

She turned back to Dante and continued, "Leroux killed my parents after my sister Marta became bonded with Leroux. She wanted to cut off all means of support to her, to us. I was young, still a cub, and I lived with them. I had to listen to the beatings she got, the mental abuse she suffered."

Zaria could hear a rumbling growl in Kenrick's chest and felt Kenrick's hand grip tighter. It gave her strength. Dante handed her a box of tissues from the table over the bed. Kindness yet again by a dominant wolf. Were things really different here?

"What happened, Zaria?" Dante asked.

"On my sixteenth birthday I found out Leroux had promised me to the pack Second as a mate. She wanted the sister of the Mater, like I was a prize. She was twice my age."

"Ovid?" Dante growled.

Zaria wiped her eyes. "Yeah."

Zaria watched Dante's eyes turn amber and her claws partially shift. Dante got up and walked over to the window.

Kenrick stood up and asked, "You know her?"

Caden nodded. "Ovid is the wolf who came into our pack, while Leroux had the elite wolves distracted, and attacked the Mater and Lena."

Dante stood silently, but Zaria and everyone else could scent the anger and fury coming from the Alpha.

Kenrick kneeled back down. "What happened then?"

"My sister wouldn't stand up for herself but she wasn't going to let me be sold off as a prize, to be treated the way she was. She and Leroux had a big argument, and Leroux beat her so badly that she couldn't shift. We waited until Leroux left our den, then packed what we could and ran."

Dante turned and said, "Where is your sister now?"

"We came running towards Wolfgang County. We were sure we would be given asylum here. My sister didn't make it. She died in a motel just outside the county line."

Everyone was silent, but when Zaria looked at Kenrick she didn't see pity in her eyes as she expected. She saw righteous anger. Why were dominant wolves being so understanding, so kind? A part of her worried that it was trick.

The pack Second, Caden, was the only one who still looked suspicious. "So how did you become restrained in silver manacles by the side of the road?"

"They found me. Since that night in the motel, I've been running from town to town, never staying in one place long enough for the Lupas to find me."

"Does Leroux know your sister died?" Kenrick asked gently.

Zaria turned to Kenrick. "I think so. I mean, I'm not sure, but Ovid knows I'm alive and has never stopped looking for me. I was her property, you see, and I ran. I don't think she will ever give up trying to find me."

"She won't get anywhere near you here," Kenrick said.

Dante, who had been quiet for the longest time, turned and said, "Is that everything? The whole truth?"

Zaria hesitated. It wasn't, but she didn't want to give away her final secret. She had to think first. "Yes."

"Caden, join me outside? Give us a moment, Zaria." Dante and Caden left the room.

"I told you that you'd be safe," Kenrick said.

"I don't trust her, Alpha," Caden said when they closed the door.

"Second, you would trust very few at the moment. Your protective instincts are on overdrive. It's hard to fake that kind of pain."

"Hard but not beyond possibility for a Lupa. They know we would be sympathetic to a wolf in need," Caden said.

Dante waved over Blaze, Flash, and Xander. "Zaria tells us she is on the run from the Lupas. My instinct is she is telling the truth, but we must be cautious."

"So what do you want to do, Alpha?" Blaze said.

"We'll give her Lena's old apartment but place guards outside, and for the moment a guard will accompany her as she moves around the pack lands."

Then Caden said, "We've been trying to coax Leroux out of her hiding place. Maybe this girl will make them break cover."

"Perhaps, but she is under our protection until she proves herself dishonest. Blaze, Xander, Flash, organize the guard rota."

"Yes, Alpha," the three wolves said in unison and left.

Caden put her hand on Dante's arm to stop her going back into the room. "Dante, did you see the way Ricky was defending Zaria?"

Dante sighed. "Yes, since we found her, I've noticed Ricky is particularly determined to take care of Zaria."

"Could it be a problem?" Caden asked.

"We'll find out. Let's go and speak to her."

Dante led the way back in and found Kenrick sitting close to Zaria. She cleared her throat and Kenrick jumped up. "Zaria, we will of course give you sanctuary for as long as you need it. We have an apartment you can use while you are here."

Zaria looked surprised. "Thank you. You don't know what this means to me. Can I go running?"

"If a guard goes with you. We have to protect ourselves," Dante said.

Zaria was about to protest when Kenrick said, "Let me do it. I'll go running with Zaria and make sure she comes back."

That was probably the worst idea, but Dante didn't want to pull rank on Kenrick in public. "Are you sure you want to do this, Ricky?"

"Yes," Kenrick said firmly.

Dante nodded and then said to Zaria, "You will have everything you need, Zaria, but if you turn out not to be what you portray, I will have no mercy. Are we clear?"

Zaria gulped. "Yeah."

CHAPTER SIX

Kenrick's wolf felt alive as she ran through the trees. The sheer exhilaration of chasing Zaria's wolf was new and exciting, and made all her senses come alive.

Since they left the hospital, Kenrick had purposely run slower so as to give Zaria some space and not make her feel pressured in any way. Zaria's wolf was beautiful, just like her human form. She was a lot smaller than Kenrick, as submissive wolves were. The markings on her back and face were black, and her undercoat and limbs were a dark honey-brown.

Kenrick picked up her speed and came level with Zaria. *There's a stream up ahead. Follow me*, Kenrick said.

She sped ahead, showing off her speed and agility with jumps over fallen logs and tree stumps. Kenrick slowed when they neared the stream and looked back. *It's here.*

When she stopped at the riverbank, Zaria was soon by her side.

This is an amazing forest. I can't tell you how good it is to run again, Zaria said.

They waded into the stream and took big gulps of icy cold water. It wasn't Wulver Loch, but it was still great. Zaria looked up at her and said, *Thank you for volunteering to take me. I feel more comfortable with you.*

I'm glad, but all the dominant wolves here are like me, Kenrick said.

Zaria gazed down at her wolf's reflection in the water as if replaying a memory in her head. *That's not how I was brought up, Ricky. It will take time to trust that.*

Take all the time you need, Kenrick assured her.

What do you do in the Wulver pack? Zaria asked.

Kenrick didn't want to lie but with Zaria's view of dominant wolves, and Alpha wolves, she didn't want to admit to anything that would intimidate her.

Whatever's needed, really. Forestry, the distillery, a jack of all trades. Why don't we get back to the hospital, and I can take you to your new apartment?

Okay. Let's go, Zaria said.

❖

Zaria followed Kenrick up a set of stairs to an apartment building. Maybe when she was left alone at the apartment, she could get away and try to find what she held most dear. As they drove from the hospital and up the main street, Zaria was amazed at what a beautiful little town it was. The Lupas were brought up being told that in Wolfgang County, only the Alpha's family and elite wolves lived in luxury, on the backs of the lower-ranking wolves.

Her grandpater had seen Wolfgang County and told them what they were taught wasn't true, and that's why she and her sister Marta ran here. But she never imagined, even from her insights gained from the Wolfgang website, that it would be like this. Now she was seeing the truth with her own eyes. Happy smiling people filled the sidewalks, cubs were playing in the playground, and shops were brimming full of produce.

Zaria stopped dead. *They lied to us. They said the wolves had nothing.*

Kenrick looked back. "Is everything okay?"

Zaria gulped down her emotion and nodded. "Yes."

She followed Kenrick up to the landing and found there were two wolves standing by the door, waiting for her. Zaria wanted to run. As if sensing her fear, Kenrick put her hand on the small of her back. She should have felt horror and panic at the touch of a dominant wolf—she always had, but not with Kenrick. Kenrick's touch calmed her wolf.

The two wolves on the door saluted Kenrick. "Your names, wolves?"

"Ryhs and Arric," the wolf on the right said.

Zaria wondered why they were saluting an ordinary wolf from another pack. Kenrick was very dominant, but still.

"I'll talk to you both once I've settled Zaria in."

Kenrick took a key from her pocket and opened the door. Zaria followed Kenrick into a large open-plan apartment. This was luxury compared to anywhere she had ever lived. Could this really be somewhere the Wolfgangs kept someone who could be their enemy?

"Welcome to your new home." Kenrick stood by the door and watched Zaria look around the apartment silently. She walked around the living room area with a comfortable couch, and then over to the kitchen. She ran her hand around the countertop and looked at the built-in oven. Still Zaria said nothing.

"Is this okay for you? The Second's mate Lena lived and was quite happy here, before they mated." Kenrick put down Zaria's bag and joined her in the kitchen.

Zaria wasn't talking so Kenrick felt obliged to fill in the gaps. She scratched the side of her head nervously and pointed to the three doors that led off from the living room. "Dante said there's a double bedroom with an adjoining shower room, a full bathroom, and office with a computer. Oh, and I'm sure Dante said she had someone fill the fridge and cupboards with food." Kenrick walked over to the large fridge and opened it up. "Aye, she has—look."

Zaria arrived at her side and stood open-mouthed at the sight of various cuts of meat, chicken, bright and colourful vegetables, and, happily, Wulver mineral water.

"I…" Zaria croaked.

Kenrick was taken aback at the emotion in Zaria's voice and looked to her side. "What's wrong?" Kenrick was shocked to see tears rolling down Zaria's face. "Hey, hey, what's wrong?"

Zaria hugged herself and shook her head. "They lied to us."

Kenrick's immediate urge was to take Zaria into her arms, but it was probably a bad idea. She balled her fists to stop herself and said, "Who lied to you?"

"The Lupa elders, Leroux, Ovid, everyone. We were brought up to think only the Alpha's family and the elite wolves shared in the Venator business millions. They told us the ordinary wolves lived in grinding poverty, and it was the duty of the Lupas to free those wolves and take over their territory and business."

"They said that?" Kenrick said. "All the wolves of the Wolfgang and Wulver packs share in the bounty of our lands, share in the kill, share in the business. That's what we live by. No one goes hungry."

Zaria tried to wipe her tears, but they kept coming and it hurt Kenrick's heart to watch her be so upset.

"My grandpater fought in one attack on Wolfgang County many years ago. He told us that the Wolfgangs weren't what we thought, but he couldn't talk about it for fear of retribution."

Every cell in Kenrick's body was screaming out to touch Zaria and comfort her, so she offered Zaria her arms and left the choice up to her.

Zaria didn't react for a second, and then tentatively walked into her embrace. Kenrick had to stop herself from growling in contentment as Zaria laid her head against her chest. She wrapped her arms around her and pressed her nose into Zaria's hair. She closed her eyes. Zaria's scent showed less fear than it did at the hospital, and she hoped her presence was giving Zaria some strength.

"I promise you, none of the things you were taught were true, not about the pack business or about how dominant wolves are expected to behave."

Zaria stiffened in her arms, pushed away from her, and wiped away her tears. "Thanks for everything, Ricky," Zaria said.

Why did she have to mention dominant wolves. She'd frightened Zaria off. There was a silence and Kenrick felt it was her time to leave. "I better go, then. Oh, I'll give you my phone number in case you need to contact me."

Kenrick took a notepad and pen and jotted down her number. "Um…the Mater said she would come around tomorrow with some clothes for you."

Zaria nodded. "That's kind of her."

Kenrick really didn't want to leave, but she had no good excuse to stay. She rubbed her hands together nervously. "I better head off."

Zaria gestured to her wrist and walked towards her. "What are these, Ricky?"

Kenrick pointed to her leather wristbands. "These?"

Zaria nodded. "They're really nice."

"Our pack tanner makes them. You get awarded a wristband at every stage of your wolf development."

Zaria took hold of her wrist and looked at each one individually.

Kenrick felt the heat from Zaria's touch spread up her arm and warm her chest and cheeks. She had never felt that from any other wolf's touch.

Zaria looked up at her and said, "You have a lot of them. You must be really important in your pack."

"Nah," Kenrick lied. "Just a jack of all trades." She didn't want to frighten Zaria and jeopardize their burgeoning friendship.

Zaria let go of her wrist and said, "Will you take me running tomorrow, or do I have to go with one of the guards at the door?"

"No," Kenrick said a little too fiercely, but she didn't want any other wolf to take Zaria running. That was her job, given by Dante, and she was determined to do it well and keep her safe. At Zaria's startled expression she continued, "Sorry, I mean, I'd like to take you. I'm going running with the cubs first thing, but I could come around eleven."

Zaria smiled. "Thanks."

"And don't worry about the guards. It's just a precaution. They won't bother you, I promise." Kenrick was going to make sure they understood Zaria's fears of dominant wolves, and make sure Zaria felt safe.

When she got the door, Kenrick hesitated and said, "Zaria, you're not on your own any more. I won't let any Lupa wolf near you, or anyone else. I promise."

"I've been looking after myself since I was sixteen, Ricky. I can take care of myself."

The thought of Zaria out in the world, on the run from Lupa wolves, with no money and no pack to take care of her, made Kenrick feel anger mixed with a need to gather Zaria in her arms.

"Ricky? Can I tell you something?"

"Aye, of course." Kenrick took a few steps back into the room.

Zaria seemed nervous and uneasy.

"I—my landlord, the one I attacked. I didn't try to kill him. I've never killed anyone in my life, but he was trying to force me...you know, and I had to get away."

Kenrick tried to keep her simmering anger under wraps. It seemed that both wolves and humans had tried to take advantage of Zaria. No one had ever been kind to her, but Kenrick was determined to show her how wolves were meant to treat each other.

"I know that, Zaria. You don't have a bad bone in your body."

Zaria furrowed her eyebrows. "How can you know? You don't know anything about me, Ricky. Not really."

Kenrick just smiled and said simply, "I know."

❖

After Kenrick left, Zaria's mind was whizzing with thoughts and emotions. Her grandpater had been right—the Wolfgangs were not what the Lupas painted, and she and her sister had been right to follow their gut instincts here.

Her stomach growled and interrupted her thoughts. Zaria hurried over to the fridge and she salivated at the gorgeous hunks of meat there. It was more than she'd ever had in her life and she couldn't wait to eat. She quickly seared a large steak on each side and sat down to her meal. It was perfectly rare when she cut into it, and the first bite was out of this world. Zaria had never tasted meat like this before. It was fresh, and so full of flavour, and for someone used to leftovers, cup noodles, and tinned soup, it was heaven.

The Wolfgangs knew meat. She cut it up into bites and dispensed with cutlery, using her fingers to eat each delicious slice of meat.

Zaria's mind turned to another hunk of gorgeous meat, Kenrick Wulver. She had astonished herself when she walked into Kenrick's arms. Her warm, reassuring scent was like the happy feeling she had running through the forest with Kenrick.

She had never found another wolf attractive before. Her natural attraction was for dominant wolves, but her upbringing had nurtured her mind to fear them, so lust and attraction had never entered her body before. Kenrick was different. She was much bigger and stronger than Ovid, the wolf that haunted her nightmares, but Kenrick's strength didn't scare her.

Zaria couldn't imagine Kenrick ever using her strength to harm an innocent wolf.

You can't trust them, Zaria chided herself. Wolf mating was about subjugation, and no matter how good an impression a dominant gave, things would always change once you had that claiming mate bite on your neck.

Zaria finished her meat and took a long drink of Wulver water.

One thing in the back of Zaria's mind bothered her about Kenrick.

Whenever she asked about Kenrick's work or her position in the Scottish pack, Kenrick became nervous and evasive. She was hiding something.

She thought back to looking at Kenrick's wristbands. There was one, bigger than the rest. It had a silver buckle on it with an engraving of two wolves with a sword underneath. One was sitting in front and one behind. Zaria was sure it meant something.

Regardless, she had to keep Kenrick onside. She was the link to her reason for keeping going all these years, and in a few days she would get out of here and find it.

❖

Dante rested her sweaty brow on Eden's stomach. "Mater, you truly inspire my wolf."

Eden smiled as she traced the gashes her claws had made on Dante's shoulders. "I told you that we needed this. Maybe now you'll believe me?"

When Leroux's pack Second attacked Eden and Lena, she took more than Dante and Eden's cub. She took an essential part of their relationship, the incredible sexual connection they shared and their need to express it.

Eden had needed to recover physically and mentally, but when she did, Dante was still afraid of hurting her and carried this immense guilt that she hadn't been able to protect her mate.

"Do you believe that I'm strong enough, Dante?"

Dante lay on her back and pulled Eden to her chest. "Considering what we just did, I'd say so. You ambushed me."

Despite Eden's constant reassurances, Dante held back from making love to her mate, wanting her to have more time to recover. But today Eden called Dante at work and asked her to come home at lunchtime. Their youngest child, Conan, was having a nap, and Eden was waiting for her in bed naked.

Eden lifted her head and looked down at Dante. "I know you were trying to protect me, Dante, but what we share when we touch each other is as essential as breathing. I began to feel maybe you didn't... after all my injuries—"

Dante cupped Eden's face with her hands. "Don't ever think that.

Ever. You are everything, Eden. You are *my* heart, the heart of our pack, and nothing makes sense or works without you."

"Then don't let Ovid or Leroux take this away from us. We need each other, Dante. I'm well, I'm recovered, and I need my Alpha to make love to me."

"I'm sorry." Dante pulled her back down into her arms and stroked her hair. "I need to find Leroux. She has to pay for what she did to you and Lena, and for taking the lives of two good wolves. I promised their families I would find her."

"You will. I have complete faith in you, but until that time, we get back to normal," Eden said.

"You're right, I know, but when I get hold of both of them, I'll rip them limb from limb. I promise you."

Eden was silent then said, "So, tell me about this young woman, Zaria. Is she genuine?"

Dante sighed. "I think so, but I'm wary. We've fallen for Lupa tricks before, but she gives a good impression of a submissive wolf in trouble and on the run, and the info Blaze got from the human police seems to back her up."

"You said her sister was mated to Leroux?" Eden said.

Dante nodded. "Leroux beat her mate, in the end, to death. Can you imagine a dominant wolf striking a submissive wolf? It's unthinkable. I would have no mercy for any wolf who did that in our pack."

"I can imagine Leroux hitting her mate, but not any wolf I know. I love your strength, Dante. It makes me feel safe, protected. I just can't picture fearing your strength."

"Ricky says Zaria has a fear of dominant wolves for that reason, although she seems to trust Kenrick."

Eden looked up with a grin. "Does she?"

Dante laughed softly. "Don't think of matchmaking with a wolf we don't completely trust. But yes, from the moment we found Zaria on the road, I noticed a connection between them. Ricky is determined to protect her."

"I said I'd take some clothes to Zaria tomorrow. I'll talk with her and get a feeling about her. I have good instincts."

Dante turned serious in a second. "Is that really a good idea? If she is in league with the Lupas…I can't risk losing you, Eden."

Eden stroked Dante's brow until her frown softened. "I won't be on my own. I'll take Vance, and maybe Kyra. She's closer to Zaria's age, plus there are wolves on her door. Trust me, Dante. It's part of my role as Mater to take care of those wolves who need some extra help."

"That's why you are our perfect Mater, but one thing you should know before you meet her. Her sister ran because Leroux promised Zaria to Ovid as a mate when she was only sixteen—a child. Assuming she is what she says, that's got to have an effect on her."

Eden shivered in Dante's arms. "Ovid is a wolf without any honour or common decency. A sixteen-year-old wolf?" Eden shook her head in disgust.

"I know, but as much as my wolf is inclined to believe her, there's something missing. Something *I'm* missing."

"Like what?" Eden asked.

"Once her sister died, why did she stay around this area? I would have gone to the other side of the country, or to a different country altogether to get away from the Lupas. Yet she stayed here, why?"

"Maybe she felt safe being near our pack? I'll try and talk to her. We've had our fair share of heartache, Dante. Now I just want to live and love."

"I've loved you ever since I could understand the concept as a cub, and there's nothing that's going to change that," Dante said.

Eden lightly traced her fingernails around Dante's nipples, making them go rock hard. "Remember our first kiss?"

Dante laughed. "It depends on what you count as our first kiss. Our first sweet kiss, or the one where we wanted to pull each other's clothes off?"

Eden laughed. "How about both?"

"Well, our first sweet kiss was when we were eleven. We were in the forest, collecting some wood and rocks for a school project. I brought you some flowers I'd collected and you leaned over and gave me a quick peck on the lips."

Eden ran her hand down Dante's body, making her growl. "You were taking so long getting round to it, I thought I should just get on with it, just like today."

"I walked around on air the whole week after that," Dante said.

Eden sat astride Dante's hips and grinned. "And our tear-your-clothes-off kiss was after your football game under the bleachers. We were fifteen and our sweet kisses became something entirely different. You won the game, and you were hot, so confident and dominant. Just watching you made something change inside me."

"What did it change?"

Eden leaned over and whispered, "I wanted to lick you all over."

Dante growled, and her hands grabbed Eden's fleshy buttocks, pulling her into a mating position.

Eden took Dante's hands and placed them on her breasts, encouraging her to squeeze.

"You came off the field, took my hand, and we went under the bleachers. We kissed like two adult wolves for the first time, and might have lost control—"

"If my mom hadn't caught us," Dante said.

Eden began to rock her hips on top of her mate's sex. Dante watched her with fascination as she closed her eyes and leaned back her head in pleasure.

"You are truly beautiful," Dante said.

When Eden opened her eyes she saw Dante's eyes had changed to glowing yellow. She missed seeing this need in her mate. Since the attack Dante had been kind, caring, and protective, but she needed her to be the sexually dominant wolf she knew only too well.

"Are you mine, Alpha?"

"Always."

As soon as Dante replied, Eden snarled and, with her wolf claws, scratched along Dante's chest leaving a bloody gash. This defiant action was meant to challenge her Alpha and make her react, and react she did. Dante flipped Eden over in a second and held her hands tight above her head.

"Submit, Mater," Dante demanded, but Eden defiantly held Dante's gaze.

One of the things the made the Alpha pair's relationship so strong was that they still loved to play together, especially these challenge and submission games. They had done this ever since they were cubs, and only in maturity did the stakes rise in intensity and seriousness.

Eden struggled and when she made no progress from Dante's tight hold, she turned and sank her wolf teeth into her mate's arm, drawing blood. Dante never flinched in pain but raised her lip into a sneer.

"You think you challenge your Alpha, Mater?"

Eden smiled back up at her mate. "As always, Alpha, it's my job to challenge you."

Dante lowered her head until her face was inches from Eden's face and made a low rumbling growl that reverberated through Eden's core and made her shiver.

"Submit, Mater."

Eden immediately bared her neck to her mate. Dante's teeth elongated and pierced the scar from the night that they first bonded in this way. Eden's sex clenched in response, ready to receive her mate again, but instead of mounting her, Dante turned her mate onto her front and began to kiss and lick her way down Eden's spine.

Eden growled in response and then howled in pleasure when she felt Dante's teeth sink into her buttock. Her instinct made her push her hips up and present her sex to her mate. Eden looked back and watched Dante with yellow eyes full of passion, teeth ready to bite, and claws slightly scratching her body.

She'd missed seeing Dante like this, hot, needy, and hungry. Eden groaned when she felt Dante running her finger over her wet sex.

"You're drenched, Mater. What do you want?" Dante growled.

Eden's sex was pounding so hard. There was something about this position that made her desperate for Dante and the orgasm she needed. It was primal.

"Fuck me, Alpha."

Dante placed herself in the mating position. Eden moaned and Dante growled. She could feel Dante and her need as she thrust into her, but she wanted more, wanted it rougher.

"Don't hold back…If you're strong enough," Eden challenged.

Dante grasped her hair, just as she wanted, and scratched her nails down her back, while her thrusts got faster. "I'm the strongest wolf and you're mine," Dante roared.

"Yes, I'm yours, Alpha. Fill me up." Eden wanted all of Dante and the essence of a dominant and her bite drove her wild. She was going to come, but Eden wanted to wait for her dominant. "Dante? Now."

Dante started to growl and moan, slow and continuously, a sure sign that her mate was coming soon. Eden was on the verge of giving in to her own orgasm when she felt Dante lean over and sink her teeth into her mate bite. They both came instantly and Eden experienced such an intense release. All the pain, worry, and fear was washed away by the orgasm that Dante had given her. They fell to the bed and held each other in a mess of sweaty limbs.

Dante kissed her deeply and said, "You are everything, our cubs are everything. Nothing will hurt you again. I promise you."

Eden believed her mate, but there was a small part of her that sensed they would see Leroux again, and this time Dante would put her threat to an end.

"I love you, Dante."

CHAPTER SEVEN

A ll right, all right, hold your horses." Kenrick and the cubs had just enjoyed a long morning run and were now in the Alpha's mudroom finishing getting changed. As promised, Kenrick gave them each a leather wristband she'd brought from back home. Marco, who had led their run today, was last, and as the others ran into the kitchen, Kenrick slipped the leather band onto Marco's wrist.

"Thanks! This is so cool," Marco said enthusiastically. "I'm like the Scottish wolves now."

Kenrick smiled and ruffled his hair. "You're welcome. You were great at leading the run today, Marco. I used to run with Flash, your pater, all over Wolfgang County when I was young."

Marco's adoptive parents, Flash and Vance, were great wolves and great parents, she was sure. Marco sat on the mudroom bench and stared at his wristband. She got the feeling he needed to talk.

"It was fun, but Dion and Nix are better at leading," Marco said.

Kenrick put her hand on the back of his neck. "You were great. Don't compare yourself to others and think you don't measure up. In the wolf pack, we each have our place, we each have our task to perform. Some lead, some follow, but no one part of the pack is more important than the other. We all depend on each other to make things work. You'll find your way, Marco. We all do."

Marco sighed. "I'm not as dominant as my pater—maybe he's disappointed he didn't adopt a different wolf. I'm not like Dion or Nix."

Flash was one of the elite wolves, and he helped Caden run the ranch and meatpacking business. He was a big tough wolf, but he was also gentle and kind. These insecurities did not come from him, she was sure.

"Has your pater ever said anything to make you feel like that, Marco?"

Marco shook his head vehemently. "No, he's the best pater in the world. I just want to be the best cub for him."

Kenrick looked him right in the eye and said, "The day your pater and dad adopted you was the best day of their lives. I know that because Flash couldn't stop telling everyone he met. You are the best thing in Flash and Vance's life."

Marco threw his arms around Kenrick's middle, and she hugged him back tightly. "Thanks, Ricky. It's good to talk to someone besides my parents."

"I'm here anytime."

Kenrick looked up and spotted Eden watching her from the mudroom door with the biggest smile on her face. She then left them to it.

"Can I ask you something, Marco?" Kenrick said.

"Sure, Ricky."

"Why was today's run your favourite?"

Marco had led them through the forest in a different direction than usual and emerged at the forest's very edge. It bordered the line between Wolfgang County and Rutherford County.

Marco's eyes flitted around nervously. "I—I've never told my parents, but sometimes I see this lone wolf. She's just sometimes there and doesn't say anything. Just watches me, then runs off."

"Do you like to see this wolf?" Kenrick asked.

"Yeah, I feel like she's kind and I've tried to talk, but she doesn't talk back."

Why would a lone wolf keep coming to the border and running away? She hoped it wasn't one of the Lupas.

"What colour is her pelt?" Kenrick said.

"Black and brown. You won't tell my parents, will you? Ever since the Lupas attacked us, I haven't gone myself, because the Alpha said cubs can't run alone, so I haven't seen her for a while."

Kenrick weighed it up. "Just don't go on your own until the Alpha has dealt with the Lupas, okay?"

"I promise. Thanks, Ricky."

When he ran off to get his friends, Kenrick thought about what Marco had said about the lone wolf. She couldn't put her finger on it, but there was something about it that niggled in her brain. What was it?

❖

Zaria finished loading the dishwasher with her breakfast plates and then poured out a cup of tea. She woke up this morning gasping for air, as she usually did. Her usual nightmares were enhanced by the guilt over her human friend's death. Chrissy died because of who *she* was, and the thought ate away at her conscience.

She sighed and opened the cupboards to find some sweetener for her tea. Amongst all the items in the packed cupboards was a bottle of honey. Perfect. Zaria took it over to her cup. As she stirred, she thought about how much her life had changed in such a short time.

A few days ago she was eating leftovers in a dump of a studio apartment, then waiting for death, shackled in the trunk of a car, and now she was making tea in the nicest apartment she'd ever seen. She dropped her spoon and shook her head in disgust. Leroux and her ancestors had lied to them all and cultivated hatred between the pack and the Wolfgangs.

Her old Lupa school friends would never believe she spent the night in a warm comfortable bed, with all the food she could dream of. Then there was Kenrick. After her initial panic of not knowing her surroundings, Zaria's next thought was of Kenrick. She had never met a dominant wolf she trusted before—or who made her stomach flip.

Zaria told herself it was simple gratitude she was feeling, but how could she explain the shiver that rippled across her body at the sound of Kenrick's lilting Scottish voice?

Everything about her was different than she was used to. Her voice, her gorgeous thick mane—and they obviously made them big in Scotland because Kenrick was as solid as they came.

Her thoughts were interrupted by a knock at the door and the sound of voices talking to her guards. She was immediately on alert. Could the Lupas have tracked her down?

There was another knock and a voice said, "Zaria, it's the Mater."

Her heart started to beat faster. If she was to pass this test and keep goodwill with the Wolfgangs; the Mater's trust was important, if only until she could fulfil her promise to her sister and make sure the cub she gave her life for was safe and secure.

Marco, his adoptive parents had called him.

Zaria opened her door to two blond women, one older than the other, and a male submissive wolf whose face she knew well, Vance Wolfgang. Marco's father.

They were flanked by the two guards at the door, who gave her a warning look.

The older blond woman, who she guessed was the Mater, said, "Hi, Zaria, I'm Eden, Mater of the Wolfgang pack."

Eden was beautiful. She and Dante made a gorgeous couple.

Eden continued and pointed to the blonde around her age. "This is Kyra, and my friend Vance."

"Hi, please come in." Zaria held open the door and Eden led the way with Kyra and Vance carrying two holdalls. Zaria led them to the couch and they all sat.

Pointing to the holdalls, Eden said, "We brought you some clothes. I hope they'll fit okay."

"Thank you, Mater. Everyone has been so kind. This apartment, the food, the clothes—I can't thank you enough."

"No need to thank us, honey," Vance said. "That's what the wolf pack does."

Zaria shut her eyes briefly. There was a part of her that wished Vance wasn't as nice as he appeared. That part of her that wished she and her sister Marta could have brought Marta's cub up themselves. The cub she took from her dying sister's arms and left on the doorstep of the Alpha all those years ago. Zaria shook that little feeling of jealousy away. She wanted Marco to have the best parents, and going by her visits to check on him over the years, he had a warm and loving home here in Wolfgang County. Marco had a life he could never have had with the Lupas. The Great Mother only knew how Leroux would have warped a young child's mind.

"Still, thank you. I really appreciate it," Zaria said.

Eden gave her the warmest smile. "You're welcome—and don't worry, I had Kyra help me pick them out. She's closer to your age."

Kyra joined in and said kindly, "Yeah, anything else you need, just let me know."

Zaria gulped back her emotions. She was overwhelmed with gratitude but racked with guilt that she wasn't telling her rescuers the whole truth.

She needed a time out. "Let me get you some tea. I'll just be a minute."

Zaria left her three visitors to talk and, after switching on the kettle, leaned against the countertop and took a few deep breaths. She scented someone approach. It was the Mater. "Sorry, tea won't be long, Mater."

"It's *Eden*, Zaria." Eden handed over a box. "We brought cakes from the diner." Eden hesitated, then said, "I sense you're feeling a little overwhelmed. It wasn't my intention. Vance is a good friend, and I thought you'd like to meet a wolf your own age. Kyra is a really nice girl."

Zaria looked back to the sitting area where Kyra and Vance were talking and laughing so freely. Everything was so different here. "It's not that. It's just, I'm not used to all this…kindness, concern. I mean, you don't even know that you can trust me."

Eden looked her straight in the eye and said, "I trust you, Zaria."

"Why? You don't know me, and the Alpha clearly doesn't trust me because there are guards on my door."

"The guards were just a precaution and will be gone by this evening," Eden replied.

"How? Why?" Zaria was surprised and confused.

"That will be my recommendation to the Alpha when I see her tonight."

Zaria couldn't believe that an Alpha would take any notice of their mate's opinions. "Why would she listen?"

"Because she trusts my judgement and we are a partnership. We lead the Wolfgang pack together," Eden said.

Zaria shook her head. "A Lupa wolf wouldn't listen to anything any submissive said."

Eden laid her hand on her arm. "Things are very different outside the Lupa pack. We don't fear our mates—we admire, love, and adore them."

Zaria took out the teabags and dropped them in the pot. That was something she couldn't believe. Maybe the Wolfgang submissives lived under that illusion, but power came from strength, and Zaria knew to her cost that dominant wolves used strength to get what they wanted.

As she poured the boiling water into the teapot, Zaria asked, "Why do you believe my story?"

"Look at me, Zaria," Eden said.

Zaria did as asked and Eden simply gazed at her. "Dante told me some of your history with Ovid."

Zaria shuddered at the mention of her name. She had only told the bare minimum of her history with Ovid, the wolf who haunted her dreams. "She did?"

Eden nodded. "I don't know if anyone told you, but I have a history with her too. Ovid attacked me and our pack Second's mate. I lost my unborn cub in that attack."

Zaria saw Eden fighting back tears. "I'm so sorry."

"Thank you. I tell you this because I know that haunted look in your eyes is from the memory of her. I know because I see the same look in the mirror sometimes. I trust you, Zaria. I just needed to look in your eyes once to know it."

Zaria was silent. She wasn't used to anyone seeing or recognizing the pain in her soul. Eden must have noticed her struggle, and said, "You don't have to say anything. Let's just enjoy our tea and cakes. Come on, every wolf has a sweet tooth, right?"

Zaria smiled and nodded. "I'll just be a few minutes."

She had never felt such warmth as she did from the Wolfgangs and Kenrick since her sister died. This pack comfort and support was everything she had missed out on, always being on the run.

Her thoughts turned to Kenrick. She had promised to take her out running today, and deep down she felt the flush of excitement.

Where are you now, Ricky?

❖

Kenrick jumped off her horse and handed the reins to one of the stable hands. "Thanks, take care of her. She did well today."

"Yes, Alpha," the stable hand said.

The name jarred inside her and made her feel queasy. "I'm not an Alpha yet, just Kenrick, okay?"

"Sorry. I'll take care of your horse, Kenrick."

Why was she constantly reminded of what was ahead of her? Becoming Alpha was like a big black hole heading for her at unbelievable speed, and she didn't want to think about it, but everyone seemed intent on pushing her in.

Kenrick walked off in the direction of the ranch office. She had been helping out Flash today, since Caden was still on baby leave, and was about to head over to take Zaria on a run.

She walked into the office and found Caden with her booted feet up on the desk and her Stetson covering her face. Kenrick approached the desk and said, "Cade?"

When there was no response she spoke a little bit louder. "Caden."

Caden jumped to her feet from sleep. "What? I'm awake, I'm awake. Not sleeping."

Kenrick held up her hands. "It's okay. It's just me."

Caden clutched her chest and took deep breaths. "Great Mother! You made me jump."

"What are you doing here, Cade? You're on baby leave."

Caden sat back down on her chair and rubbed her tired looking eyes. "Lena kicked me out."

"What?" Kenrick said.

Caden took a big drink from her water bottle. "Just for the day. She said I was fussing and getting in the way. Can you imagine that?"

Kenrick laughed. "Aye, I can. How's the bairn?"

"He's the most precious thing in my heart, but he's so loud. We're hardly getting any sleep. Lena has the worst of it with feeding and everything, and I'm hovering, I know—I'm just frightened to let anything happen to him. He's so fragile."

"So since you were kicked out, you thought you might as well come here for a sleep?" Kenrick said.

"Something like that. I'll give Lena a few hours to cool off, then go back home. Every instinct I have tells me to be around our den guarding them. I'm so lucky they're mine."

"You deserve it, Cade."

Caden stretched and then looked more alert. "So, what's happening today?"

"I was out checking the cattle with Flash and Ripp. They rode on over to the meatpacking plant, and I'm heading back into town to take

Zaria out for a run." Kenrick pulled her T-shirt to her nose and added, "I better get a shower first, actually."

Caden clasped her hands and sighed.

"What is it? Something wrong?" Kenrick asked.

"Don't you think it would be better if I got someone else to take her out?" Caden said.

"What? Why? Dante gave me the job. I'll take her out until the Alpha says differently," Kenrick said with force in her voice.

Caden sat back in her seat. "Exactly because of that anger in your voice. Dante and I have noticed your protective instinct towards her since she arrived here."

"Of course I feel protective. She's a submissive wolf who's been hunted since she was a child, with no wolf pack to protect her. It's our duty to care for her."

"We don't even know if her story is true. Zaria is a Lupa and could be here to betray us."

Kenrick felt anger and energy coursing through her body, but she didn't want to fight with her old friend, so she took a breath and tried to calm herself.

"I know she's not here to harm us. My wolf trusts her completely," Kenrick said firmly.

Caden nodded. "You must understand my and Dante's fear. The Lupas attacked our mates."

"I understand." Kenrick did get it. She would feel the same if her mate was Lena or Eden—or Zaria? Kenrick shivered and shook that feeling from her body.

"Remember, you're only here for a few weeks, Ricky. You've got a whole new life waiting for you when you get home to Wulver Forest."

"What are you saying, Cade?"

"Don't get attached."

CHAPTER EIGHT

Kenrick went back to the Alpha's den and got a quick shower and change before driving over to Zaria's apartment. Caden's words weighed heavily on her mind. Was she getting attached? The excitement in her stomach and heart as she drove to her destination confirmed that fact.

She parked Dante's truck outside Zaria's apartment and turned off the engine. She ran her hands over her ponytailed dreadlocks and tightened the leather band that held them together.

Was this a bad idea? Was everyone right? She wasn't here for long and yet she felt an emotional attachment, and her wolf felt territorial over Zaria. Her wolf was telling her it was her job to take care of Zaria the way no other wolf had. It was always to wise follow your wolf.

Kenrick looked up at Zaria's apartment windows and— remarkably—saw Zaria looking back. Zaria smiled sweetly and Kenrick felt like Zaria's bite was sinking deeply into her heart.

I need to know her. No matter what, Kenrick determined. She got out of the car and hurried upstairs. The two wolves on the door saluted.

"Everything okay?"

"No problems. The Mater, Vance, and Kyra were here earlier."

"Good." Kenrick knocked on the door and heard Zaria tell her to come in.

She walked in and immediately growled low and deep in her throat. Zaria was wearing a short denim shirt dress with a brown leather belt. Zaria must have noticed her staring silently, because she looked down at her dress and brushed the front with her hands. "Is everything all right? Is the dress okay? The Mater brought some clothes for me."

Kenrick found it difficult to form words. Her body was on fire, and it felt like there was a big neon sign pointing down at Zaria saying, *This is your wolf. The one you've been searching for.*

How could she be feeling this, and so soon? Kenrick's mother had often told her that the Great Mother didn't like to waste time. When she put your mate on your path, you'd know it.

"I know it," Kenrick said.

"Ricky? What are you saying?" Zaria said.

Kenrick shook herself. *What are you playing at?* "Sorry. Ignore me. You look really bonnie, Zaria."

Zaria smiled. "Thank you. Are we going running now?"

"No...yes...well, later. I thought I could take you for lunch then get an ice cream and walk down to the lake," Kenrick said.

Zaria folded her arms defensively. "That sounds nice, but I don't have any money and I can't let you pay for it."

Kenrick marched over to Zaria. "Why not?"

Zaria sighed and hugged herself. "Because dominants control submissives with money, and I promised myself I'd never be in debt to a dominant." Zaria regretted her words when she saw the look of hurt on Kenrick's face.

"What do you mean by that? A dominant wolf provides the meat for their family's table, but there's no debt involved. It's the wolf's duty."

Zaria couldn't look in Kendrick's hurt eyes any longer, so she walked over to the window and gazed out at lots of happy looking wolves and cubs coming and going. "Maybe things aren't as bad here in Wolfgang County, but I've been in debt to a wolf before, and I've seen my sister controlled by money."

Zaria could feel Kenrick approaching. Kenrick's scent sent shivers all over her body. She should not be reacting like this. She had to stop it.

"Zaria?" Kenrick's Scottish accent sent shivers over her ever-warming skin.

Zaria didn't move, but she could feel Kenrick's warm, reassuring presence.

"Please, turn around."

After a few seconds she did. Kenrick held out her open hands. "I know that what you've been through has coloured your opinion about dominant wolves, but please, give me a chance. We are not what you were brought up with." Kenrick reached out to Zaria's hand. "May I take your hand?"

Zaria was surprised. No wolf had ever asked permission to touch her before. She nodded and Kenrick took her hand and placed it on her chest.

"Can you feel my heart?" Kenrick said.

"Ricky—" Zaria protested.

But Kenrick was determined. "No, please. Feel my heart and look at me."

Zaria did and found herself falling into the deep blue eyes she found there.

"Zaria, I have never in my life hurt, physically or mentally, any submissive wolf. My mother would have flayed me alive. Buying you lunch or ice cream does not put you in my debt. It gives me the company of a beautiful lassie to share a meal with. Nothing more. Look in my eyes and feel my heart. I would rather cut off my own arm with a rusty blade than hurt you."

Zaria couldn't help but smile. "Lassie? Do people actually say that?"

A smile crept up on Kenrick's face. "In Scotland we do."

"Okay then, Highlander."

❖

Kenrick and Zaria walked from her apartment down Main Street. It had taken a monumental effort on Kenrick's part just to get this far. She watched Zaria look around nervously and check behind her quite often. It saddened Kenrick that even here, where she was safe, Zaria was still haunted by her past.

She would love to get her claws on Ovid and Leroux and see if they could frighten someone of their own size. It went against everything she was taught to harm others for no good reason, but Ovid and Leroux gave her every reason to tear them limb from limb.

"Zaria, no one is going to hurt you. You're safe here. I'm at your side." That last sentence betrayed as much as she was able to admit for the moment.

Zaria sighed. "It's hard to switch off when you've been doing it for most of your life. Where are we going anyway?"

"Well, there's either the Big Bad Wolf Diner for something more basic, or the New Moon Bar and Grill. What would you prefer?"

Zaria looked down at her feet. "Not the diner. Too many bad memories."

"Aye, maybe. The New Moon it is then. Let's go. It's just across the road."

When they reached the edge of the sidewalk, Kenrick automatically reached out to take Zaria's hand. Just as they touched, Kenrick realized what she was doing and pulled back.

"Sorry, sorry. I just acted out of instinct. I should have asked—" Kenrick blabbered.

"It's okay, Ricky. Really. No one's ever asked permission to touch me before, so you're different from anyone I've ever met."

"I'd never touch you without permission. I promise you."

Zaria smiled. "Let's just get across the road, huh?"

Kenrick smiled back. Zaria's smile made her head turn to mush. Was that supposed to happen? "Aye, let's go."

After managing to navigate the quiet road, they entered the New Moon Bar and Grill. The wolves already in the bar all looked suspiciously at the Lupa wolf they had no doubt heard about through pack gossip, but when Kenrick looked all around with equal fierceness, they went back to what they were doing.

She found a booth near the back so Zaria would have some privacy.

"This is a nice place," Zaria said.

"Yeah, the younger wolves mostly go to the Big Bad Wolf, but this is for us adults," Kenrick told her.

"We never had anything like this in the Lupa pack lands. It makes me sick that they actually had us believing the other packs lived in poverty."

"I'm sorry you were lied to, but you're here now. We can show you what being in a pack is really about."

Before Zaria could respond, a waitress Kenrick recognized came over holding menus. When she got to the table, she put her hand to her chest in salute.

"Hi, Kenrick, it's a pleasure to have you here with us again."

Shit. Why do people have to do that? Kenrick decided just to ignore it and carry on. "Hi, Judy, this is Zaria. She's staying with the pack for a while."

Judy didn't disappoint her and gave Zaria the biggest smile. "Glad to have you here, Zaria. Take a look at the menu and let us feed you."

They each took a menu and Judy left. Kenrick studied her menu, hoping Zaria wouldn't say anything about the saluting. She could feel Zaria's eyes staring at her, waiting for an explanation. "What looks good to you? I think the meat feast platter looks brilliant."

"Ricky?" Zaria asked.

Kenrick still didn't look up. "Hmm?"

"Why does everyone keep saluting you?" Zaria asked.

"Do they?" Kenrick tried to deflect the question.

"Yeah, they really do. You must be someone really important in the Wulver pack."

Kenrick finally needed to look up. "Me? No, it's just because I'm a visitor, I think. A cultural thing, a way to show respect to another pack."

Zaria searched her eyes for a while, then thankfully looked down at the menu. "Look at the prices, Ricky. I'll just have some soup, and water."

"Don't look at the prices. You said you'd let me buy us lunch. Please?"

Just then Judy came back over. "Have you decided yet?"

Zaria start to say, "Just s—"

But Kenrick cut her off. "Two large meat platters, large fries, and two lime Wulver Spring waters."

"You got it," Judy said.

She walked away and Zaria said, "Why did you do that?"

"Because I want to have a nice meal with you and you're being stubborn. I have money and no one to spend it on except myself. I think I can spend it on a meat platter for two without me claiming any rights over you. You told me you trust me."

Zaria closed her eyes and took a breath. She was fighting every instinct inside herself. She knew in her heart that she trusted Kenrick, but it was so hard to make her head understand this wasn't a Lupa wolf trying to get something from her.

She opened her eyes and said sarcastically, "The Wulvers must pay their jack of all trades well."

Kenrick smiled, clearly knowing she'd won this round. "Aye, they do."

When their meal came, they became relatively quiet. Both were enjoying the meal so much. Zaria had never eaten meat like this. It was so juicy and there was so much of it, and she allowed herself to let go and enjoy it. A few times she felt Kenrick's gaze on her as she ate. Kenrick looked away immediately but Zaria saw it unmistakably.

Zaria should have felt threatened, but Kenrick didn't make her feel like when Ovid ogled her, or any other Lupa wolf. It didn't feel wrong or make her feel objectified in any way. Kenrick's appreciative glances were sweet, especially her red cheeks when she realized she'd been caught.

It also made a thousand fresh spring forest leaves flutter in her stomach, and who could blame them? Ricky was gorgeous and different to any other wolf she had seen. She was like some kind of rock god, with a physique hewn from the wild Scottish mountains, and a wildness infused in her by the ancient Caledonian forest in which her ancestors had made their home.

Her mane of dreadlocked hair was crying out for Zaria to touch it, and at one point she got a flash of holding on to it as Kenrick lay on top of her. She shivered. Attraction and the urge to mate was a new emotion and she would need some time to process it. Luckily she wouldn't be here for long to be tempted.

CHAPTER NINE

K enrick led them down to the lake, and they sat on the sandy beach that bordered the water. At the ice cream shop, Zaria had been overwhelmed with all the choices, so Kenrick just ordered the biggest ice cream cone they did, with all the sprinkles and added extras for both of them.

She looked to her side and watched Zaria hungrily licking her ice cream. Kenrick felt a deep hunger low down in her sex at the sight. She was glad they got ice cream because it might cool her body down.

Kenrick forced herself to look away, which went against all her instincts. It was the same in the restaurant. She had never found a woman eating meat to be a turn-on before, but now it was, and Zaria caught her looking a few times.

It was the last thing she wanted. Zaria had spent her life being appraised sexually and being made to feel like a sexual object by the dominant wolves she knew, and now she was appraising her too. She had to show Zaria she was different.

"This lake is beautiful," Zaria said. "Is it as big as Wulver Loch?"

"No, Wulver Loch is bigger, but this is pretty enough in its own way, and it's *loch* not *lock*."

"Huh?" Zaria asked.

"People outside Scotland get the word wrong. Imagine you've got something caught in the back of your throat when you say it."

Zaria laughed. "You paint a lovely picture, wolf."

"Try it," Kenrick said.

"Loch."

"Hey, you got it." Kenrick gave her a high five.

Zaria pointed up to a point across the lake and halfway up the mountain where cars were parked. "What's up there, Ricky?"

"It's the lookout. Tourists park there to go on some of the walking trails, but the teenage wolves use it for something quite different." Kenrick winked at her.

Zaria smiled. "You mean a make-out spot?"

"Maybe," Kenrick replied coyly.

Zaria took a few licks of ice cream and said, "So, you're related to the Wolfgangs?"

"Yeah, all the British and Irish packs are. We take pride in our blood connections, and in our wolf pioneers who left to set up new packs in the New World, as it was at that time."

"The Lupas don't really have that kind of extended family. We come from a mix of Eastern European and West Asian packs, but we never kept up our history or connections. We had countless battles and wars with them in the past, that's all I know."

Kenrick would bet that Zaria got her genetics from West Asian packs, going by her darker colouring, and her deep brown hair and eyes. She was the most utterly beautiful woman Kenrick had ever seen.

"Can I ask you a question, Zaria?" Kenrick asked. Zaria continued licking her ice cream, making Kenrick almost forget her question. "Um…what happened before we found you?"

Zaria looked down and ran her free hand through the sand beneath them. "I made a mistake. Since I was sixteen, I've always moved around from place to place, job to job, never settling in one place too long, so Leroux and Ovid couldn't find me."

Kenrick finished her ice cream and rubbed her hands together. "Why is Ovid so determined to find you? You never became mated."

"No, but it was announced in the pack, and Ovid thinks I still belong to her. She's hunted me since I went through the rush, but I was protected until I was sixteen."

Kenrick sensed there was a lot of pain surrounding that incident, so she shifted the conversation back to what happened after that. "So, you were working in a diner?"

Zaria let out a breath. She was probably relived she wasn't being asked about Ovid.

"Yeah, it was a nice place and I became friends with the manager. She was so kind, giving me extra shifts because she knew I need the money, and I always got the leftover food. I became too comfortable and stayed too long."

"The Lupas found you?" Kenrick asked.

Zaria nodded. "I suppose the Alpha did her research and told you I attacked my landlord?"

Kenrick nodded. "Yeah."

Zaria discarded what was left of her ice cream in the paper bag that sat between them, ready for the trash bin. "I never wanted to hurt him. I never want to hurt anyone. I hate violence."

"I know that, Zari," Kenrick said affectionately.

"He tried to—I mean, he wanted to take his rent out of me in another way."

Kenrick growled. "Fucking bastard, preying on young women. I'd like to see him trying that with me. I wouldn't have just put him in hospital like you did. He'd be missing a few vital organs." Kenrick's wolf was raging that anyone tried to touch Zaria. She wanted to protect her and make sure something like that never happened again. "Sorry about the language. My ma would kick me up and down Wulver Loch for talking like that."

That brought a small smile to Zaria's face. "That's okay. No one's ever been angry or stuck up for me before, except my sister."

"I'm here for you, Zari, if you want me to be." Maybe Kenrick had said too much. After all, she hardly knew her, but her wolf was very clear about what she wanted. Kenrick felt an electricity whenever they were close, and she wondered if Zaria felt it.

Zaria looked at Kenrick's hand sitting between them, and then just went back to her story.

"He had me up against a wall. I partially shifted and pushed him. He flew across the room and hit the wall. I ran. I knew then that I would have to leave the area, so the next morning I went to the diner to get my pay and let my friend Chrissy know I had to leave. The Lupa wolves arrived, and I fought, but I wasn't strong enough against two dominants. They cuffed me, shoved me in the trunk, and—" Zaria's voice cracked as tears came to her eyes. She tried to keep control but the thought of what a horrible death the Lupas gave Chrissy overwhelmed her.

Kenrick turned around and opened her arms, and for only the second time in her life, Zaria went willingly into another wolf's arms.

Kenrick's reassuring scent was so calming. She felt safe and she couldn't help pressing her nose into her neck. "Chrissy died because of me, Ricky. I heard her screams."

"It's okay, bonnie lassie. No one can get you now. Her death is on the Lupas, not you," Kenrick said.

It would be so easy to fall for Kenrick's charms. So, so easy. She found her fingertips stroking the hairs at the nape of Kenrick's neck. Zaria pulled back and gazed into Kenrick's eyes. and Kenrick's eyes turned yellow, a clear sign of wolf attraction. She assumed her eyes were the same.

As their lips got closer, Zaria saw a flash of Ovid's face coming at her. She jumped up and brushed the sand off her.

"Zari, are you okay?" Kenrick got up quickly.

"Yes, can you take me home?"

"What about our run in the forest?" Kenrick asked.

Zaria felt panic spread all over her body. She had to get away from Ricky. She couldn't allow this growing attraction to take hold of her. She had to leave tonight.

"I'm tired. I just need to go home, please?"

Kenrick looked really confused and a bit disappointed. "Aye, all right then. Let's go."

❖

When they got back to the apartment. Zaria found no guards, just as the Mater had said. Her Alpha listened and took her advice? Again Zaria's guilt at deceiving these good people ate away at her. If they knew that she wasn't being honest…

She stopped at the door and said, "I'd like to be on my own if you don't mind, Ricky."

"Oh, okay," Kenrick said with disappointment.

She felt terrible for hurting Kenrick this way, but she promised herself she would never be owned by a dominant like her sister was. That was the purpose of mating and a mate bite. And as kind as Kenrick was, she couldn't risk losing her heart to this handsome wolf—she had to protect herself. Tonight, she had to finish her task here and leave.

Kenrick stuffed her hands in her jeans pockets and stared at the floor. "If you want to go running tomorrow, I probably won't be able to go till the evening. I'm starting my first day at Venator with Dante."

"Why are you working there?" Zaria asked.

Kenrick ran her hand over her dreadlocks nervously. Whatever this was for, it stressed Kenrick out.

"I told you I'm a bit of a jack of all trades in the Wulver pack…"

Zaria nodded and Kenrick suddenly found her leather wristbands very interesting. It was strange and kind of sweet to see a dominant so unsure of herself. Zaria felt even more guilty at what she had to do tonight.

"Well, I've got a new job in the office to start when I get home. Kind of a new life, and my pater thought it would be good for me to come here and shadow my cousin. Get used to working with figures, and staffing, that kind of thing."

"And you're not looking forward to it?"

Kenrick looked up at her and, almost like a child, said, "I have to wear a suit."

Zaria had the biggest urge to pull Kenrick into her arms then. There was something so innocently sweet in Ricky's character.

"And a suit's bad?" Zaria said.

Kenrick held out her arms. "Do I look like I would fit in an office? I've been dreading it—it's not me."

"Then don't take the job. Stick to the jack of all trades thing you enjoy."

Kenrick closed her eyes and then shook her head. "It's not an option. Kind of a duty sort of thing. Anyway, you don't want to hear me complaining. I'll leave you to it. Night."

"Night, Ricky."

Zaria ached inside as she watched Kenrick walk away. Kenrick had given her so much comfort and support since she arrived, and Zaria couldn't do the same for her.

She went into the apartment and locked the door. When they left the lakeside, everything felt so clear to her. She had to get away from the biggest temptation she'd ever faced, a big hunk of a wolf, who was kind, generous, sensitive, and incredibly good-looking.

Zaria couldn't understand how she had come so close to kissing her. Since she went through the rush, she had associated the urge to mate and attraction to other wolves as something bound to end in pain. Nothing good ever came of giving over that part of yourself to a dominant wolf, but here she was nearly kissing one. Maybe it was living in this strange wolf pack where submissive wolves walked around with smiles on their faces, not haunted looks, and cubs were happy and anxiety free.

Zaria let her head fall against the back of the door. *It can't be what it seems, could it?* Behind closed doors surely relationships were different?

"I have to get out of here."

She hurried to the bedroom and packed the clothes that the Mater had given her, ready to leave as soon as she got back. The Lupas might be out there, but staying here and risking letting her emotions take hold of her was not an option.

Zaria finished with the bag and waited for the dark of night to come. Then she headed for the window. She might not have guards on the door anymore, but she wasn't completely trusted, and suspicions would be raised if they saw her wolf leaving by the front door.

She took her clothes off, left them in a neat pile, and opened the window. She climbed out and down the fire escape. Once she was at the bottom and was sure she was alone in the back alley, Zaria shifted, and her wolf ran off, trying her best to keep away from the populated areas.

About ten minutes out of town, Zaria reached a large house on the edge of the forest. She had never been this close before, never been this close to the reason that made her life of hiding, running, and barely making ends meet worthwhile.

Her sister's cub, her nephew, a child Leroux thought died along with her mate.

Zaria crept around the back of the house quietly. She passed the kitchen window and quickly hid behind a tree when she saw Flash and Vance by the kitchen table. Zaria watched them for a while. They were drying some dishes together, and then Flash pulled a laughing Vance into his arms and they danced together. Vance was a submissive, but he didn't seem to be the least bit fearful of his dominant partner. Everything was so different here, so apparently perfect, but it couldn't be.

While they were engrossed in each other, Zaria's wolf made a dash for the side of the house from the tree she was hiding behind. She looked up to the bedroom window above her and gulped hard. Up there was the purpose for her life—Marco. Never in a million years did she think all those years ago when she ran to the Wolfgang County border with her newborn nephew in her arms, that he would have such a safe, comfortable life. She and her sister took a risk and trusted their instincts that the Wolfgangs were good wolves and would look after the boy and keep him from his pater—Leroux.

Zaria had promised her sister she would always look out for her son, and she had, keeping close, checking in on him, and even when Leroux kidnapped Marco and the sheriff's daughter Tia, she had followed them and helped lead the Alpha to them.

Thank the Great Mother Leroux had no idea the significance of one of the cubs she had kidnapped. Over the years, Marco had spotted her wolf checking on him from the edge of the forest. He seemed to be drawn to her and to instinctively know they had a connection. He spoke to her every time, and it hurt so badly not to respond to him, her only family in the world.

It was better Marco didn't know about her or his past, lest Leroux work out her great secret. But now might be the time to move on. Marco was safe and protected, but now that Leroux's wolves were very active again, her presence might lead her to him. Or was that just an excuse?

Zaria's wolf pawed the gravel beneath her paws. She had never felt so unsure of her purpose in life. Coming to Wolfgang County and seeing first-hand how they lived as couples, families, and a pack had opened her eyes. Then a certain big Scottish wolf bounced into her life and woke up her bruised, broken heart. Zaria was afraid of what would happen if she stayed. She would hurt Ricky by just leaving without saying goodbye, but otherwise Ricky might convince her to stay, even though Ricky was only here for a few weeks, and she might say yes. That was what worried her so much.

This had to be goodbye. She looked up to Marco's window and let out a soft whine, hopefully not loud enough to alert Flash and Vance. Zaria repeated the call a few times, and finally Marco came to the window. The biggest smile came to his face when he saw her. Zaria's heart filled with joy to see him. He was a good-looking boy with so much of his mother in him.

It was worth it. Even if I died tomorrow, my life would have been worthwhile.

Marco opened the window and shouted down. "It's you. Don't move, please. I'm coming down."

As soon as he shut the window and began to run downstairs, Zaria knew she had to leave.

I love you Marco. Have a good life.

❖

Leroux felt like she had a new lease of life as soon as she received the enchanted ring. She was full of energy and vigour. She hadn't felt this good since before she fought with Dante for the first time.

Tonight she was doing her favourite kind of hunting, hunting for female humans. While on a night run in the wooded area behind their base, she caught the scent of a human female out jogging, and as fit as the human was, she couldn't outrun a wolf.

Leroux's black wolf streaked through the trees and as she gained on the human, she tripped on a branch.

I have you now, human.

The human seemed to have injured her ankle because she couldn't stand and could only drag herself away. Leroux shifted back to skin and the woman screamed. The scream and fear she scented gave her such a thrill. She could have any submissive wolf she wanted—a few had joined them from their pack lands when Leroux established a base in Knoxton—but Leroux wanted more of a challenge.

Leroux wanted fear, power, and control and she got that by hunting women down. This pretty blond human backed up against a tree trunk.

"Please don't hurt me. Please let me go."

Leroux was breathing heavily, full of hunger for sex and dominance. "I don't think so, human."

She flashed her eyes and bared her teeth. The human screamed and held her hands protectively over herself.

❖

Ovid met her Alpha by the back door to the house. Leroux's black wolf shifted back to skin and Ovid saw blood coating Leroux's face and neck.

She handed Leroux a change of clothes. "We have the seer, Alpha."

Leroux pulled on the clothes quickly. "Good. Send someone to do a clean-up in the forest. We don't want any extra human attention."

They walked through the kitchen, and Ovid said to Cera, "You—clean-up in the woods. Now."

"Yes, Second."

Leroux grabbed a towel as she passed through the kitchen. "Where are they?"

"She is in the cellar," Ovid told her.

"She? Nice." Leroux grinned.

She walked into the office and over to the safe in the corner. The safe turned out to be pretty handy—she had only obtained the combination from the previous owners thinking there might be money kept in it, but now it housed the enchanted ring. She didn't trust anyone in her pack anywhere near it while she was in pelt, so it stayed here.

Leroux took out the ring and slid it on her finger. Every time she put it on she got a rush of power, and she couldn't wait to use it on Dante.

"Why did you want a seer, Alpha?" Ovid asked.

Leroux sat on the desk. "Because something is bothering me. There's a connection between the Wolfgangs and Zaria, and it might be crucial to our plans. Why has Zaria stayed around this area since she ran? There are plenty of places she could have gone where it would be nearly impossible for us to find her."

"That's true," Ovid said.

"I know, so let's find out." Leroux lifted the laptop they had recovered from Zaria's studio and walked downstairs to the basement.

Before she walked through the door, Ovid said, "The seer has a little brother with her. Might be useful as an incentive."

"Well done, Second." Leroux entered the cellar and found a young woman, maybe twenty if that, and a little boy on her lap.

The appearance of blood on Leroux's face appeared to put fear into the woman and boy. "Let us go, please?"

"If you help me, I will, so let's not play games. Just get down to business. I understand you need an object to connect to another person?" Leroux said.

"Yes, that's right."

Leroux handed her the laptop and said, "Put down the boy and answer my questions."

❖

Sometime later Leroux and Ovid came up from the cellar. Leroux couldn't believe Zaria had managed to keep this secret all this time.

"Marta had the cub?" Ovid said.

"Yes, it seems Zaria likes keeping secrets." Leroux felt sick at the thought of her flesh and blood being brought up as a Wolfgang.

"When we retrieve Zaria, do you want to take your cub?" Ovid asked.

Leroux roared angrily. "He's a Wolfgang now and no cub of mine. No doubt weak and pathetic, but we can use him to our advantage."

"How?" Ovid asked as they walked into the office.

Leroux twisted the ring on her finger. "I want to draw Dante out of Wolfgang County, not fight her on her on land with her whole pack behind her. They are taking care of Zaria for some reason. If I tempt Zaria out, Dante might follow. In fact, I'm sure she will."

"As long as *I* get Zaria. What did you have in mind?" Ovid asked.

"I need you to get hold of a phone number, Second." Leroux grinned.

CHAPTER TEN

K enrick felt like an idiot. An idiot in more ways than one. She took one last look at herself in the mirror and stuffed her tie in her pocket. This suit her mother had bought for her was everything she feared. Uncomfortable, constrained, and just not her.

Her second reason for feeling like an idiot was her whining like a little cub to Zaria last night about it. Zaria didn't need to hear her problems. Kenrick didn't normally share her fears with anyone, but Zaria was different. She felt she could tell her anything.

Kenrick hesitated at her bedroom door and thought back to yesterday by the lake. She had nearly kissed Zaria—like there was a magnetic pull, with her wolf egging her on to kiss her. At first she thought Zaria was responding, but then she recoiled in fear and Kenrick felt guilty.

She knew Zaria had issues with mating and dominant wolves, and she obviously wasn't ready for that. She was trying to be as gentle and careful as she could with Zaria, but every moment Kenrick spent in her company, her heart filled with want and a need to protect her.

I'm only here for a few weeks and I'll be gone. Stop thinking like this.

Kenrick shook off her thoughts and opened the door. Dion and Meghan shot past her at the top of the stairs.

"Morning guys," Kenrick said.

Meghan doubled back and gave Kenrick a hug. "Good morning, Ricky. We're late for school."

Meghan ran off and Dion said, "Hey, Ricky, will you play video games with me tonight?"

"Aye, I'd love to. See you after school."

Kenrick walked downstairs just as Eden was seeing the two kids out the front door. "Remember to give your teacher your field trip money."

Eden sighed when she shut the door.

"Busy morning?" Kenrick said.

Eden rolled her eyes. "You could say that. We all slept in." Then Eden's face lit up. "Come and let me take a look at you in your suit."

Kenrick trudged towards her like a cub. Eden brushed some fluff from her shoulder and gushed, "You look so handsome and smart."

"I feel like an idiot," Kenrick replied.

"I know it's not you, Ricky, but you do look good in it from where I'm standing. Dante did say you didn't have to wear one."

Kenrick pulled herself together. "No, I don't want Dante's staff or clients to think she has some uncivilized Highlander working for her."

"Where's the tie?" Eden asked.

"In my pocket. I…it looked stupid," Kenrick said.

"I was thinking," Eden said, "why don't you ask Zaria to Lena and Caden's cub celebration on Friday? You got on so well yesterday."

Kenrick would have loved to, but with how frosty Zaria was last night, she didn't think Zaria would agree. "I'm not sure if she'd want to, Eden. Zaria doesn't do well in large groups of dominant wolves."

"All the more reason to bring her. She has a warped sense of what wolf relationships should be. We need to show her she's wrong, and what better way than a gathering full of happy wolves, couples and cubs, celebrating a new arrival."

Kenrick nodded and looked at her shoes. "Aye, you're right. I'll ask, if I see her."

Eden narrowed her eyes and said, "You like her, don't you, Ricky?"

Kenrick was about to speak but was interrupted by Dante running down the stairs, frantically trying close her briefcase.

"We're late, Ricky. Let's go."

Eden growled and pulled Dante to her by the lapels. "Not before I get my kiss, Alpha."

Dante growled and they kissed each other passionately. Kenrick felt she was intruding on their moment.

"I'll wait outside at the car, Dante."

As she walked outside, she prayed to the Great Mother to bless her with a mate and cubs. Nothing would make her happier. Then Zaria's face floated across her mind.

"Zari," Kenrick said wishfully.

❖

Wolfgang executives and heads of departments filed out of the Venator conference room. Dante sat at the head of the table with Kenrick beside her, taking notes on an iPad.

"So you made it through your first day. How do you feel?" Dante asked.

"It's different, but I've got lots of new ideas from the way you do things. My pater is from a different generation, and everything isn't as streamlined as it could be. I think for the business to grow, I need to modernize. Upgrade computer systems and equipment. That way I can keep a better handle on the business."

"You're already thinking like a business wolf," Dante said with a wink.

Kenrick laughed. "I don't know about that, but I want keep growing the Wulver brand and make my pater and grandpater proud."

Dante closed her folders and said, "Don't be hard on yourself—it takes some time to adjust. I think it took me about a year working in here before I got on top of things. My heart was always out there, in the fields with Caden, working with the cattle."

Kenrick tapped her fingernails on the table. "I just hope I don't disappoint my pater. I want to make him proud."

Dante smacked her on the back. "You know you will. You've done enough for one day. I've got a couple of calls to make before I head home, but you go ahead."

"Thanks."

"Oh, how is Zaria doing? I hear you took her out yesterday," Dante said.

Kenrick sighed. "Yeah, I did. She's so damaged, Dante. The Lupas have really scarred her, especially Ovid. She hasn't told me any more than she told you, but you can guess. Thanks for taking the guards off her door."

"The Mater trusts her, that's good enough for me, but I will remain cautious. Also, the Lupas will know she is here now, and if they want her, there's even more reason to attack us."

Kenrick growled. "They'll only get near Zaria over my dead body."

❖

Zaria walked down Main Street, her head down, still looking over her shoulder. She didn't think she'd ever get over that impulse. She couldn't quite believe she was still here. Last night after seeing Marco, she returned to her apartment, picked up her bag, and started walking to the county border. As she walked, she couldn't get Kenrick's face out of her mind. She felt like she was betraying Ricky and all her kindness. Zaria had stopped at the border and asked her heart what she should do, and without further hesitation she turned back. She had to at least tell Kenrick face to face that she was leaving.

So here she was, making her way to Venator to meet Kenrick after her first day at the office. She knew this was a big deal for Kenrick and wanted to be there for her after brushing her off last night. She could at least give Kenrick some support before she told her she was leaving.

A familiar voice roused Zaria from her deep thoughts. It was Kyra, the wolf who came with the Mater and Vance to bring her clothes and welcome her. She'd really enjoyed Kyra's company. She'd never had friends since she left the Lupa pack lands, and it was nice to have someone her own age to talk to. This time Kyra had a dog with her. It was highly unusual for weres to have dogs. The dogs tended to get spooked by them, but this one looked quite happy, and all the wolves that passed Kyra stopped to pet it.

She walked across the road to the front of the Big Bad Wolf Diner, where Kyra was standing. Kyra immediately gave her a hug. Another new thing to her was the close reassuring touches from fellow wolves. Wolves thrived on close community and Zaria had been alone for a long, long time.

"Hi, Zaria. Let me introduce you to our dog, Storm."

She held out her hand to let Storm sniff and suss her out. "Hi, Storm. He's a handsome boy."

Kyra smiled brightly. "He sure is. So, how are you settling in?"

"Slowly, I guess," Zaria said. "I'm not used to being in a wolf pack, but everyone has been so kind."

"Great. My friend Lena—you know, the pack Second's mate?"

Zaria did remember. Caden was the most suspicious of her. "Yeah?"

"Well, she and Caden are having a party for their new cub on Friday. Lena wanted me to invite you. She really wants to meet you."

Zaria felt panic. She'd be in a room full of dominants, and that gave her such fear. "I don't know, Kyra. I'm not good in crowds, and besides I'm not a Wolfgang."

Kyra grasped her hand. "You don't have to be frightened of anyone any more. You're one of us now, no matter what you think. At least think about it?"

"Okay, I will."

"Fabulous, now I need to run. Wedding planning with Ripp." Kyra then rummaged in her bag and pulled out an envelope. "I almost forgot. This is for you. See you later." Kyra handed her the envelope and ran off.

Zaria opened it and pulled out an invitation to Kyra and Ripp's mating ceremony.

She closed her eyes and sighed. This wolf pack was being so nice to her, and she was lying to them. Eventually, she'd either have to come clean or run. But which?

❖

Kenrick walked down the steps outside the Venator building. Wolves saluted her as they passed. Zaria was going to find out who she was eventually, but should she tell her now or wait until she'd gained more of her trust?"

At the bottom of the stairs she spotted Zaria siting on the last step, waiting for her. Kenrick's heart soared. She stopped for a second and just gazed at Zaria.

The afternoon sun shone on her and amplified that imaginary arrow she thought the Great Mother was showing her. Kenrick was just mesmerized by Zaria's long dark hair. She couldn't see her eyes from here but could remember every detail of them. Kenrick could lose herself in Zaria's deep brown eyes. She had fallen asleep last night thinking of those eyes and wishing that Zaria could feel how she did.

Kenrick walked up to her and said, "Zari?"

Zaria stood up and looked her up and down. "You look good in your suit."

Kenrick took off her suit jacket and put it over her shoulder. "It just feels wrong to me."

"Maybe it's what it symbolizes that bothers you," Zaria suggested.

Did Zaria know? Had someone told her? "What do you mean?"

"That you're giving up the life you love for another, working in an office environment, I meant."

"Oh, okay." Kenrick breathed a sigh of relief. "So what brings you here?"

Zaria looked away quickly. "I just wanted to see how your first day went and thought we could talk."

"Why don't we go for a run? I can't wait to get out of this and feel the ground beneath my paws."

"Sure," Zaria said.

Kenrick's spirits lifted. Running with Zaria sounded like the best thing in the world. "Let's go."

She took Zaria's hand without thinking but was so happy when Zaria didn't pull away. That was a big thing. Zaria trusted her.

They walked along the lakeside slowly on their way to the edge of the forest, chatting about Kenrick's day as they went. Zaria didn't know when to bring up that she was leaving. Kenrick was full of energy and excitement about their run, and she didn't want to kill the moment.

"So, tell me about your pack, the Wulvers, and your family," Zaria said.

"There's not much to tell really. We live a pretty quiet life in Wulver Forest. There's the distillery, the first part of our business and the most important."

"Is it true that the Wulvers can drink alcohol?" Zaria asked.

Kenrick smiled. "Yes, we and the Irish Filtiaran pack can. It's in our blood. We've built up a tolerance to it, a bit like snake handlers can build up a tolerance to some poisons."

Zaria shook her head. "I always assumed it was a myth. I mean, even coffee gives me a buzz I can't handle. Tell me more."

"Um...the two most important things to the Wulvers are the loch and the forest." Kenrick stopped and turned to her. She put her hand on her heart and said, "The spirits of the loch and the trees are written on our hearts, and even though I'm so far away, if I close my eyes, I can still smell the fresh clear loch water, and the pine of our deep forest."

Kenrick had closed her eyes and appeared to be lost in the moment. She was so beautiful like this, so beautiful that Zaria had to stop from reaching out and touching her.

"That was beautiful, Ricky. Wulver Forest sounds perfect," Zaria said.

Kenrick opened her eyes. "It is, and I'm missing it, but now that I've met you it was all worth it."

The tension hung heavily between them. Zaria couldn't believe her wolf was making her feel this way. Having fought against attraction since she left Lupa pack lands, to feel it now with a wolf who she had to leave was maddening.

Why her?

Because she is the one, she felt her wolf tell her.

Stop it. Zaria had to change this atmosphere between them. "What about your family?"

A slightly melancholy look came across Kenrick's face. She started to walk again and Zaria caught up quickly.

"Ricky? Don't you want to talk about your family?"

"What? No, of course I do. There's my pater, Fergus and my ma, Elspeth." Kenrick was growing ever more nervous at Zaria's line of questioning.

"What do they do exactly? You said your pater worked in the office end of the Wulver business."

Tell her. Tell her now, Kenrick told herself. The lie was only going to grow and grow, but she couldn't bear the thought of losing Zaria's trust.

So she lied again, and then changed the subject. "Aye, administration. Nothing exciting. My best friend is called Rhuri. We do everything together."

"Are they a submissive?" Zaria questioned with an edge to her voice.

Did Zaria really care if anyone had a claim over her? "No, dominant. She's unmated but takes care of her niece. Her sister was killed and her cub was brought back to us. It's hard for Rhuri on her own, she's not exactly the mother type, and her niece Milo is half witch, but no one loves that child more than Rhuri, and the whole pack chips in."

"That's really nice. She sounds like a kind wolf," Zaria said.

Kenrick could sense Zaria's sadness. She knew what it was like to be a young cub on her own.

"We're not all bad, Zari. Dominants, I mean. We care, we love, we respect. I wish you could understand that."

Zaria didn't reply and they walked on in silence.

When they got under the cover of the trees, Kenrick threw her jacket on the ground and immediately began to pull off her shirt and kick off her shoes.

Zaria hungrily appraised Kenrick's naked torso and arms. She was so solid, so strong, and whereas she always had seen strength and muscles as weapons that could be used against her and other submissives, Kenrick's strength made her feel safe, excited, horny, hungry—all the things she had never experienced before. Was this normal in other packs? The sweet story of Kenrick's best friend made her want to think it was true, but it was so hard to fight against her fear.

As Zaria gazed at Kenrick's body, she felt her wolf's teeth breaking through her gums, and saliva filled her mouth. Zaria's wolf told her to go over there and sink her teeth into Kenrick's shoulder and claim her.

Zaria closed her eyes. *Stop it. I can't.*

When she opened her eyes, Kenrick was standing right in front of her, and Zaria couldn't take her eyes from Kenrick's torso. Her small breasts and hard nipples were just in front of her, and she had the urge to scratch her claws right across her chest, then lick the wound she had made. The very thought made her sex wet and ache so very desperately.

"Are you okay, Zari?" Kenrick asked.

Zaria quickly gathered up Kenrick's discarded clothes and put them in a pile. "You can't just throw your clothes anywhere, Ricky."

"Relax, lassie. It'll be fine."

By the Great Mother, Zaria thought. Every time she opened her mouth, Kenrick was sexy. That accent did things to her. Why did she have to be so perfect?

Kenrick took a big breath of air. "Smell the scent of the forest, Zari. It makes you feel alive. Not the same as Wulver Forest, but still." Kenrick hadn't shifted but she ran and grabbed a tree branch. She vaulted up into the tree and clambered up higher.

"Ricky? What are you doing?"

"Having fun. I love to play in trees. Watch," Kenrick said.

Kenrick climbed higher up the tree then walked out onto a long branch. She balanced liked a tightrope walker. Zaria had never seen a wolf so at home in her human form and enjoying it as much as her wolf form.

"Be careful, Ricky," Zaria shouted up.

Kenrick looked down at her with the biggest smile on her face. "I don't need to be careful. I grew up jumping through the trees."

She stopped in the middle of the branch and leapt high in the air. Zaria gasped, but Kenrick landed perfectly back on the branch with only the slightest of shakes.

"Come down, Ricky," Zaria shouted.

Kenrick jumped off, swinging round the branch with her hands, and summersaulted, landing right in front of Zaria, breathing hard, her eyes yellow, her teeth bared.

Zaria was lost for words. She had never seen anything so erotic as Kenrick after her physical display of strength and skill. Her muscles were taut and a slight sheen of sweat covered her skin.

Kenrick growled, low and wanting, and on pure instinct Zaria responded with her own growl and walked the few steps to Kenrick. Her hand shook as she placed it between Kenrick's breasts on her chest, and then her nose followed Kenrick's dizzying erotic scent to her neck. She didn't touch but ran her nose all over the crook of Kenrick's neck and shoulder.

Zaria moved to Kenrick's cheek and whispered, "You could have hurt yourself, Ricky."

Kenrick touched her cheek gently to Zaria and rubbed her scent on her. "I'm a big wolf, Zari. I can look after myself."

Kenrick's scent was everywhere now swarming around her head, entering her body. The scent of lush, wet forests and sex had a dizzying effect on her, almost the way humans described being drunk. Then her mind threw cold water over her hot, hungry body. Drunk on love. Every young wolf had heard adults describe the need, the want, the desire for their mate as drunk on love, and Zaria felt it for the first time in her life.

She pulled away sharply and saw Kenrick had tight balled fists, her knuckles white with the effort of staying put. *She wanted to touch me. She feels it too.*

In that instant Zaria saw what this was becoming. Kenrick was trying to be the best-behaved dominant she could be so as not to frighten Zaria, but that could never last, and she was not going to be subjugated by any wolf, no matter how kind and gentle they appeared at first.

"No, Kenrick." Zaria held her hand up, putting distance between them.

"No what?" Kenrick took her hand. "Can't you feel this? I have since I found you lying in the road."

Zaria pulled her hand back. "No."

"I don't believe you. I know you can feel it. We have a connection, Zari."

"Ricky, I'm sorry. I met you at Venator because I wanted to talk to you," Zaria said.

Kenrick's body was thrumming with energy. She wanted to get closer to Zari, get to know everything about her and explore this connection between them, but she kept pushing her away. "What did you want to talk about?" Kenrick asked.

"I came to tell you I'm leaving Wolfgang County. It's time to move on."

"No," Kenrick said fiercely. She immediately regretted it when she saw Zaria taking a few steps back from her. "I'm sorry, Zari. I didn't mean to shout, but you can't leave. The Lupas are out there, just waiting for you."

"They always have been and I've always looked after myself," Zaria said.

"But they know your exact whereabouts now. Once you step over our border, they'll be waiting for you."

Kenrick felt panic in every cell of her body. She couldn't bear the thought of Zaria leaving and Ovid or any other Lupa getting their hands on Zaria.

"Besides, you have no money or anything. Why not bide your

time, get a job at the diner, and save some money? At least until I go home in a few weeks."

Zaria sighed and covered her face with her hands. Kenrick knew she was getting through to her.

"Please think about it, Zari. You know I'm right. If you make some money here with us, you don't have to be looking over your shoulder."

Kenrick would use any more time she had with Zaria to persuade her that they were meant for each other.

Finally Zaria said, "All right, but just until I've made money—and if the diner will give me a job."

Kenrick mentally punched the air. "Let's go run."

CHAPTER ELEVEN

Zaria had nearly finished working her first week at the Big Bad Wolf Diner, and she had to admit that it was fun as well as satisfying that she was earning her keep in Wolfgang County.

She piled empty coffee cups onto her tray and walked through to the kitchen with them. Dezzie was back there cutting up a cake for display out front. It was one made from a recipe Zaria had given her. A recipe handed down from her grandmother.

"Hey, Zaria, your cake is a huge hit. This is the last of the original batch. Mom is going to make a few more this afternoon."

"I'm glad people like it," Zaria said.

"Like it? They're crazy about it," Dezzie said. "I'll see you out front." Dezzie walked out to the front of the diner.

Dezzie, who helped her mom run the diner, had been so kind to her. Since the first day she had come in and asked for a job, they had taken her under their wing. It would be so easy to give in and sink into the welcoming warmth of the Wolfgangs. They were kind and gave her shelter, food, and medical care, all whilst knowing she was born a Lupa.

She put the dishes in the dishwasher and headed back out to the front. Dezzie was chatting to Kyra at the counter, her mom was cooking on the grill behind the counter, and the sound of laughter and chatter emanated from the customers sitting at the tables.

This pack was like a dream—everyone was happy and productive, it all seemed too good to be true, but every day that passed made that thought seem silly. If she stayed here, she could have a safe, comfortable life, not looking over her shoulder, but Zaria couldn't handle seeing Marco every day and not telling him who she was.

Then there was Kenrick.

Zaria saw Kenrick at least once a day. She came into the diner each morning and they ran together most nights. Since the day at the forest when she nearly gave in to her need, and they nearly touched and kissed, Zaria had kept her distance emotionally and physically. Kenrick hadn't pushed their obvious attraction, thankfully, but every part of her was aching to lie in the safety of Kenrick's arms. Leaving Marco and Kenrick was going to be so hard.

"Zaria? Come here." Dezzie waved her over to where she and Kyra were standing.

"Hey, morning, Kyra," Zaria said.

"Are you coming to the cub celebration tonight? Lena can't wait to meet you," Kyra said.

"I don't think her mate Caden trusts me that much," Zaira said.

Dezzie let out a laugh. "Don't worry about Caden. She's in full wolfie protection mode because of the cub."

"Yeah," Kyra said. "Besides, Lena will keep her on her leash."

It never ceased to amaze her how relaxed these Wolfgangs were about their dominant partners. Saying something like that, even as a joke, to a Lupa wolf would get you a black eye, if not more.

"So Ripp and I will pick you up. No arguments," Kyra said.

Zaria was just about to respond when the bell on the diner door rang and Dezzie said with a conspiratorial growl, "Unless a big hunk of Scottish prime beef wants to take you."

Zari looked up and her heart and everything else in her body fluttered. It was Kenrick.

"On that note, I better run," Kyra said. "See you tonight."

Kyra spoke to Kenrick as she passed, and then she walked over to the counter.

"Morning, Ricky," Dezzie said, then whispered, "I'll leave sexy wolf to you."

"No—" But Dezzie was gone, and Kenrick was standing in front of her with a big smile on her face.

"Morning, Zari. How are you?"

One simple question, but even Kenrick's voice turned her on. It caressed her skin and made her hot.

"I'm okay. What can I get you?" Zaria said. *Concentrate on what she wants and now how much licking her neck would make more sense.* "Two decaf cappuccinos and two muffins, please. Dante's waiting outside for me."

Zaria was happy to get behind the coffee machine and have some distance between them. Not that it helped much. Kenrick's close proximity made goosebumps erupt all over her body. "Sure, I'll just be a minute." She had to find a polite way of stopping their nightly runs, because each night spent in Kenrick's company made Zaria want her all the more. They had a bond without even trying, and each night before falling asleep she imagined Kenrick kissing her, touching her body, and making love to her, but as she was enjoying these erotic thoughts, Kenrick's face was always replaced by Ovid's, hurting and violating her.

Zaria couldn't give in to her attraction—the cost of mating was too high. She handed Kenrick the two coffees and opened a bag to put the two muffins in. "So, what are you up to today at Venator?"

Kenrick sighed. "We're going to have a working lunch with one of the supermarket chains that Venator supplies. Dezzie's sending over sandwich platters and cakes."

"Why are you sighing?" Zaria asked.

"The phrase *working lunch* makes me shiver. It's so corporate, so constrained, so not me," Kenrick said.

The corners of Zaria's mouth rose. "Is that why you've got the tie on today?"

"Aye, I thought I better make the effort," Kenrick replied like a little boy forced to wear a suit on Sunday.

Before Zaria could stop herself, she reached over and straightened Kenrick's tie. "You'll do great, Highlander. Believe in yourself." Kenrick grinned like a cat who got the cream. It was a simple but intimate act and she shouldn't be giving Kenrick any encouragement.

"Aye, thanks. I better go." Kenrick grabbed the coffees and bag of muffins, walked backward whilst never taking her eyes off of Zaria, and bumped into a table and chairs. "Shit. Eh, sorry. I'll see you at our meeting point for our run, and then I'll take you to the cub ceremony, that okay?"

"Yeah, I guess." She couldn't say no to Kenrick's face.

Zaria screwed up her eyes in disbelief as on Kenrick's way out she managed to bump into more chairs and then the door frame on the way out. Was this the same wolf who jumped around in trees like a monkey?

"Drunk on love," Dezzie said as she walked up beside Zaria.

"What?" Zaria asked.

"The bad coordination. She's drunk on love for you, honey."

Zaria turned to her and said, "What? I didn't do anything."

Dezzie chuckled. "Of course you did." She imitated Zaria leaning over the counter to straighten Kenrick's tie. "That kind of attention and telling them they're great turns dominants to mush."

"But we're not—"

"Well, you both sure look as if you're heading towards some wolfie love, and she's such a great catch, Zaria. Being Alpha and all," Dezzie said.

Zaria did a double take. "Alpha? What do you mean?"

Dezzie narrowed her eyes. "Surely you knew she was going to be Alpha of the Wulver pack in a few weeks? Her pater is stepping down."

Then suddenly everything made sense. The saluting everyone did, the nerves over a new job that Kenrick had, and the reluctance to talk about it and her family.

She lied to me.

❖

Kenrick was worried. She had waited at the forest meeting place for Zaria for an hour, and she wouldn't answer the phone in her apartment. She quickly drove over to Zaria's apartment, worried that something had happened to her.

She ran upstairs and knocked on the door. "Zaria, it's Ricky. Are you okay?"

There was no response, but Kenrick could scent that she was in the apartment and hear her moving around.

"Zaria, I can hear you're in there. What's going on?"

Finally she heard Zaria walking towards the door. When she opened it, Zaria looked different. Fearful, distrustful. Almost like when they had first met.

"Is everything all right? You never came to meet me."

"Who was I supposed to meet? Ricky or the new Wulver Alpha?" Zaria said.

Kenrick's heart sank. Someone told her.

Then Zaria clicked her fingers and said, "Oh, that's right. They are one and the same. Funny that everyone knew but me. Kenrick Wulver, Alpha to be of the Wulver pack."

Zaria was angry she could see, but Kenrick had to defuse the situation. "Please let me explain. Can I come in?"

Zaria walked inside and left the door open but didn't invite her in. Kenrick followed her in and desperately tried to think of how best to explain.

Zaria stood by the kitchen counter and crossed her arms defensively. "Well?"

"I didn't intentionally lie to you, I just didn't tell you," Kenrick said.

"Is there a difference?" Zaria said angrily.

How could she explain this? Kenrick scratched her head and tried to order her thoughts. "The truth is that my pater sent me here to shadow Dante, before I become Alpha in a few weeks. I wasn't sure of myself—well, you know this."

"So why lie?" Zaria asked.

Kenrick looked up and sighed in exasperation. "I didn't lie. When I first met you, you didn't even want to be in the same room as a dominant—you were terrified of them. How could I gain your trust if you thought I was the most dominant wolf in my pack? The more I learned about your history, and your sister being mated to an Alpha who abused her and you, I just couldn't, and after that I didn't want to ruin the trust we had with something I thought would scare you."

Zaria's anger started to dissipate as she listened to Kenrick's desperate explanation. "You're right, I wouldn't have trusted you, but at least you would have been honest." Then a thought hit Zaria. She was keeping something from Kenrick too. Marco.

Kenrick took a step towards her, but naturally Zaria took a step back. She wasn't just looking at Kenrick anymore, she was looking at a dominant Alpha. The hurt look on Kenrick's face nearly broke Zaria's heart.

"Please don't be afraid of me. Because I'm an Alpha doesn't change who I am," Kenrick said.

"Of course it does, Ricky. You are everything I've feared my whole life." Zaria turned around and felt tears come to her eyes. Part of her was calling her an idiot for even considering fearing Kenrick, and another was telling her to run.

She felt Kenrick step behind her. "Zaria? Look at me. Please?"

Zaria turned around slowly.

"Am I stronger than you?" Kenrick asked her.

"Obviously," Zaria snapped.

Kenrick gave her a determined look. "Have I ever used that strength to hurt you?"

Zaria could only answer honestly. "No."

"Well then, it's not the strength that you fear. It's the person using that strength. Strength can be used for good as well as bad. My ma told me that with great power comes gentleness, tenderness, care, and love."

As she had once before, Kenrick took Zaria's hand and put it on her chest. "If you don't have those things, power will corrupt your soul. I've lived my life according to those words, and I know you're fighting a whole load of fear that Ovid and Leroux have given you, but you know in your heart that I'm not like that. Trust me, lassie."

Zaria felt like she was standing on a precipice. She was either going to run out the door or run into Kenrick's arms. After a few seconds she threw her arms around Kenrick. "It's just so hard. I've seen so much violence."

She felt Kenrick breathe a sigh of relief. "I know that, and I promise, no more secrets. You know everything about me."

The guilt of what Zaria was holding back churned inside her. She had to tell Kenrick everything. She pushed back from Kenrick and said, "But you don't know everything about me."

Kenrick looked at her strangely. "You're the wolf Marco sees when he's out running, aren't you?"

Zaria nodded. "I'm Marco's aunt. I brought him here as a baby."

Kenrick pulled up in front of Dante and Eden's den and switched the engine off. She could scent the fear and trepidation from Zaria in the other seat.

"Everything is going to be okay. Dante will understand," Kenrick said.

Zaria said nothing. She was reverting to her fears of dominants and Kenrick could understand why.

When Zaria explained how she brought baby Marco to Wolfgang County, how she had given up her life to protect Marco, and why she kept it secret, Kenrick understood. But she also knew they had to tell the Alpha as soon as possible. She called Dante and explained the situation, and Zaria was summoned to the Alpha's den, to explain her story to the Alpha and Marco's parents, Flash and Vance. That was really worrying Zaria.

Kenrick took her hand. "I'll be there with you, lassie. Everything will be all right."

Zaria looked at Kenrick. "If I was in Flash and Vance's shoes, I don't think I would be okay with it."

"Why didn't you tell us? Did you want to take our boy?" Flash shouted.

Kenrick was growling over him in seconds. "Don't shout, wolf."

"Sit, both of you, and let Zaria talk," Dante ordered.

Eden had sent the kids off to her friend Stella's and ushered them all into their living room. Dante listened calmly but Flash and Vance were shocked when they found out who she was. Flash was on the edge of anger most of the time, but Vance tried to calm him.

"Tell us why, Zaria," Vance asked.

Zaria was nervous but she got strength from the arm that Kenrick wrapped around her waist. Everything about Kenrick made her feel stronger, even though she now knew she was destined to be an Alpha.

"At first, when I woke up in your hospital, I didn't think it was worth causing you both worry. I was going to check on him one last time, then leave. No problems for you both, for the pack, nothing. Then you all looked after me, encouraged me to stay a while longer, and I just couldn't repay your kindness with the terrible truth. I was going to leave so many times. One night I got as far as the county line, but I turned back."

Eden, who was sitting next to Dante, asked, "Why didn't you?"

Zaria looked at Kenrick quickly then turned away. "Something always pulled me back, but I promise you that I never wanted to interfere with Marco's life or you as his parents. I've seen what a happy life he's had."

Vance said, "You know what this means, Flash? Leroux is—"

Dante said firmly, "Flash is Marco's pater, Vance, and she will never get near your cub."

Flash took Vance's hand. "I'll rip her apart if she tries."

Vance nodded and turned back to Zaria. "Tell us about his mother, his birth."

Zaria clutched at her stone pendant, and Kenrick rubbed the small of her back soothingly. "Marta was the kindest, softest wolf you could meet, and when she became pregnant, she was so happy but also scared of how Leroux might hurt her baby. Luckily Leroux lost interest in her—when she found out Marta was pregnant, she met her needs elsewhere. I tried to talk Marta into leaving, running away, but she had been so beaten down by her mate that she didn't have the confidence to think she could. She was scared."

Zaria noticed that Eden and Vance snuggled further into their mates at that point.

"When did that change?" Dante asked.

Zaria's free hand start to shake as she relived the memory.

"Hey, it's okay," Kenrick soothed her. "They can't hurt you now."

Zaria nodded, but Kenrick sensed that she didn't quite believe that.

"Leroux told her that she had given me to Ovid. Ovid met me at school that day and—"

Tears started to roll down Zaria's face. Eden came straight over and pulled her into a hug. Kenrick was pleased that the Mater was caring for her but frustrated because that should be her job. Just contemplating about Ovid's dirty paws touching Zaria made her want to rip everything in the room apart. Struggling to control her anger and aggression, she got up and walked to the window.

Vance took her place next to Zaria and brought a box of tissues. "You poor girl."

Flash didn't look quite as convinced. "Van."

"Stop it, Flash. You can see what she's been through."

Dante sat forward. "Can you tell us more?"

Zaria dried her tears. "When Marta saw me, she was so angry, and for the first time in her life she said no to Leroux. It was a mistake.

She beat Marta so badly that she couldn't shift. She told me to pack our things, and we stole one of the cars. I drove us away."

"How pregnant was she?" Eden asked.

"Seven months," Zaria replied.

Kenrick could hold her words no longer. "Leroux deserves nothing less than to be ripped apart by a whole pack. She's a disgrace to the name wolf."

Dante got up and put her hand on her shoulder, then said in a low voice, "Let the submissives take care of each other. The story will come out in its own time. Calm your wolf."

Kenrick looked over at Eden and Vance comforting Zaria and took her point. They were making Zaria feel safe. She nodded. "You do believe her story don't you?"

"Yes, but Flash needs a little more time. It's his cub and he's feeling protective. He needs to be sure."

Zaria continued, "We got as far as a motel just outside the county. Marta had nothing left to give, and she went into labour. She made me promise to take the cub to the Wolfgang Alpha's doorstep. At least there he would have a chance. She kissed him goodbye, and I ran."

Eden and Vance were now in tears.

"I hid in the trees and watched you and the Alpha come out for him, Eden. I knew he would always have a good life here," Zaria said. "When I got back, Marta was dead." Zaria hesitated. "After that I moved around, the Lupas were always looking for me, but I kept close to Wolfgang County."

"Why?" Flash asked pointedly, and Vance gave him a look.

"Because I promised my sister that I'd always look out for him," Zaria explained.

"What about when Leroux kidnapped Marco and Tia, the sheriff's daughter?"

Zaria gave him a steady stare. "I couldn't stop them on my own, but how do you think you had a convenient scent trail leading to where they were?"

"That was you?" Dante said.

"Yeah. I followed them. I knew you'd need a Lupa scent trail. I was the Lupa wolf to give it to you."

Flash got up and Kenrick tensed when he got closer to Zaria, but he surprised everyone when he said, "Thank you, Zaria."

❖

Zaria felt emotionally drained, but a large load had been taken off her shoulders. The Alpha understood why she kept it to herself, and more than importantly, Flash and Vance understood.

Kenrick was frustrated and angry, she could feel it. While Dante called Caden to tell them that they would be a little late for the party, Eden made tea, Flash and Vance were deep in quiet conversation on the other side of the room, and Kenrick sat in the armchair and stared down at the floor, her anger simmering close to the surface.

Kenrick's reaction was both wonderful and scary. No one had cared that much about her since Marta, but with that care came mating, and Zaria didn't think she was capable of letting anyone that close.

Vance came back over and sat beside her. "Flash and I were talking, and we think we should tell Marco the truth about his past, his mother, and about you. Maybe tomorrow you'd like to come and see him?"

"Really?" Zaria was overjoyed. She'd watched Marco grow up from afar, but to actually talk to him would be a dream.

"Yes," Flash said. "You've sacrificed a normal life to keep him safe. We think he needs to know what his aunt has done for him."

"Thank you, truly," Zaria said.

Eden walked back in with Dante carrying the tea tray.

"What have I missed?" Eden said.

Vance squeezed Zaria's hand and said, "We're going to tell Marco the truth, and Zaria is coming to visit Marco in our den tomorrow."

"That's wonderful. Dante told Caden we'd be late, so let's have a cup of tea and calm down after all that emotion."

Dante sat in the seat opposite Zaria. "Leroux doesn't know the baby survived, does she?"

"No, she must have assumed that the baby died," Zaria said.

Vance shivered. "To think that she kidnapped Marco and Tia and never even realized who he was. If she had—"

"Don't think about that, Van," Flash said. "He's safe with us and now that we know about his past, we're going to be extra vigilant with him."

Dante sighed with frustration. "We need to find Leroux and put a stop to her once and for all. After what she did to Eden and Lena, and our two guards, she deserves to die, but Marco and Zaria deserve to be able to live without looking over their shoulders too."

Flash growled. "Leroux's been hiding like a coward. We have wolves checking contacts, trying to find out information, but getting nothing."

A new thought trickled into Zaria's mind. It was dangerous, but she would do anything for Marco. "Alpha, I have an idea. Ovid and Leroux want me, so if I leave Wolfgang County, they will come to me. Then you'd have her."

Kenrick, who had been silent all this time, said firmly, "No, that is not going to happen."

"Excuse me?" Zaria said sharply.

Kenrick looked at her with a hard stare. "You heard me. That is not going to happen."

Zaria felt utter fury rise up like a volcano inside her. She jumped and exclaimed, "You have no say in my life, so I can do what I want."

Kenrick got up and walked over. "I'm telling you, I'm not letting you do it. No matter what you say. It's not safe, and I don't want Leroux or Ovid anywhere near you."

Zaria gave a hollow laugh. "Well done. You've shown your true dominant colours. I can't believe you got me to think you were different."

Dante stood up and said, "Let's all calm down here—"

But Zaria didn't want to listen. She pointed her finger at Kenrick. "Let me make this clear. You are not my mate, and you do not make any decisions for me. I've had dominants who wanted to control me all my life. I thought you were different—apparently not."

With that she stormed out of the house.

As soon as the front door slammed, Kenrick smacked herself on the forehead. "Why did you say that, idiot."

"Ricky, you should have let Dante say no," Eden said. "She's fighting years of being controlled, but she would have taken it from Dante."

"And I would have said no. It's far too dangerous," Dante said.

"I was just trying to protect her. Fear just made me say it like that. I love her—I don't want to control her."

"Does she know you feel like that, Ricky?" Vance asked.

"No, I haven't told her," Kenrick replied.

Vance shook his head. "Then go after her, wolf, and explain."

"Okay, Eden, will you give my apologies to Caden and Lena? I really need to sort this out."

"Sure, go get her," Eden said.

Kenrick ran out the door but didn't see Zaria. She must have been walking home alone. She jumped into the car and drove out of the Alpha's gated den. When she spotted Zaria further up the road, she caught up and put the window down.

"Zaria, wait."

Zaria just kept walking, so Kenrick slowed to a crawl beside her. "Please, Zari. I didn't mean what I said."

"I'm not interested. Go away, Kenrick," Zaria said.

Kenrick was panicking. She couldn't let Zaria think she was anything like the dominants she grew up with. "Look, I was scared, okay. I was scared to death that you'd get hurt, and I acted like an idiot."

Zaria stopped walking and sighed.

"Please, Zari. Forgive me?" Kenrick pleaded.

Zari turned around and said, "A dominant has never told me they were scared before."

Kenrick stopped the car. "Well, I was—I am, I mean. You are really important to me, and I—" She wanted to say *love* more than anything, but she was certain that would scare Zaria. "I care about you, a lot. I don't want you to get hurt. Please get in the car and I'll take you home," Kenrick said.

Zaria walked around the car and jumped in the passenger seat. Kenrick breathed a sigh of relief. "I'm sorry, really."

"I know," Zaria said. "It was probably a bad idea, but now that I've found Marco, I want to bring this to the end. I want to stop running and for Marco to be safe."

Kenrick reached for her hand. "It will be over. Just give Dante time. She will find Leroux."

Zaria nodded. "Will you take me home? I'd like to go back to my apartment. I'm so tired."

"Aye, of course. Do you want me to stay on the couch or something?" Kenrick asked.

"I'd rather have some time to myself."

Kenrick wanted to be close, protecting Zaria, but she wasn't going to make a mistake again. "Aye, sure."

CHAPTER TWELVE

The next day Zaria finally got to meet Marco. Kenrick picked her up and drove her over. Once they'd said their hellos, Vance suggested she take Marco out to the backyard. It was a big grass yard with lots of sports gear and playground equipment. Marco led her over to the swings.

They swayed together in silence for a minute, and then Marco said, "When my wolf saw you out running, it felt I knew you."

"I'm sorry I didn't talk to you, Marco, but I didn't want to disturb your life," Zaria said.

"It's okay. I get it. When I got taken with Tia by Leroux—" Marco stuttered.

"Take your time, Marco."

"She was so nasty, like a villain in a movie. Do you think I'll turn out like her?" Marco said.

"Never. You have too much of your mom in you," Zaria reassured him.

"What was she like? My mom, I mean."

Zaria took a picture out of her pocket and handed it to Marco. He scanned it quickly.

"She looks beautiful."

Zaria felt joy in her heart that she hadn't felt in a long, long time. "Marta was the most beautiful wolf in our pack, but she was beautiful inside too. Everyone loved her gentleness and kindness, and she taught me everything I know."

Marco was crying. "I wish I could have known her, Aunt Zaria."

Hearing the word *aunt* out of Marco's mouth made the tears flow for her too. "She would have been so proud of you, and happy that you have such a good life with your dad and your pater."

"They are the best," Marco agreed, "but why did she have to die?"

"Only Leroux can answer that question, but she died protecting you and me and made sure you got a good chance in life."

Marco got off the swing and looked a little unsure of himself. "Aunt Zaria? Thank you from bringing me here when I was a baby."

Then he hugged her tightly. Zaria had been waiting for this moment since she left Marco on the Alpha's doorstep.

We did it, Marta. He's safe and happy.

Kenrick watched Zaria sleeping on the couch and felt her heart fall even more in love with her. After reconnecting with Marco, Kenrick got them takeout and brought it back to Zaria's apartment. The day had been so emotional for Zaria that after dinner she went straight to the couch and fell asleep.

I'm in love with her, but what do I do now?

She would be heading back to Scotland soon, and she couldn't bear the thought of Zaria not being with her.

Zaria's eyes fluttered open and she stretched. "How long have I been asleep?"

"An hour, I think," Kenrick said.

Zaria yawned. "I'm sorry to just check out on you. You should have gone home."

"Nah. I'd rather be right here. What did Vance say to you before we left?" Kenrick said.

"He asked me to go on a run with them tomorrow morning."

Kenrick sat forward. "Well, that's great. You're building a relationship with your new family. But you don't look so sure."

Zaria tied her hair back in a ponytail. "It's complicated and awkward. I don't want to step on Flash's and Vance's toes and hover over them."

"You're not. You're just getting to know Marco and Flash and Vance."

"I don't know what comes next, that's all," Zaria said.

"Me neither," Kenrick said sadly.

Zaria narrowed her eyes. "What do you mean?"

Kenrick didn't want to say she loved Zaria and wanted her to come to Scotland, so she just said, "You know, becoming Alpha and stuff."

Zaria came over to sit beside her. "Why are you worried about that?"

"Because I don't know if I should be," Kenrick said.

"Why? You're really dominant, your pater is Alpha—why not?"

"I had a twin brother. I was born first, I was bigger and stronger, but I failed him." Kenrick's voice cracked.

Zaria put her hand on Kenrick's knee. "How could you fail him?"

"He was attacked by a vampire," Kenrick said emotionally. "I couldn't find him in time."

"I'm so sorry, Ricky. What age were you both?"

"Ten." Kenrick cleared her throat trying to control her emotions.

"You can't blame yourself, question your fitness to lead, over what happened when you were ten. It was for the adult wolves to take action."

"They did find him, but he was drained of blood." Kenrick couldn't stop the emotions this time.

Zaria put her arms around her and hugged her. When she rubbed her back, Kenrick pressed her nose into Zaria's neck and Zaria moaned.

Kenrick didn't want to make any mistakes, so she pulled back and looked at Zaria. Her eyes were glowing yellow.

"Ricky?" Zaria said then pressed her lips against Kenrick's.

Kenrick gave a soft growl and melted into her lips. It was pure bliss kissing Zaria and every cell in her body was demanding, wanting, needing, but she had to go slow for Zaria's sake.

When her teeth erupted, Zaria ran her tongue over her canines. That was too much for Kenrick. She had to either take things further or slow down.

She pulled away and rested her forehead against Zaria's. "Are you ready for this, lassie?"

Zaria took a few moments and calmed her breathing. "Slow, Ricky. I need to take it slow."

Kenrick wanted to show Zaria she always had the right to control what they did together. Ovid and Leroux took what they wanted, but

Kenrick wanted to be given the honour of touching her love when she said so.

"Your decision. Always."

❖

Zaria felt the exhilaration and excitement of new possibilities. She lay in her bed and relived the feel of Kenrick's lips and the sensation was like coming home at last. But Kenrick had a big future ahead, she was leaving for Scotland soon, so what was the point of a week-long romance? Kenrick hadn't mentioned those problems after they kissed.

There was no point in thinking about new possibilities when they were only dreams. Kenrick's life was in Scotland. She was an Alpha and she needed a Mater, and Zaria was not a Mater.

Her excitement had been overcome by a feeling of depression. Why did the Great Mother make her fall for such an unattainable wolf?

Zaria nearly jumped out of her skin when the apartment phone rang. She looked at the clock. It was one o'clock in the morning. Kenrick wouldn't call at this time, would she?

She sat up and lifted the phone. "Hello?"

"Hello dear sister." The voice sent fear and chills through her bones. "It's been such a long time."

Zaria jumped out of bed, her whole body shaking. "It—it can't be."

"I can hear the joy in your voice, sister. Yes, it's your Alpha, Leroux."

The last time she spoke to Leroux, she was sixteen years old, and the voice took her back to that scared child.

"What do you want?" Zaria said.

"Isn't it obvious? I want my family back, and Ovid wants her mate."

The sentence made her want to throw up. "I'm no one's mate."

Leroux laughed. "We'll see about that. I think you've gotten too comfortable with the Wolfgangs and learned some of their submissives' bad habits. You don't talk back to a dominant, especially your Alpha, Zaria."

Zaria stayed silent. She wanted to hang up and call Ricky and Dante, but she was too scared to do anything.

The silence ended when Leroux said, "As I said, I want *all* my family back."

Zaria's heart sank. No, not Marco. "I don't know what you mean," Zaria said in a tiny voice.

"I'm talking about my sister-in-law and my son, Marco. Your little secret is out. You and your sister have tried to keep me from my son."

Zaria held her fist against her forehead. She was experiencing true panic. "Please, Leroux, leave Marco out of it. He's happy, he has a new family."

"But he's my son," Leroux said. "But—"

"But what?" Was there room for negotiation? "I'll do anything if you promise to leave Marco alone and forget about him."

Leroux's voice turned deadly serious. "If that is the case, then you pack your things and walk to the county line. My wolves will be waiting there to bring you home to us."

"I have your word that you'll never go after Marco?" Zaria said.

"You have my word, if you behave and accept me as your Alpha, and Ovid as your mate."

Zaria closed her eyes and let her heart answer. "I'll come."

"Good wolf, maybe Ovid will make you behave better than Marta ever could. Be at the county line in one hour."

Leroux hung up and Zaria collapsed to her knees.

"I'm sorry, Ricky. I love you."

❖

Dante couldn't sleep. Her mind was racing with ideas and plans to smoke out Leroux. She had to be found, or Marco and Zaria would never be safe.

She turned to watch Eden sleeping peacefully and stroked her fingers down her bare arm. "I will find her, I promise you, Mater."

Dante got up and pulled on some boxers and a T-shirt. Maybe a drink of water would clear her head. She walked downstairs to find Ricky sitting at the kitchen table nursing a glass of whisky.

"I wish I could have one of those," Dante said.

"Aye, well, it's not helping too much."

Dante got a bottle of water from the fridge and sat down. "It was a big day for Zaria, huh?"

"It was. She was knackered by the time she got home. Fell asleep on the couch, but she had a great time with Marco. Flash and Vance are being really generous to her."

Dante took a drink of water and said, "They're good wolves. So what's got you drinking at this time in the morning?"

"We kissed," Kenrick said with a little smile.

"That's great. I know she's got a lot to deal with, but you two look good together."

"But what's next? I love her, Dante. She's my wolf, I know the Great Mother sent her to me, but I'm going home in a week."

Dante raised her eyebrows and nodded. "Yeah, there's that."

"I want to ask her to come back with me, but that's a huge thing to ask. A new country, a new pack, leave Marco behind? I don't know what to do."

"It's her decision, Ricky. You just have to be brave enough to tell her you love her and give her a choice. Show her she could have a future with you in Scotland—then it's up to Zaria. What do you think Aunt Elspeth and Uncle Fergus would think of her?"

Kenrick laughed softly. "My ma would love her and cluck around her like a mother hen, and my pater would charm her."

Dante smiled. "I think you're right. So ask. You'll never know if you don't try."

Kenrick stretched her long, tired body. "There are more logistical problems though. Zaria has never had a passport in her life. It would take too long to get her one."

"I think I might be able to help you there." Dante winked. "I know a few people."

"Really? That would be amazing. You're a good pal, Dante, and a cousin."

"True," Dante said. "Let's make plans then."

Zaria stared at the picture of Marco that Vance had given her today and knew in her heart that she was doing the right thing. If it meant a lifetime of abuse at Leroux's and Ovid's hands, or death, it would be worth it knowing Marco was safe.

But she would think of Kenrick every day of her life. She only hoped that Kenrick could make her new life and find the right wolf for her, although the thought killed her.

She stuffed the picture of Marco in her bag, and as she did one night before, jumped out of the window and made her way to the edge of Wolfgang County. Only this time there was no turning back.

As she approached the *Welcome to Wolfgang County* sign, she saw a truck sitting with its lights on. Her heart started to beat faster and faster. When she got closer, two wolves in black clothing stepped out. The female wolf was the one who tried to abduct her from the diner and killed Chrissy.

She stopped in the road at the county line.

"Well, well, well. Ready to give up at last, Zaria?"

"Let's just get on with it." Zaria stepped over the line and the female wolf grabbed her and threw her up against the truck.

"You are lucky my Alpha and Second want you alive—otherwise I'd tear your throat out. You got my friend killed."

Zaria felt the spit hit her face as she snarled at her. She was then thrown in the back of the truck. As they drove away from Wolfgang County, away from Kenrick, she thought: It was always going to end like this.

Chapter Thirteen

D ante whistled as she walked upstairs from the war room.
"Someone's cheerful," Eden said.

Dante put her arms around her middle and kissed her. "Despite everything we have going on, Eden, it makes me happy to help true love."

"What do you mean?" Eden asked.

"Kenrick and Zaria. I was making a few phone calls to try and get Zaria a passport quickly, through unofficial means. Kenrick is asking her to go to Scotland with her."

"Oh, that's great news." Eden squeezed her mate in a hug.

"That's where Kenrick is now, asking Zaria," Dante said. She heard someone running up their drive at full speed. She put Eden behind her and opened the door. It was a frantic Kenrick, half shifted, enraged, and holding a piece of note paper.

"They've got her. Leroux and Ovid, they have her," Kenrick roared.

There was no time for talk—they had to get Zaria back and quickly. All the elite wolves gathered in the Alpha's driveway, including Caden, Flash, Ripp, and Joel. Dante had learned her lesson from the first time Leroux tricked the elite wolves out of their pack lands, and she was leaving Blaze and Xander to take command at home, to place lots of guards around their borders and dens.

Kenrick paced around, encouraging them all to hurry packing their equipment into the trucks.

"Come on, we don't have time for this," Kenrick urged.

Dante walked over and held her by the neck. "Calm yourself—we will find her, but we have to be prepared. The Lupas are armed with silver bolts—we have to be too."

"Dante, if Ovid gets her paws on Zari, there's no telling what harm she could do. I need to find her."

When Kenrick had gotten no answer at Zaria's apartment, she broke down the door and found the note Zaria left. Kenrick cried out in physical pain when she read that Zaria had willingly given herself up to save Marco.

"This is like my brother all over again. I'm not going to get there in time. I'm going to fail again." Kenrick was starting to be overcome with panic.

"No, it's not," Dante said. "We will find her. You lead the hunt, be the Alpha I know you are, Ricky."

A feeling of steely strength came over Kenrick. No one was going to take her mate. Not ever.

"Wolves, listen up," Dante said. "Kenrick leads the hunt today."

"Right, let's go now," Kenrick shouted. "Me, Dante, and Caden will lead the way in the first truck. The rest of you, follow behind. Keep on your paws. Good hunting, wolves."

"Good hunting," they all replied.

Zaria was pulled out of the truck and was surprised to find herself in the grounds of a mansion.

"Where are we?" Zaria asked the wolf she now knew was called Cero.

"The outskirts of Knoxton. I hope you'll like it." Cero shoved her forward and was guided into the house. Zaria presumed the human family that lived here were now no more.

Ovid walked out from the hallway and grabbed her by the arms. "I have you at last." She pushed Zaria up against the wall and pulled her T-shirt to the side. Zaria felt sick that this disgusting creature was touching her again.

"Where's the mate bite I gave you?" Ovid said with fury.

Zaria felt angry for the sixteen-year-old girl who could do nothing against this much older wolf. She thought of Kenrick and the strength she had given her and used it now.

"It healed after one shift because you're not my mate," Zaria said.

Ovid got so close she could smell her breath. "Then I'll just have to make a new one. Come with me."

Ovid dragged her towards the stairs but stopped when she saw Leroux coming down.

"Put my sister-in-law down, Ovid. We have no time for that. The Wolfgangs will be here within the hour. This is our chance and we are not going to mess it up. Plenty of time to fuck your mate after. Hi, Zaria, I'm glad you've come home at last."

When Leroux walked past, Ovid sniffed all around Zaria's face and neck. "Who is that wolf I can smell on you?"

"A wolf that would rip your spleen out. A real wolf," Zaria sneered.

Ovid punched her to the ground. "Make sure you have a shower before you come to my bed."

Zaria clutched her face and caught the blood dripping out of her nose. She might be in pain, she might be scared, but Leroux seemed to think that the Wolfgangs were coming. Maybe there was the slightest bit of hope.

"Cero, watch my mate, and don't lose her," Ovid said.

"Yes, Second."

❖

"I have a bad feeling of déjà vu," Caden said to Kenrick and Dante.

"Yes," Dante said, "Leroux is making it easy with a nice clean trail. Pull in here and call Blaze. Check if everything is okay at home."

While Caden called, Kenrick pointed at the big white house up ahead. "I think that's where the trail is leading."

"Leroux is coming up in the world. The last time we found her, she was in a dilapidated old shithole."

Caden reported, "All our borders are secure."

"Then let's get Zaria, kill Leroux, and get out of here," Dante said.

They all got out of the trucks, and Kenrick led them up to the wall that ran all around the property. She crouched down and whispered, "Let's get over the wall, assess the property, then shift."

The wolves leapt over the wall with ease—luckily there were trees for cover. Kenrick indicated she and Dante would go to the edge of the trees and take a look.

What they found surprised them both. Leroux, Ovid, and all her wolves were standing outside the house waiting for them.

Kenrick shook her head in disbelief, and then Leroux shouted, "Bring your little gang of mutts out here, Dante. I know you're there."

Dante gave a signal to hold back, but then Leroux pulled Zaria out front and placed a silver bolt gun to her head.

Kenrick didn't stop to think. She ran out there and straight for Leroux.

"I wouldn't do that, stranger. Do you know what a mess this bolt will make of my dear sister's brain?"

Kenrick stopped dead and put her hands up. "Don't hurt her."

"Ricky, don't…" Zaria pleaded with her eyes for Kenrick to calm down.

Dante led her wolves out of the trees with their hands up. Leroux shoved Zaria at another wolf, and Kenrick knew by the way she touched Zaria, and by the fear in Zaria's eyes, that this was Ovid. She growled a loud warning. "I'll kill you."

Ovid sniffed the air and a look of fury came over her face. She grabbed Zaria's hair and pulled it back. "Is this wolf the one I could smell all over you?"

Kenrick roared, "As soon as you put the coward's bolt gun down, you are mine, wolf. I will pay you back for every misery you gave Zaria."

When Ovid went to respond, Leroux shouted at Ovid, "Calm down, Second. We don't have time for this."

Ovid did pull back, but Kenrick stared at her and pictured all the ways she could pile pain on this disgusting animal, including ripping her organs out one by one.

Dante walked forward. "What's the game this time, Leroux? I know my borders are well guarded."

"Don't worry, there are no wolves in Wolfgang County, apart from my son," Leroux joked.

"He's no son of yours," Dante said.

"True, he's probably been polluted by the Wolfgang weakness by now. No, I want to finish this problem once and for all. A fight to the death. You and me. How about it?"

Dante laughed. "I'm bigger and stronger than you, and I've beaten you easily twice before."

"Three time's the charm, Dante."

"Fine, let's do this. Shift."

"No, no shifting. Let's see if you're strong enough to kill me in human form," Leroux challenged.

"Have you lost your mind, Leroux? You'll stand even less chance."

"Humour me."

Both Kenrick and Caden approached Dante. Caden said, "This is a trap. It must be."

"Let her have her moment," Dante said, "I'll destroy her. Watch my back."

Dante approached Leroux, who had dispensed with her shirt, to fight. They circled a few times, and then Dante flew through the air and kicked Leroux to the ground. She raised her fist to punch. "This is for my mate and my baby cub."

Leroux caught her punch, headbutted her, and threw her back about five feet. She stood up and laughed. "Come on, big Alpha, is that the best you can do?"

Kenrick looked at Dante gasping for air and spitting out teeth as blood poured out her mouth.

"Dante?" Kenrick said.

Dante stood up and walked forward again. Leroux appeared to be infused with new energy. Kenrick could tell by Leroux's poor build and physique that she shouldn't be that strong.

Dante punched and aimed a knee to Leroux's middle. Leroux took the assault, then grabbed Dante's hair and gave her a kick to the abdomen.

Dante was panting and bleeding. Not only was Leroux stronger, but Dante was getting weaker by the second.

Caden edged over to Kenrick. "We have to do something."

Dante groaned. "Something's happening—my strength…"

Kenrick spotted a ring on Leroux's finger. It flashed and sparkled with every movement or blow Dante tried to make.

Leroux called out, "Lupas, attack the rest, Dante is mine."

"Cade," Kenrick ordered, "get Zaria to safety if you can. I have an idea."

"Will do."

As the Lupas shifted and attacked, so did the Wolfgangs. Fights started all around Kenrick, but she had a hunch, and one goal: to get that ring off Leroux's finger.

Confusion reigned around the front of the mansion—fights erupting all over, wolves tearing flesh, and Zaria screaming as she watched—but to save Zaria, Kenrick had to keep single-minded.

Dante was rolling on the ground, blood pouring from her face, and Leroux was just walking slowly around her, taking great pleasure in kicking her when she was down. When Leroux bent down to grab Dante's head, Kenrick spotted her chance. She shifted and ran at Leroux, grabbed on to her arm, and bit down with everything she had.

She heard the bones snap, heard Leroux scream, but Kenrick didn't let up. She ravaged Leroux's arm and severed her forearm right off.

Leroux's arm lay on the ground, and Kenrick bared her bloody teeth over her. Blood dripped onto Leroux's face.

"Please don't kill me, please."

She heard breathing behind her and stepped back. A bloody Dante had regained some of her power when the arm was severed. Kenrick had been right. The ring had been drawing Dante's power somehow.

"Kenrick's not going to kill you, Leroux. That right is mine," Dante said.

Kenrick's wolf stepped back and looked around for Zaria. She was standing behind Caden's wolf, who was fighting with Ovid.

"Go to your mate, Ricky. I'll take care of this mutt."

As Kenrick charged over to Ovid, she heard Dante say, "*This* is for my mate, my cub, and Marta, sister of Zaria."

Then a satisfying howl of Leroux's pain and the crunching of bones.

Kenrick's focus was now killing Ovid. *Caden, guard Zaria. This one's mine.*

Caden stepped back and the two wolves clashed in mid-air. Kenrick's power knocked Ovid over. *Let's see if you enjoy fighting me as much as hurting little submissive cubs.*

Zaria's mine and she always will be, Ovid replied.

Ovid made a move, but Kenrick dodged it easily and struck Ovid across the face with her claws. Ovid howled as her face was ripped apart. Kenrick taunted her. *Come on, wolf. You like hitting submissives, strike me. Come on!*

Ovid's face was a mess, her eye displaced and fur ripped. Ovid looked around, then obviously seeing the fight was done, turned and ran for her life, scrambling up the wall and over.

Kenrick went to chase her. She wanted to kill her for what she'd done, but then she heard Zaria call, "Ricky, leave her. She's gone. Stay with me."

She looked back to Zaria and then back in the direction Ovid took. There was only one choice. She padded over to Zaria quickly.

Zaria wrapped her arms around Kenrick's wolf and stroked her. "It's over, Ricky. It's over."

Kenrick shifted back to skin and held Zaria close.

Caden left them and went to check on the Alpha.

"You came for me, Ricky."

"I always will, Zari," Kenrick said.

"Leroux?" Zaria asked.

Kenrick looked over at the mess that was Leroux's body and said, "It's over. She's gone."

Zaria burst into tears. "She's gone, she's gone at last, Marta."

Kenrick saw the other Wolfgangs shifting back to skin after disposing of their opponents. Caden was helping Dante back to her feet. When Dante did stand up, she threw her head, covered in blood, up to the sky and howled in victory. All the wolves joined her, including Kenrick.

She had gotten there in time, she had led the pack, and she had helped Dante to victory. For the first time in her life, she truly felt like the Wulver Alpha.

The drive back to Wolfgang County was in silence. Zaria couldn't speak or think—she just lay in Kenrick's arms in the back seat. But in Kenrick she sensed the high, the buzz of victory coursing through her bloodstream, and despite all she had been through, it was awakening her wolf. All the wolves in their hunting party were projecting their need for their mates.

Each wolf was amplifying the group's need and hunger for sex, and Kenrick and Zaria were no different. Zaria appeared connected to Kenrick and programmed to mate, but they weren't mates, and now she was even more confused about her future.

Dante and the other wolves had taken time to dispose of the Lupa bodies, so that they wouldn't arouse suspicion from the humans. One strange loose end remained in the aftermath of the fight. Dante had ordered they bring the ring Leroux had worn back home, but when they checked the severed hand, the was nothing there.

Kenrick scented witch around that area, so someone must have taken advantage of their preoccupation, and stolen the ring. They would probably never find out where it came from, but at least Dante knew enough to spot it in the future and how to deal with it.

Caden pulled up in front of Zaria's apartment. "Do you want us to wait for you, Ricky?"

"No, go home to your dens. I'll be staying here."

Zaria was glad. She didn't want to be on her own. They walked upstairs and Zaria saw her door lock broken.

Kenrick scratched her head. "Sorry about that. When I didn't get any answer from you yesterday, I was worried there was something wrong."

"There was," Zaria said softly.

When they walked into the apartment, Zaria had a flashback of Leroux calling her, frightening her. "This was my sanctuary. Dante gave me this safe place, after all these years, and Leroux violated it."

Kenrick grasped her shoulders lightly. "She hasn't. No one will get near you again. I'll fix this door in the morning, but in the meantime I'm here, and I will always keep you safe, if you let me."

Kenrick was right. She was safety, Zaria's safety. The first wolf to give her that, to care about her thoughts and feelings. The dread inside her, the dread that Ovid put back in her, had to be banished, and Kenrick was the only one who could make it better.

Zaria pulled Kenrick to her, growled, and kissed her, grazing Kenrick's lip with her canines. Kenrick, already hot and hungry from the battle, didn't need any more encouragement. She kissed Zaria back and ran her fingers through her dark hair.

She felt Zaria ripping her T-shirt, raking her claws down her chest.

Her sex burned so hot after the battle that she wanted to claim Zaria, proclaim to every wolf that they belonged to each other.

Kenrick lifted Zaria and she wrapped her legs around Kenrick's waist. Kenrick walked them back to the front door and pushed Zaria up against it. She felt Zaria's claws dig into her neck.

It felt so good. Kenrick had been dreaming of this since she met Zaria. This was her mate—Zaria was her future.

She pulled back from the kiss, then grasped Zaria's hair and pulled it to the side to expose her neck. Kenrick rubbed her scent up and down her neck, then started to kiss it.

Zaria went stiff and dropped her arms and legs. Kenrick stopped and moved her head back. Zaria looked like a frightened deer, her breathing was shallow, and there were tears welling in her eyes.

"Zaria, what's wrong?"

Zaria stared straight ahead as if she was reliving something in her mind. Kenrick cupped Zaria's cheeks and looked directly into her eyes.

"Zari? Look at me. It's Ricky, concentrate on my eyes."

Zaria closed her eyes tightly and when she opened them, she was back. "I'm sorry, I'm sorry, I can't—"

"You don't have to do anything, lassie. Tell me what *I* did wrong," Kenrick said.

Zaria struggled through her tears to speak. "When I got to the Lupa base and I walked in, Ovid was there, and the first thing she did was grab me, push me against the wall, and try to bite my neck. She was angry that the mate bite she gave me all those years ago was gone."

"Is that what she did to you when you were sixteen years old?" Kenrick couldn't believe an adult wolf could ever behave that way to a child.

Zaria nodded. "That and more. She could use my body, but the Great Mother chooses your mate, and it wasn't Ovid. The mate bite healed the very next time I shifted. Today the only reason she stopped was because Leroux interrupted her."

Kenrick bowed her head and shook it. "I'm so sorry she did that to you, and I'm sorry for trying to—"

"I kissed you, Kenrick. I'm sorry, the emotion of today just got to me, but I wasn't ready," Zaria said.

Kenrick took a big step back to give her some space. "I should have known better, after all you've been through today. You need to get to bed and get some sleep."

"Not in the bedroom," Zaria said. "Leroux called me there. I'll sleep on the couch."

"Do you want me to go?" Kenrick asked.

Zaria grasped her hand. "No, stay with me."

Kenrick settled Zaria on the couch with a blanket, while she sat on the floor beside her and held her hand.

Zaria fell asleep quickly and Kenrick guarded her and thought of all the ways she'd like to kill Ovid.

Chapter Fourteen

One week had passed since Leroux had been killed at last, and it gave the Wolfgang pack extra cause to celebrate the mating ceremony of Ripp and Kyra. Zaria was standing with Vance and Marco watching the ceremony, and sweetly Marco held both her hand and Vance's.

Kyra looked beautiful standing at the dais in a flowing green gown, and Ripp was handsome in her green cloak.

Dante, who was presiding over the ceremony, gave the couple their oathing stone. "The oath you take today is indivisible. Do you both swear in front of your pack to never break the vows you make today, and to keep them till death and beyond, when you enter the Great Eternal Forest?"

Zaria looked over to Kenrick, who was standing by Ripp with the other dominants. She imagined standing there with Kenrick, but that was only a dream. Kenrick went back to Scotland tomorrow, and she would be left with an aching heart.

Eden had hinted that she should go with Kenrick, but Kenrick had never asked her, and even if she did, there was no way she could be Kenrick's Mater, in another country. Zaria had never been brought up in a normal pack, and she had no wolf social skills. Their brief romance, if that's what it was, was coming to an end.

Kenrick turned her head and looked straight at her, making Zaria's heart thud. The week that she had spent recovering from her ordeal with the Lupas had given Zaria time to think about what came next. Dante and Eden had offered her a place here in the Wolfgang pack, but she felt it would be awkward for Flash and Vance to have her hovering over their shoulders. Now that Leroux was dead, maybe it was time to make a fresh start.

Ripp and Kyra finished taking their oath, and Dante said, "Today we celebrate the love of Ripp and Kyra, but we also give praise to the Great Mother for guiding us and helping us hunt down our enemies. Leroux is no more, and we have avenged the destruction she brought to our pack. We can look forward to a safe, happy future, for our cubs and grandcubs."

Dante threw back her head and howled. The rest of the pack joined her.

❖

While Ripp and Kyra went to place their oathing stone by their ancestors' sacred tree, the guests moved on to the reception. Banks of tables on a large grassy area beside the ceremony site were laden with food and drink. In the middle, boards had been put down for dancing and many already were.

Zaria sat at a picnic table with Eden, Lena, and baby Chase. "He's gotten so big already, Lena," Zaria said.

Lena rolled her eyes. "It's not surprising. He never stops eating."

Eden laughed. "You might be tired just now, but give it a few months, and you'll be wanting cub number two."

"I've already got cub number two—her name is Caden," Lena joked.

Eden and Zaria laughed, and then Zaria felt Kenrick walking towards her.

"Watch out, Zaria," Lena said. "Your hunky Highlander is on an intercept course."

Eden leaned in and said, "Whatever she has to say, give her a chance."

Kenrick appeared at Zaria's side and saluted both Eden and Lena. "Zari, will you dance with me?"

"Sure."

Kenrick took her hand and Zaria followed her to the dance floor. The started to sway slowly to the music.

"How have you been, Zari? I haven't seen you the last couple of days," Kenrick said.

"I've been okay. I just wanted time to think, you know?"

"Aye, I know. Listen, Zari, I go home tomorrow, and I need to know, will you come with me?" Kenrick asked.

There was the question. Zaria's heart said yes, but her head said, *You'll never be Mater material.*

Zaria sighed and it broke her heart to refuse but she had to. "I'm sorry, I can't."

"If it's because of Ovid, then I'd never treat you like—"

Zaria cut Kenrick off. "I know you wouldn't, it's me. I'm a stray wolf, Ricky. I can't just join your pack and become Mater. I'm not a Mater. I don't even know what I am. I've never had the space to find out. I've always been hunted. Now Leroux's dead, Ovid's probably dead after the beating you gave her, and the Lupas have melted away, so I'm finally free. Do you understand?"

"I don't. You're not a stray and my pack would love you," Kenrick said with anger in her voice. "I love you, and I'm offering you a future. You know in your heart the Great Mother has destined us to be together. You have to come with me."

"I want to make my own decisions for once in my life. I won't be pushed into something I can't do. I'm not the mate of an Alpha. I can't, Ricky."

Kenrick looked as if she was gulping down her emotions. "And I'm not Leroux and you're not Marta. You're letting your past stop you from having a happy future."

"You'll find the right Mater, Ricky."

Kenrick dropped her hands suddenly and took a step back. "I already have. You are my Mater, but you won't admit it. I love you, Zari."

Kenrick walked away and left her standing there alone. *She really loves me.*

"Aunt Zari?" Marco appeared at her side. "Can I dance with you?"

Zaria did her best to smile even though her heart was aching. "That would be nice." Marco danced her around the floor beautifully. "I think you've been practicing dancing, Marco."

He gave her a bright smile. "I have, we all have."

Zaria looked around the dance floor and saw Dion dancing with Tia and Nix trying to dance with Meghan but constantly standing on her toes. It was so sweet. What a happy, comfortable life Marco would have here, the complete opposite of her childhood.

"Your mom would be proud of you, you know?"

"Thanks, I try my best. I'm not confident like Dion and Nix, but Ricky has really helped me."

Zaria was surprised. "Ricky has?"

"Yeah, right from when she came here, she talked to me and helped me understand stuff better. All the cubs love Ricky. Look, she gave us these bands."

Zaria saw the same type of leather band as Kenrick wore on her wrist. She looked around and couldn't see Kenrick anywhere. She had hurt her by turning her down.

Why did you have to be so perfect, Highlander?

That night Kenrick drove to Zaria's apartment. It was probably in vain, but Eden told her to fight for her, to fight for the woman she thought was destined to be her Mater. She knocked on Zaria's door and a few seconds later heard the lock come off, then open. Zaria stood there looking pensive and stressed.

"Hi—um, can I talk to you?"

Zaria leaned her head against the door, clearly weary from all the emotional upheaval that she had been going through. Kenrick wanted to take her into her arms and make everything feel better, but she was part of the emotional upheaval, so that wouldn't be the best idea.

"Is there anything else to talk about? My head hurts from talking and everyone giving their opinion on my future. Eden, Lena, Kyra, Vance, all telling me what I should do."

This was Kenrick's one last shot, so she had to make it good and not seem like she was forcing Zaria into something.

"Just five minutes. Please? I leave at six tomorrow, so it's my last chance to talk to you." The truth of that sentence made Kenrick feel sick. Tomorrow morning she had to turn her back on the love of her life, her mate, her one true Mater. How would she ever find the strength?

But Kenrick was sure she saw pain in Zaria's eyes. Her words clearly had an effect on Zaria too.

"Okay, sure." Zaria opened the door and Kenrick followed her in.

Zaria stood by the sofa and said wearily, "What do you want to say?"

Okay this was it. Her one shot at convincing her mate they had a future.

She took a deep breath. "The last time I talked to you I was wrong."

"The last time we argued," Zaria corrected her.

"I know, I know. I was—" Kenrick pinched the bridge of her nose. "I was panicking at the thought of losing you. I'm not perfect. I am a dominant, and it's written in every cell of my body to look after the ones I care about, but I understand that it can come across as controlling sometimes."

Zari sighed. "I know you mean well, Ricky, but I vowed I'd never let any wolf make my life choices."

Kenrick took a step towards Zaria and put her hand on her heart. "I don't want to make them for you. I want to offer you choices. They are freely offered and it's your decision if you take them or not."

"Ricky—"

"Please, let me just say my piece and get it all out."

Zaria nodded.

"You've lived your life here in the States, and it's a huge decision to go to the other side of the world with me. A new country, a new pack, new wolves to meet, and on top of that being with me as an Alpha and all that means. I don't want you to think of it like that, like your future is set in stone if you come with me."

"What do you mean?" Zaria said.

Kenrick took out the plane ticket she had printed before she left Dante's den. "I booked this ticket for you to use if you want it. It's an opened-ended return ticket. You can come and meet my pack for a week, two weeks, a month, or whatever, and come back to America any time you want."

"I don't even have a passport," Zaria said.

"You have now. Dante was able to pull a few strings with her contacts." Kenrick placed the ticket on the coffee table. "It's all in your hands. You can stay here and live as you have been all these years, stay in Wolfgang County with Marco, or come with me and return whenever you want. I'm giving you choices. Which one you choose is up to you."

Zaria rubbed her forehead. "Why are you doing this, Ricky? You're making this so hard."

Kenrick took Zaria's hands. She didn't want to say it was because they were meant to be. That would scare Zaria, she guessed. "Because I love you, because I want you to have a better life than you've had up till now, because I want to see what this bond we have for each other can become, and because I care enough to let you go—if that's what you want. But just know that you don't have to be alone any more."

"Ricky, I don't know what to say."

Kenrick cupped her face and smiled. "I don't want you to say anything, lassie. Just think about it overnight. I'll be leaving for the airport at six. If you want to join me, come to the Alpha's house. If you're not there, then I'll have my answer."

Before Zaria could respond, Kenrick leaned in and kissed her. She then leaned her forehead against Zaria's and said, "No matter what, no matter how far apart we are in the world, you'll always be my true mate. I'll never care about anyone like I do about you."

One more kiss and Kenrick walked out of Zaria's apartment and didn't look back. Her heart and her wolf were screaming to go back and be with Zaria, no matter the cost, but she had to give her this choice, and she had an obligation to her pack. She was the Wulver Alpha, and her destiny was to lead.

Next morning, Kenrick brought her bags downstairs. She hadn't slept a wink, knowing she was most likely leaving without the love of her life. Eden and Dante waited for her at the bottom of the stairs. She had said her goodbyes to the cubs the night before. It was too early for them to be up.

"I've got the truck ready," Dante said.

"Is she…?"

Dante shook her head. "Sorry, Ricky."

Kenrick gulped down her emotions and nodded. Dante took her bags and went out to the truck. Eden took her hands.

"Don't give up hope, Ricky. I know she loves you, but she's fighting a lifetime of fear. Maybe with a few weeks' separation she'll come to you."

"She's not coming. I can't live hoping that Zari will change her mind. Will you make sure she's looked after, whether she stays here or leaves Wolfgang County?"

"Of course I will, Ricky," Eden said.

It killed her to think of Zaria alone, outside the protection of Wolfgang County, with Ovid still on the loose.

"Oh." Kenrick took out an envelope from her back pocket. "I went to the bank yesterday and opened an account for her. The details are in here, if you could give it to her. I'll always keep it topped up with money. She'll probably refuse, but I can't think of my mate out there with nothing, no food, no shelter—I should be providing that."

"Don't worry. I'll give it to her."

"No matter what she says, my wolf thinks of her as my mate, and I need to do something to help her," Kenrick said sadly.

"I know. You better go or you'll miss your flight. Safe journey, Ricky," Eden said.

"Thanks for having me."

Kenrick trudged to the truck. Each heavy footstep felt like a stamp on her heart. She got in and Dante said, "You want to wait five more minutes?"

Kenrick shook her head and said gloomily, "No, there's no point in dragging it out. She's not coming."

Dante nodded and started the engine, and as she pulled away, Eden came running from the house, waving her hands.

"Wait, Dante."

Kenrick got out of the truck and saw the best sight of her life coming running up the road—Zaria with her rucksack over her shoulders.

Kenrick's heart started to thud with excitement. Could it be? Could it be true that Zaria wanted to come with her?

Zaria got to the truck and dropped her rucksack. She was breathing heavily. "I didn't think I'd make it. Is your offer still open?"

Kenrick could hardly believe this was happening. Zaria wanted to come to Wulver Forest with her. She pulled Zaria into the biggest hug and said, "Thank the Great Mother. I didn't think you'd come. Aye, the offer is always open for you, lassie, and you can come back whenever you want. You know that?"

Zaria smiled. "I know. Show me your beautiful forest."

Kenrick kissed her on the lips. "Let's go, lassie."

Eden had joined them by this time and hugged them both. "Good luck, you two. Keep in touch."

"We will, and tell Marco I'll call him soon," Zaria said.

"I will. Safe journey."

Dante smiled when they got in the truck. "Let's get you to the airport, or that plane to Scotland will leave without you."

It was happening. Kenrick's dream was actually coming true.

CHAPTER FIFTEEN

Zaria held Kenrick's hand tightly, reminding herself why she was taking this chance, why she was leaving everything she knew, and why she was in a plane thousands of feet above the ground.

She looked around the airplane and it wasn't as packed and cramped as she expected. She and Kenrick had lots of room to breathe, thankfully. Kenrick had booked them in first class, yet another reminder of the gulf between them. Kenrick came from a proud pack that owned a large international business, and she came from a pack that had lied, cheated, and stolen their way through history. What would Kenrick's parents think of her?

These were amongst all the millions of things that she had lain awake last night worrying about. Before she met Kenrick, she never would have imagined in a million years that she would trust a dominant at all, far less go halfway around the world with them, but the thought of letting Kenrick go was just too much to bear. She had no expectations for this trip, maybe she would fly home in a week or two, but she had to know if she could build something with this wolf the Great Mother seemed to be pushing her towards.

"Are you okay?" Kenrick asked.

"What?" Zaria smiled at Kenrick. "Just a bit tense. I've never flown before."

"We'll be there before you know it. I can't wait to show you my home," Kenrick said.

"How much longer?"

"A few hours. Not long. Then my pal Rhuri will pick us up from

Glasgow Airport and take us to Wulver Forest. It should take us around three hours and bit. We'll get home in time for a big steak dinner at my ma's," Kenrick replied.

Zaria sighed and tightened her grip on Kenrick's hand.

"What's wrong?" Kenrick asked.

Everything, Zaria thought. *I've never felt so inadequate in my life.* "Did you tell your mom you were bringing someone home?" Zaria asked.

"Aye, I phoned at the airport. Don't worry, my ma is the nicest woman and Mater you could meet, and my da is a gentle giant."

Zaria smiled. "Like you, you mean?"

"I'm gentle enough with my kin and those I care about, but I can be the fiercest wolf you'll meet when I need to protect them."

"I know, I saw that when you helped kill Leroux, but it feels like you're bringing home a Lupa waif and stray."

Kenrick wanted more than anything to kiss Zaria again and make her feel secure. So she inched forward and whispered, "You were never a waif and stray. You're the strongest and bravest wolf I know to have been alone for so long. My parents will see that strength in you because I do. You're only a Lupa by birth, you share nothing with them, and I want to offer a new pack, a new family name, but it's your choice."

Zaria searched Kenrick's eyes and saw nothing but truth, love, and want. She parted her lips and invited Kenrick to kiss her, and she did with such tenderness that Zaria let go of all the tension she was feeling.

Kenrick pulled away and smiled. "Better?"

"Better," Zaria replied.

"Good. I need to thank you too. I was dreading this journey home, not just because I was leaving you."

"What else?" Zaria asked.

"I was dreading it because I was coming home to be Alpha, and my life was set out for me. I didn't believe in myself or my abilities until I met you. When you ran to the Lupas, all the abilities I didn't think I had rose to the surface, and I led the Wolfgangs to you. I know now that I was born to lead."

Zaria caressed her cheek. "Of course you were. You'll be the best kind of Alpha, kind, gentle, understanding, but fierce when you're defending your own and your pack lands."

"Thank you. That means a lot," Kenrick said.

Zaria noticed they were getting a few glances from the humans around them. "I think we've caught everyone's attention."

"Nah. It's not you. You can pass for a human female, a beautiful one at that, but still human. It's me who stands out wherever I go."

Kenrick smiled and pointed at her dreadlocked hair. "The hair, the build, the height—it all challenges the human constructs of gender. To them, I'm abnormal."

Zaria gave a low growl. "Human gender rules are stupid. You are everything a wolf should be, Ricky." Zaria truly meant that, but she'd never admitted it out loud before. Kenrick was perfect, her dream wolf, but could the life she could offer Zaria be her dream too?

"Thank you, lassie," Kenrick said, then looked around quickly, "Let's play spot the paranormal."

Zaria laughed softly. "Spot the paranormal?"

"Aye, have you never played it before? We can't be the only non humans on the plane."

"No, I can honestly say I haven't."

"Well, let me tell you the rules. You spot a Vampire—ten points. Witch and fae—five points, shapeshifter and wolf—one point, cause that's an easy spot."

Zaria giggled. "Okay, game on, wolf."

Kenrick was happy to see Zaria looking excitedly out of the plane window as it was coming to a halt on the runway. Zaria had been nervous for most of the flight until they had their talk, but now at least she was starting to treat this as an exciting adventure. Kenrick had to keep reminding herself that it wasn't certain that Zaria was going to stay with her, even though she felt like she was bringing her Mater home to her pack. This was only a chance, a choice she had given Zaria. Zaria had to feel free to make her choice or she'd never be settled here.

"Look at the rain, Ricky. It's bouncing off the runway."

Kenrick smiled. "Welcome to Scotland. You'll be seeing lots of rain."

After twenty minutes they were finally ready to disembark. "This place is so busy," Zaria said. She had never been somewhere so packed with people and it was a bit overwhelming.

Kenrick, who was carrying their hand luggage, said, "Just hang on to my arm tightly."

They eventually made their way to customs, and Zaria held her breath while the customs officers checked her passport, but she got waved through quickly. Dante's contact was clearly good at what they did.

"I thought my heart was going to burst," Zaria said.

"Don't worry. I trust Dante, and if she thinks someone is good at their job, then I know they will be. Let's get the cases."

Kenrick pushed the trolley, heavy with luggage, out into the foyer of the airport.

"Which one is Rhuri? There's so many people."

"Look for someone with hair like me, except dyed bright red," Kenrick said.

Zaria scanned the hundreds of figures in front of them. "I'm never going to spot someone—" Then she did. Tall, well built, and with extraordinary hair like Kenrick, but a little different. Her dark brown hair was shaved on the sides, with the same Celtic symbols as Kenrick's scalp, but on top she had a mane of obviously dyed flame-red hair. "Wow, you Scottish wolves sure like to stand out like peacocks."

Kenrick laughed and Rhuri, spotting them, waved her hand. "Let's go introduce you to my best friend."

Zaria's nerves came back. She was sure Kenrick's friends and family wouldn't be ecstatic about a Lupa wolf arriving in their pack lands. She followed Kenrick, and Rhuri came towards them, meeting them halfway.

Rhuri had a huge smile on her face. She thumped her chest in salute to Kenrick and engulfed her in a hug. "Welcome home, pal. Did ye have a good journey?" Rhuri asked.

"Aye, excellent. Let me introduce my friend, Zaria. She's going to stay with us for a few weeks at least."

Rhuri inclined her head respectfully. No dominant wolf had done that except Kenrick. "Welcome Zaria. I'm glad to meet ye," Rhuri said.

Rhuri had a broader Scottish accent than Kenrick, and she had to concentrate on the words to make she understood, but her voice's beautiful sing-song quality was the same as Kenrick's. She wore the same leather wristbands on as Kenrick but had different ear piercings.

Hers were black horn shaped ones piercing through her ears. Going by these two, Wulver wolves had their own unique look.

"I hope you'll love Wulver Forest as much as we do," Rhuri said.

"I'm sure I will."

Kenrick and Rhuri packed the Land Rover with the luggage while Zaria gazed around at her first look at the city of Glasgow. It wasn't what she expected. When Zaria thought of Scotland, she imagined rural villages and farmland, but from all the large buildings and built-up area around the airport, Glasgow could match many big cities.

Kenrick took her hand and said, "What are you thinking?"

"I wasn't expecting a city like this. I thought rural villages and small towns," Zaria said.

"This is the west of Scotland, lassie. It's very different in the Highlands. I can't wait to show you."

Kenrick was right. It didn't take too much driving time on the freeway, or the motorway as they called it here, for the large towering city buildings to give way to rolling fields, sheep and cows grazing, and mountains in the distance.

"It's beautiful, Ricky."

"This is only the start." Kenrick smiled.

As they left the airport Zaria felt like someone was watching her. She turned around quickly but there was no one there.

Strange.

❖

Rhuri had been driving them for a few hours and Kenrick was delighted that Zaria was loving the scenery around them. Kenrick was proud of her home, and also very proud of her friend Rhuri being so welcoming to Zaria.

She chattered non-stop to Zaria and took a very gentle approach to her. In Kenrick's quick phone call home, she had briefly explained Zaria's difficulties. She wanted her to feel as comfortable as possible.

"I'm glad you came to visit us, Zaria. All the pack is excited to meet you. It's a great time to visit too, with Ricky's Alpha ceremony next week."

Zaria gazed at Kenrick with what Kenrick hoped was pride. "I'm looking forward to it, Rhuri."

As their journey continued, Kenrick pointed out the mountain range in the distance that surrounded Wulver Loch.

"So has your loch got a monster like Loch Ness?" Zaria said with a smile.

"Aye, we have. The Water Kelpie," Rhuri said excitedly.

Kenrick facepalmed. "By the Great Mother, don't get her started on the Water Kelpie."

Zaria laughed. "What's a Kelpie?"

Rhuri said, "I saw it when I was eight years old. It was amazing."

Kenrick shook her head. She had heard this story a million times from Rhuri and a few other believers in the pack, and then there were the human tourists who came to catch a glimpse.

"It's different from the Loch Ness Monster. The Kelpie is a mythical water spirit, sometimes called a demon. It's supposed to be able to shapeshift, take many forms—like a horse, a naked woman—but it's only a myth."

Zaria nudged Kenrick and said with a cheeky smile, "Surely a werewolf would have a more open mind than that?"

Rhuri piped up from the driver's seat, "You never said a truer word, Zaria. I've been telling her that for years, but will she listen?"

Kenrick chuckled. "I guess I'm outvoted then. Well let's see if you spot this Kelpie while you're here."

Zaria winked at her and squeezed her hand. Kenrick was delighted to see Zaria comfortable enough to poke fun at her. There was such a difference in her since they first met.

Hopefully it would continue.

"Drop us here, Rhuri. I want to show Zaria the loch," Kenrick said.

The car stopped by what looked like a pathway into the forest. But the entrance was guarded by a car barrier and two big dominant wolves.

Zaria wondered why the forest needed a guard, but before she had a chance to think about it for too long, Kenrick had opened her car door and offered her hand to help her out.

As she did, Rhuri said, "Will I take all the bags to your den?"

Kenrick looked to her and said, "You don't mind sharing my den do you? There are two bedrooms so you'll have your privacy."

Zaria didn't want to be on her own in a new place where she was a stranger, so that suited her perfectly. "I'd like to be close to you."

Kenrick gave her the biggest smile, and the smile warmed her heart. This was the first time in her life making another wolf feel good and happy meant something to her—apart from her sister.

"Good. Let me show you our beautiful loch."

Zaria got out and was hit by the freshest scent. She filled her lungs deeply. There were notes of rain, water, wood, pine, and a distinctive earthy smell that made her shiver.

When she turned to Kenrick, she had her eyes closed taking everything in.

"I'm glad to be back home," Kenrick said.

Rhuri drove away and was let through the barrier. The trees around the checkpoint looked almost designed to cover what was behind them.

The loch was much bigger than the lake in Wolfgang County and was surrounded by a mountain with rolling hills. Zaria could imagine how the loch was hewn from the mountainside by the great glaciers, millennia ago.

At the end of the loch, not too far from them, was a large white stone building with *Wulver Whisky* painted in black letters on the side. It was so near the loch that the water lapped at the sides of the walls.

"Look, this is the one of the best views. You can see right down to the end of the loch."

Zaria was awed at the natural majesty of the loch and the quaint white cottages and small buildings that followed its contours, right down to the other side of the loch. Each building looked old but all of them had solar panels on the roofs. Clearly the Wulvers were ecologically aware.

Lots of humans milled around the buildings and stood by the loch's edge, with children running around playing. It was a busy place.

"Is that where you live? Those buildings down there?"

Kenrick chuckled. "Nah, that's for the benefit of the tourists. There are sweet shops, tea shops, gift shops, that kind of thing. We have steady stream of human visitors here. The adults love to come and tour the whisky plant, and the kids love the water, the adventure play park we have further down, and watching out for that Water Kelpie."

Zaria smiled. "Sounds great. So where do your wolves live?"

Kenrick winked. "You'll see." She pointed to a large silver building down at the other end of the loch. "That's Wulver Spring bottling plant. We have the freshest, clearest water in the world, I think. Come and try."

Kenrick jumped down from the wall onto the stone beach and held out her hand to Zaria. She took her hand and jumped. Kenrick led them over to the water's edge. Zaria could see how clear it was. No wonder Wulver Spring was so popular.

Kenrick crouched down and cupped some water into her hand and drank it quickly. She let out a long sigh. "Ah, Great Mother, I missed that taste when I was gone. Here, try some."

Kenrick cupped some more water with both hands and brought it up to Zaria. The water dripped through her hands but there was plenty still in there. Zaria put her hands around Kenrick's and lowered her lips to lap up the water. Kenrick wasn't exaggerating. It was the clearest, freshest water she had ever had, and the deep, cold temperature made it seem as if you were drinking the water of the melted glacier that first sculpted this landscape.

Zaria drank a little more, then looked up at Kenrick with a smile. "That was delicious."

Kenrick let the rest of the water drip onto the stone beach. "Just imagine how much better it tastes after your wolf's had a long run in the forest."

Zaria noticed a sparkle in Kenrick's eyes, as if they were more alive somehow, and it totally captivated her. "You look different here, Ricky. More vigorous, vital, and alive."

Kenrick took Zaria's hand and placed it on her chest. "Our pack has been here a very long time, and we've become connected to the air, the water, the earth, the trees. They sustain us and we sustain them. I can't wait to show you and tell you our story."

Zaria was certain that whatever the story was and whatever Kenrick showed her, she was only going to fall deeper and deeper for this remarkable wolf.

❖

Kenrick offered Zaria her hand and was delighted when she took it without question. She could feel how nervous Zaria was and wanted to make things as easy as possible. They walked up to the security barrier and the two wolves on duty saluted.

"Jansen, how's things?" Kenrick said.

"It's been pretty quiet around here. Good trip?" Jansen asked.

Kenrick smiled at Zaria and then looked back. "Excellent. This is Zaria. Let everyone know she is to get full access."

"Yes, Ricky. Nice to meet you, Zaria." He turned to the other wolf and said, "Raise the barrier."

They walked through and straight in front was a road that went up and around a bend, but they walked to the left to a wall of tall pine trees.

"Are you ready to see our marketplace?" Kenrick asked Zaria.

Zaria looked at the dense wooded area. "Your marketplace is through there?"

Kenrick nodded. "We like our privacy. The humans think we live out front at the shore, but this is the real Wulver Forest."

Kenrick led Zaria though the trees on a well-worn path. After a few minutes' walk they reached a high wooden post fence which had a gate with a security entry on it.

"Does this fence run around the whole of Wulver Forest?" Zaria asked.

"No, it's too big. Just this end to try to keep the nosey humans out." Kenrick raised her wrist to the security entry. "Our wristbands let us in."

The large wooden gate opened and Zaria gasped. "It's beautiful."

It was truly a marketplace. Two lines of shops ran on either side of a wide wooden walkway. Every so many yards there were benches and small trees. Wolves and cubs went in and out of the shops with full shopping bags. Some stopped to chat with one another and others sat at tables enjoying coffee.

Baskets of flowers and plants hung from every shopfront. On each roof were solar panels.

"It's like the perfect little ecological village," Zaria said.

Kenrick smiled brightly. "I'm glad you think so. That's what the Wulvers live by, being as in tune with nature as possible." Kenrick led them into the marketplace, and she got salutes and waves from the other wolves as they strolled. "We recycle everything, use material from the forest, get as much energy as we can from our solar panels, but the sun isn't always so good in bonnie Scotland, so we have a water turbine at the other end of the loch, next to the bottling plant."

Kenrick led then to the front of one of the bigger shops. "This is our food store."

Zaria peeked in the store and saw bright, colourful produce and smelled good meat. "That smell is making my mouth water."

Kenrick laughed. "We'll eat soon. The shops down the left side all back onto the shops the humans use on the shore front. That's how we get our deliveries in."

Zaria turned around in a circle, trying to take all this in. "It's amazing the humans don't know there's another world back here."

"You've arrived on a good day. It's not raining just now, but look up," Kenrick said.

There was a large mechanical system high up above the stores. "What is that?"

"Retractable roof. If it starts to rain, we can cover the marketplace to make things a bit more pleasant, and if it's really hot in the summer we can close it and put the solar panels to good use."

"Wow."

"Let's walk down to the far end."

Everyone they passed smiled at Zaria. There were no strange looks or bad vibes, as Zaria had worried. She followed Kenrick to the end. They walked down a ramp off the wooded marketplace. Up ahead was a stone bridge, and to the right was what looked like a small wooden amphitheatre.

"What's that, Ricky?"

"It's our wee theatre. We show movies and the young people put on shows. It's really popular with the cubs."

Zaria shook her head and laughed softly. "Ricky, I can honestly say I never expected anything as wonderful or beautiful as this. I'm blown away."

Kenrick winked. "We haven't even gotten started yet."

After they crossed the stone bridge, Zaria followed onto a well-maintained stone path. They were now in the real Wulver Forest, Zaria guessed, surrounded by huge, ancient looking, towering trees. The scent was wonderful, exciting, and new, and made her wolf anxious to run.

"This is where you all live?" Zaria asked.

"Aye, we each have a large piece of land. There's plenty of space for us all, but we have to go a bit deeper into the forest to get to my den," Kenrick said.

"What kind of trees are these? The scent is amazing."

Kenrick stopped by one thick-trunked old tree. She put her hand on the bark and took a moment, silently connecting to everything about her. These wolves were true forest dwellers, Zaria realized, much more than the Wolfgangs or other North American wolf packs she knew of.

"This is a Scots pine, one of the main trees in our forest. There's also Douglas fir, oak, ash, beech, chestnut, and so much more."

"Beautiful. How far is your den?" Zaria asked.

"It's a pretty walk with lots to see, maybe fifteen minutes, or five if we shifted. Which would you prefer?"

Zaria knew immediately. She took Kenrick's hand and smiled. "The long scenic route, I think."

"Aye, that sounds best," Kenrick said. She felt Zaria loosening up and relaxing with every minute they spent in her home, and Kenrick was getting more excited by her response to Wulver Forest. She tried to temper her joy. It didn't mean Zaria would stay, but she was going to give it her best shot. If the long scenic route was what it took to win Zaria's heart, then she would do it.

As they walked along, Kenrick told Zaria about the different trees, plants, and animals. Luckily it wasn't raining, so Zaria could see the landscape at its best.

Soon they were a few yards from Kenrick's den. "We just take the path to the left up here."

Zaria walked down the path between the trees and gasped when it opened out onto a clearing. In front of her was a huge wood-framed house, held high up in the trees by ancient looking, thick, solid tree trunks that passed through the balcony around the house up into the leafy canopy above.

"This is your den? This is how you all live?" Zaria gasped.

Kenrick was full of smiles at her reaction. "Aye, we live in the trees. It's the Wulver way."

"This is why you were so good at climbing trees back in Wolfgang County."

"Yeah, we enjoy climbing. You like it, then?"

It was obviously really important to Kenrick that she liked her den, and she did. "I love it."

A walkway started at the foot of the trees and spiralled around until it reached the house at the top. She followed Kenrick up the stairs, and as they got higher, she realized there was another walkway that led through the tops of the trees away from Kenrick's den.

"Is that how you get from den to den?"

"Aye." Kenrick smiled. "Although I prefer to climb."

Zaria raised an eyebrow. "Are you a werewolf or are you a weremonkey?"

Kenrick laughed. "We Wulvers are just good climbers. Let me take you up."

When they got to the top, Zaria realized why the Wulvers liked living so high up off the ground—the beautiful view of the loch and Wulver mountain.

"It's breathtaking, Ricky."

Kenrick gently pulled her hand and said, "There's more. Come with me."

She opened the doors and led Zaria into a large open-plan living space. In the middle was a kitchen area with all the usual appliances, and off to the side there were doors to what she imagined might be other bedrooms or bathrooms.

Up at the other end of the living area was a large bed, pressed against a far wall of glass. "Is that your bed?"

"Aye, I like to sleep looking over the forest. Come and see."

When she got closer, Zaria realized this side of the den overlooked a medium sized river, and the wall of glass windows was actually two sliding doors that could be opened so you could walk out onto the balcony or lie in bed and watch the stars and listen to the sounds of the river.

To the side, doors opened up to the balcony, and on the right-hand side there was an outdoor shower with a wooden grid underneath that let the water flow back down to nourish the earth.

Zaria was lost for words. She could have never imagined wolves living like this, in happy family communities, and in such a stunning landscape.

"What do you think, Zari? It's important to me that you like it," Kenrick said.

Zaria tried to find the words. "I think…I couldn't have imagined a more beautiful den or pack lands. It's no wonder you don't want to leave here."

Kenrick couldn't have looked happier at her response. "That means a lot." The she suddenly looked at the clock on the wall and said, "It's almost light-up time." Kenrick took her hand and guided her onto the balcony.

"Wait, what's light-up time?"

"You'll see. Watch." Kenrick stood close behind her.

The evening darkness was falling, and she could sense a change in the atmosphere of the forest. Then it happened. The evening gloom was lifted by the pretty glow of countless fairy lights. She hadn't noticed in her walk up the spiral staircase that the lights were entwined around it, but now they were lit up. The wooded walkways that Kenrick said joined all the tree houses together were also lit up in the darkness and could be seen, linking tree to tree, far off in the distance.

"It's magical," Zaria said.

Kenrick rested her head in the crook of Zaria's neck. "It gets dark early here, so it's practical as well as pretty. I've missed this. It's good to be home."

Zaria took Kenrick's hands and wrapped them around her middle. She could see now how much a part of Kenrick these lands were. She was connected to the very essence of this forest and had become even more alive and vibrant since they got here.

Zaria could see how easily she could fall in love with this place, as she was with Kenrick.

"I can't wait see the rest, Ricky. The scenery is just…beyond words."

Kenrick whispered in Zaria's ear, making her shiver. "Thank you for coming and giving me a chance, lassie."

"Anytime, Highlander." Zaria smiled.

CHAPTER SIXTEEN

K enrick was so full of excitement and energy having Zaria here. She was everything she always wanted, and a bedroom might separate them just now, but Zaria was here, in her country, in her pack lands, and in her den. Now she just had to prove her love to her and show Zaria that she could be a Wulver and leave her Lupa past behind.

Kenrick woke up at four thirty and couldn't get back to sleep. Her instinct was to go on a long run, but she had planned that for Zaria's first morning, then breakfast at her parent's den.

She lay in bed listening to the dawn chorus of the birds and the forest wakening. She felt an absence—something was missing. She should have Zaria in her arms.

Zaria was getting more used to her touch and their kisses, and hugs and hand-holding were getting more frequent, but they'd shared nothing like that night in Wolfgang County when they both lost control.

Ultimately, though, it had been too soon and Zaria had become scared. When Kenrick touched Zaria she wanted to be as gentle as she needed and never echo anything that Ovid had done to her. To do that, she would dampen every dominant instinct she had.

Wolf mating was complex and Zaria didn't have good role models, something good for her to base her feelings and expectations on. Maybe Kenrick could speak to her ma about it. The absence she felt now, here in her bed, was not about sex. All she wished was that she had Zaria in her arms listening to the forest awakening and starting a new day.

She couldn't lie here any longer, so she got up and pulled on the pair of jeans she'd discarded last night and walked over to the kitchen to make a hot cup of lemon water. It was her favourite morning drink, with the added sweetness of a drop of honey.

Once she made her drink, she listened for any movement from Zaria's room, but there wasn't a sound. She would just have to be patient and wait for their day to start.

❖

Zaria's eyes fluttered open and she was hit with a warm feeling in her chest when she remembered where she was. In her sleepy state, she reached to her side and was disappointed to find the space empty.

"Ricky," she said out loud.

Her wolf, her body, her subconscious expected and wanted Kenrick to be beside her in sleep. That was new and unusual for her. Never had she wanted to be physically close to another wolf. Her natural wolf bonding instinct had been destroyed by her upbringing and by Ovid's cruelty.

Not having to look over her shoulder, even though habit still made her at the airport—that was another new sensation. But now, thanks to the Wolfgangs and Kenrick, she was safe for the first time in her life, and that was a lot to take in and believe. Leroux and Ovid were dead and the rest of the Lupa wolves were chased away.

Last night, Kenrick got them some food from one of the village restaurants while she unpacked, and then they called Dante and Eden back in the States and set her up with an email account so that she could contact Marco.

After that, she just needed to sleep and now she felt so rested—in fact, more relaxed and rested than she had ever felt. Never in a million years would she have believed she'd end up here in Scotland with the Wulver pack, when she ran from the diner and the Lupas.

Zaria sat up, yawned, and ran her hand over the crisp white sheets on Kenrick's spare bed. She could get used to living in such comfort. She stretched then walked over to look out of her bedroom window. The view wasn't as good as Kenrick's, but still wonderful.

After a visit to the bathroom, she threw on a work shirt of Kenrick's that she'd given her and walked out of the bedroom in search of her. She found Kenrick's bed empty and no trace of her in the den or out on the balcony.

"Ricky? Are you here?" Maybe she went on a run?

"I'm over here," she heard Ricky shout.

Zaria looked around, then followed the sound of Ricky's voice out onto the balcony beside her bed. She wasn't anywhere on the balcony.

"Ricky?"

"I'm just here," Ricky said.

Zaria walked to the edge of the balcony and saw Kenrick sitting precariously on one of the branches of the tree that supported the balcony. Her first thought was Kenrick's safety. They might be werewolves, but they could still get hurt. It was very high off the ground.

Then, when Kenrick smiled at her and said in her sexy lilting voice, "Morning, lassie," safety went out of the window.

Kenrick was only wearing a pair of jeans which were unbuttoned, had bare feet and a bare chest, and her mane of dreadlocked hair hung loose around her shoulders. Kenrick looked so undone that it undid Zaria. She felt her chest heat up and lost the words she meant to reply. Wolves were used to nakedness. It was a natural consequence of shifting to and from their wolf form, but it was a long time since she had been part of a wolf pack, and she had always felt nakedness was a vulnerability that could be taken advantage of. Ovid had always leered at her as she shifted, and in the human world it was the same. It would take some getting used to, being in a pack that didn't objectify her.

She couldn't take her eyes off Kenrick. She was so sexy, such a magnificent example of a dominant wolf. She was strong and powerful looking, but her eyes shone with such gentleness that it disarmed Zaria.

That was the killer combination that sneaked in through her barriers. As she'd grown older, Zaria knew the need to mate would tempt her, so she built up her defences and vowed to never fall for a dominant wolf, but she had not expected one like Kenrick.

Kenrick leapt up onto the branch and walked along it without a hint of a wobble. "Zari? Are you okay?"

"Would you come onto the balcony, please?"

"Aye." Kenrick vaulted onto the balcony beside her. "Is something wrong?"

Zaria couldn't take her eyes from Kenrick's muscled stomach and her gaze fell to the open buttons of her jeans. Kenrick clearly wasn't wearing any underwear. Heat immediately flushed all across her body, her teeth broke through her gums, and the heat had turned into a deep ache and want in her sex.

Every cell in her body was telling her to scratch Kenrick across the chest and mark her as her own, challenge her. It was so hard to fight her nature. She closed her eyes, knowing they would have probably changed to yellow. After a few deep breaths, she opened her eyes and looked up at Kenrick. "You shouldn't sit out there. It could be dangerous."

Zaria didn't know if Kenrick bought her explanation, but she just laughed and said, "I'm a weremonkey, remember? I sit there every morning. It's peaceful."

"It just makes me nervous," Zaria said, desperately trying not to respond to the sexual tension between them.

"Did you sleep well?" Kenrick asked.

Zaria let out a breath and the tension started to dissipate. "I don't think I've ever had a more peaceful sleep. Thank you." She could see how happy that reply made Kenrick. It seemed that Kenrick just wanted to make *her* happy, and that was a nice sensation.

"That's great." Kenrick leaned in and kissed her on the cheek. "If you're happy, I'm happy."

That sentence blew Zaria away. She'd been brought up to believe submissives were there to keep dominants happy, to take care of them in any way they needed. She had learned in Wolfgang County that wasn't the case, but she found it hard to believe. Now Kenrick was starting to make her believe.

"I'll make you a hot drink. Do you want tea? Lemon water with honey?" Kenrick asked.

"Lemon water with honey would be nice. What are we going to do today?"

Kenrick squeezed fresh lemon into a cup and poured on hot water. "I thought we'd go running this morning and I'd show you a couple of interesting places, then Ma and Da have invited us for breakfast. After that I'll show you around some more—I've got lots to show you—and you could take some pictures to email to Marco."

Zaria smiled. "That would be nice."

She wasn't lying but meeting Kenrick's mother and pater made her really nervous. Why would they want a Lupa stray in their pack?

❖

Kenrick didn't want to make Zaria feel uncomfortable in her nakedness, so she told her she would meet her at the bottom of the stairs to shift. It took a conscious effort to remind herself that Zaria felt self-conscious and protective of her body. It hurt Kenrick deep inside that such twisted wolves had made a young wolf like Zaria take something as innocent as shifting from skin and make it sordid.

This morning Zaria seemed focused on Kenrick's body. She could feel Zaria's wolf call to her, her scent show her readiness to mate, but she forced herself not to gaze at how sexy Zaria looked dressed in her shirt. She never ever wanted to look at her like Ovid did.

She heard Zaria coming, but she kept her eyes facing front.

"I'm ready, Ricky," Zaria said.

Again Kenrick didn't turn around. "Okay."

She felt Zaria's bare arm brush hers and she shivered.

"Is everything all right?" Zaria asked.

Kenrick's body was thrumming with excitement. She was about to go on a run with the woman she loved. Normally two wolves involved in mating would run, play, tease, test each other's boundaries, but she couldn't do that with Zaria. Zaria was different.

Kenrick turned around and didn't dare look down at her nakedness. "Aye, you ready to go?"

Zaria smiled. "Yes, I can't wait to feel the earth beneath my paws."

Kenrick would just have to run her feelings off. "Let's go." Kenrick shifted quickly and stretched out all her limbs. Zaria shifted and surprised Kenrick by nuzzling her snout.

Before Kenrick could respond, Zaria shot off into the forest saying, *Catch me if you can!*

Kenrick growled. *She tricked me.*

She sped off into the forest after Zaria's wolf. Kenrick was faster than Zaria by a long way and soon caught sight of her brown and black fur up ahead. The exhilaration of the chase was taking over, and all that mattered was tracking Zaria and catching her.

They darted through the trees, Kenrick gaining on Zaria with every step. Kenrick had the advantage of knowing every tree in the forest and took a few shortcuts. She eventually got to a few yards behind Zaria.

You can't catch me, wolf, Zaria teased.

She's challenging me? Kenrick thought.

Kenrick had never had so much fun. She forgot about all the rules she had imposed on herself and followed her wolf play instincts. Kenrick leapt through the air and knocked Zaria's wolf onto her back. Zaria lay submissively, panting while she stood over her.

Kenrick's heart was pounding, her body surged with energy—and then she remembered Zaria's issues and fears. Kenrick jumped straight off her, leaned her front legs down, and lowered her head.

I'm sorry, Zari. I was just playing. I didn't mean to frighten you.

Zaria jumped up. *You didn't. We were just playing. You don't need to submit to me, Ricky. Stand up.*

I don't want to frighten you, Ricky replied.

Zaria padded closer. *I challenged you, Ricky. You did nothing wrong. Let's have fun.*

Kenrick stood up tall and gave her a lick on the snout. *Okay, sorry.*

Zaria lifted her head up high and took a big sniff of the air. *You're right about your forest, Ricky. It's different.*

What do you scent? Kenrick asked.

Wood, leaves, pine needles, lush wet raindrops on green leaves, and safety.

Kenrick was filled with joy at Zaria's description. She scented what Kenrick did. Safety and hopefully home. *Follow me and I'll show you more,* Kenrick said.

This time they padded on together, side by side.

Zaria slowed her speed to keep pace with Kenrick as they came out from the trees to a clearing. She saw a waterfall cover the mouth of the small cave and fall into a shallow pool that washed away into the river. The unusual thing about it was the water was red, and the stones that the water washed upon were red.

What is that, Ricky? Zaria asked.

The humans call it the Devil's Cave. There's a whole folklore going back generations. They say that witches, fae, demons, Vampires, and werewolves are seen here.

Not weremonkeys? Zaria joked.

Just the wolves. Of course, over the years we've had all kinds of paranormal creatures visit us here, but not to consort with the devil. We never discouraged the rumours, though. They kept a few humans who would want to hunt us away.

Are there any natural wolves here? Zaria asked.

No, they were hunted to extinction in Scotland. They say the last one was killed in the seventeenth century, but my pater and I have been campaigning the Scottish government to let us reintroduce them on our private land. It would be good for the balance of the environment.

Sounds like a good idea. So what turns the water red? Zaria said.

Kenrick snorted. *It's just the red sandstone underneath that gives it the red colour. Perfectly natural, but try telling a superstitious human that.*

I'd love to get a picture of this for Marco.

We will. If you've had enough running for just now, why don't we head back. Ma will be expecting us for breakfast.

Great! Zaria said with false enthusiasm. Tension and nervousness painted a more accurate picture of what she felt.

❖

Zaria had a shower, then looked through the clothes she had brought with her. Eden, Kyra, and Lena had been generous, but these clothes weren't her own. She hadn't earned the money or served a useful purpose in the pack to earn them.

The thought depressed her. She owned nothing and had nothing to offer. She was going to meet Kenrick's parents in borrowed clothes. Even if she was brave enough to stay and have a life with Kenrick, she was never going to be good enough. How could she be a Mater of such a wonderful pack, which ran multinational businesses, when she didn't even have her own clothes?

Why did I come here? She'd raised Kenrick's hopes that she'd make a life with her. She sighed and closed her eyes. Ovid's face burst into her mind. *I'm spoiled goods.*

"No. I'm not," Zaria told herself firmly. She stood up angrily and picked one of the dresses Eden had given her. For however long she was here, she would give the best impression she could.

Zaria dressed and applied some light make-up. She looked at herself in the mirror and brushed down her dress. *I'll have to do as I am.*

She walked out of her bedroom and turned around to look for Kenrick. What she found made her lose the power of her legs. Kenrick was naked, standing under the outdoor shower, eyes closed and soap suds running down her wet body.

Zaria was instantly wet, her teeth erupted, and her mouth watered. She had never seen anything more erotic in her life. Kenrick was massaging shampoo into her dreadlocks and squeezing them out like a sponge.

Her eyes fell to Kenrick's buttocks. They were muscled and powerful, and Zaria couldn't help but imagine herself slipping in front of Kenrick under the shower. She could see in her mind Kenrick's wet, soapy hands grasping her breasts, thrusting those gorgeous buttocks into her, while she sank her teeth into her neck.

I'm not good enough for her. Maybe Kenrick secretly knows that, her demons said.

She had thought that showing up at Dante and Eden's that morning was enough to show Kenrick that she wanted to see what they could be to each other. But since they'd been in Scotland, Kenrick had only given her pecks on the cheeks or lips, and she purposely didn't look at her or her body the way Zaria looked at Kenrick's. Maybe now that they were back in her pack, Kenrick realized Zaria wasn't what she wanted.

She gasped and opened her eyes quickly. *Get a grip of yourself.*

Zaria then noticed Kenrick was watching her. Did Kenrick know what she was thinking about? She didn't know what to say or do, so she just walked over to the kitchen to get a bottle of water. She took a long sip of water and started to cool down.

Kenrick came into the kitchen wearing just a towel. "Zari? Are you all right?"

Touch me, touch me now, Zaria said like a mantra. She didn't want to make the first move and get it wrong.

"Zari? Look at me."

Zaria turned around slowly. It was worse than she imagined. Her eyes were level with Kenrick's breasts, water dripping down them in the sexiest way. She had her eyes fixed on one drop that had made its way to her nipple and was begging Zaria to lick it off. She covered her face and said with exasperation, "Stop, don't, the water, the drips—it's just too much."

Great Mother, what did I say that for?

When she took her hands away from her face, Kenrick was looking at her with confusion.

"Water? What do you mean?" Kenrick said.

Zaria closed her eyes and centred herself. "Sorry, I'm not making much sense. I'm nervous about meeting your family, your pack."

"Don't worry about that, lassie. They're going to love you. I promise."

"I've never been in a loving family pack like yours, like the Wolfgangs. I don't know what to expect, I suppose."

Kenrick took her hands and squeezed them. "I'll be holding your hand." Then she leaned in and kissed her on the cheek and whispered, "I'll be there and so will Rhuri. Don't worry. You look beautiful in that dress, by the way. You're so pretty."

"Thanks," Zaria replied.

"I'm just going to get dressed in your bedroom, okay? I won't be long," Kenrick said.

Zaria took her bottle out to the balcony. Why did Kenrick want to get dressed in the guest bedroom? Zaria felt like Kenrick was either holding back that natural dominant side of herself, or definitely wasn't as interested as she had been. They had to talk about these things if they were to have any future together.

Zaria took a sip from her bottle and then heard some scrabbling noises from below the balcony. She walked to the edge and saw a child climbing up the tree as high as the branch Kenrick had been sitting on.

"Hey, take my hand, quickly. Get onto the balcony before you fall," Zaria said in panic.

"I'm okay."

The child climbed as nimbly as Kenrick. Zaria grabbed her when she was close and pulled her over the edge of the balcony.

"Thank the Great Mother you're safe," Zaria said.

The child gave her a big smile. "I'm good at climbing, just like Aunt Rhuri and Ricky."

Then it clicked. "You're Milo?"

"Yeah, are you Ricky's new mate? The one from America?"

Was that what everyone in the pack thought? "No we're just friends, but I am from America," Zaria said.

"The way you talk is cool."

Milo was a beautiful child. Around ten years old, she had warm brown skin, darker than hers, a mop of brownish-blond loose dreadlocks, and light blue eyes.

Zaria smiled. "Thanks."

Milo's speech was a mixture of English and Scottish with a hint of a French accent, a nod to her heritage before she came to live with her aunt.

"Does your aunt Rhuri let you climb this high?" Zaria asked.

Milo's eyes danced all around the room. "Yeah, she does...but not *this* high. Granny says if she catches me she'll bite my bum."

"Who's your granny, Milo?"

"The Mater. My aunt's my only real family, but the Mater looks after me lots when Rhuri is working. I've called her Granny since I was wee."

Zaria smiled at the Scottish showing itself at the end of that sentence. This cub was adorable. "Well, you should listen to your granny. You might get hurt," Zaria said.

Milo nodded. "Is Ricky here?"

"Yes, just getting dressed." At that moment Kenrick came out of the bedroom. She was looking so good, wearing jeans, a vintage looking Guns N' Roses T-shirt, and boots, and her hair looked amazing as usual.

"Ricky!" Milo said.

Milo ran over to Kenrick and she swept her up into her arms. "Hey, little cub. How are you?"

"Great. I missed you loads." Kenrick turned Milo around and held her upside down.

Milo giggled and laughed as Kenrick walked over to Zaria. "Have you met this little cub then?"

"Not little." Milo struggled and giggled in Kenrick's hands.

"Yes, I did. She climbed up the tree. Another weremonkey."

Kenrick laughed and let Milo down. Milo staggered and then found her balance. "Tell me about Wolfgang County, Ricky."

"I will, once we get to Granny's, I promise, but she'll bite our behinds if we're late," Kenrick said.

Zaria was amazed at how good Kenrick was with cubs. She was a natural, both with the Wolfgang cubs and Milo. She would be the perfect parent.

She caught herself rubbing her abdomen. It was a biological impulse triggered by Kenrick, something she'd never experienced before. The needs and wants of mating had never come up in her life before, and now here she was, wishing she could give Kenrick a cub.

They hadn't even made love yet, but Zaria's body, her wolf, was pushing her in that direction. But Kenrick wasn't giving her any of the dominant wolf signs that she wanted sex. They had to talk soon.

CHAPTER SEVENTEEN

Milo ran ahead of Kenrick and Zaria. Kenrick held Zaria's hand tightly. She wanted to make her more relaxed, although she was feeling tense herself. She wanted Zaria to be her Mater and be accepted by her pack.

Kenrick had no doubt that her parents and friends wouldn't let her down. She just wanted everything to be perfect for Zaria, and to make sure Zaria had what she'd never had before—pack, family, and love.

"Your mom and dad's house is much bigger than yours," Zaria said.

"Yeah, it's about three times as big, but it's well supported by some of the oldest trees in the forest," Kenrick told her.

Milo ran up the walkway ahead of them to the front door. She knocked at the door and disappeared inside. Kenrick felt Zaria grasp her hand more tightly as they got closer.

"Don't worry, please, Zari. They won't bite."

When they neared the bottom of the stairway, Zaria pulled them underneath the house.

"Are you sure you told them I was a Lupa?" Zaria asked with panic in her voice.

"Aye, I told them, and I told you that you had nothing to worry about. My parents are good people."

Zaria placed her hand on Kenrick's chest. "I'm sorry. I didn't mean they weren't. It's just that I come with a lot of baggage."

Kenrick covered Zaria's hand with hers. "I'm strong enough to help you carry that baggage, we all are, and my pack will help you throw that baggage away. I asked my ma to only invite close friends, and they won't judge you." She leaned in and kissed her cheek.

Zaria touched her face. Again with the peck on the cheek. Zaria was ready for much more, and she guessed it would have to be her that brought it up.

"Come on," Kenrick said.

Zaria followed her up the walkway and tried to steady her breaths. When they got to the top, Kenrick knocked at the door and opened it straight away.

They walked into a large living room, beautifully decorated with natural stone and wooden sculptures. The living room was huge, almost as big as Kenrick's whole den, but she supposed the Alpha and Mater would have a lot of wolves to fit in, when entertaining. There was the most comfortable leather couch that looked like you would just sink into it bordering the area. Rhuri and another couple she didn't know were on the couch, together with Milo and a little boy.

They all stood up and had huge smiles on their faces. Rhuri greeted her first. "Hi, Zaria. Good to see you. I hope Ricky's been showing you around and looking after you?"

"Hi, Rhuri. Yes, she has. Wulver Forest is just beautiful."

Then a smiling woman with the most gorgeous long auburn hair walked forward and opened her arms to her. "Hi, I'm Heather. Welcome to Wulver Forest."

Zaria was surprised but happy by this warm welcome. "Thanks. It's great to be here."

Heather pulled back and indicated to the tall man beside her. "This is my mate, Callum."

Callum gave her a warm smile and a small nod of the head. Dominant wolves would rarely greet a submissive physically, not when they had a mate or suspected the submissive was mated. He had the appearance of a Viking with long braided hair and a big beard, but he gave off the aura of a most gentle person.

"Good to meet you," Zaria said.

Heather added, "And that little boy down there is our son Glen. Glen, say hi to Ms. Zaria."

He looked up and smiled. "Hi, Zaria. Cool name."

Zaria chuckled. "I never knew I had a cool name."

She felt Kenrick's presence behind her, and she shivered when she put her hands on her shoulders.

"Callum is going to join the elite wolves when I'm made Alpha on Saturday, and Rhuri will be my Second."

She could imagine them both being so supportive to Kenrick, and it was clear Rhuri was second most dominant wolf behind Kenrick, just by her demeanour.

"Life's about to change for all of you then?" Zaria said. Could it change for her too?"

Just then an elegant, smiling older woman came into the room. She looked younger than her years. She had fashionably silver hair tied up in a chignon, and wore jeans, a soft sweater, and an apron with the same coat of arms she'd seen in Wolfgang County.

"Where's ma big bairn?"

She heard Kenrick groan and then walk forward to hug her mother. "Ma, not the bairn stuff. I'm a grown wolf."

Zaria leaned over to Heather. "What does bairn mean?"

Heather grinned. "Child, baby. Ricky pretends to hate it, but secretly I think she likes it. She'll always be her ma's bairn."

Kenrick's mother hugged her tightly then gave her a kiss. "Your pater will be here in a second." Then her eyes lifted to Zaria and Zaria's heart started to thud. "Introduce me to the beautiful young wolf you've brought home with you."

Both Kenrick and her ma walked towards her, and the rest of the people in the room thumped their chests in salute.

"Ma, this is Zaria. We met in Wolfgang County. And Zaria, this is Elspeth, my ma, and the Mater of the Wulver pack."

Zaria went to salute but before she could, Elspeth engulfed her in a hug. "I'm so happy to meet you, Zaria. You have a beautiful name."

Zaria was a bit overwhelmed at her welcome. This pack seemed as warm and loving as the Wolfgangs. "It's great to meet you, Mater," Zaria said.

Elspeth stood back. "It's Elspeth. You are most welcome here in our pack lands."

"There's my big wolf." Another voice behind Elspeth said.

A handsome silver-haired man with a neat beard walked in holding a whisky bottle and glasses. He was unmistakably the Alpha.

Kenrick gave him a quick hug and said, "This is Zaria, Da, and Zaria, this is Fergus, Alpha of the Wulver pack."

"Only for a few more days," Fergus said with a grin. He was clearly looking forward to his retirement. The changeover between an Alpha and their heir was never as happy as this in the Lupa pack. Leroux had killed her mother in combat to become the Alpha, but in the Wulver and Wolfgang packs it was a happy occasion, a celebration of a changeover in leadership. It was amazing.

"Pleased to meet you, Zaria. We're glad to have you."

"Thank you, Fergus."

Fergus uncorked the bottle and poured some whisky into each glass he'd brought. "Let's drink to new friends and new beginnings."

"Isn't it a bit early, Fergus?" Elspeth said.

"We are welcoming a new guest. You can only do that with a wee dram, Mater."

"Da, Zaria's pack can't tolerate alcohol," Kenrick said taking both their glasses from her dad.

"It's okay, Ricky. I can take one little drop for the toast," Zaria said.

Once everyone had their glass full, Fergus said, "We welcome our guest Zaria to Scotland and hope your time will be happy here. Slangevar."

"Slangevar," everyone repeated.

Zaria dipped her finger in the amber liquid and dabbed some on her tongue. It burned pleasantly, and when she gulped, a whoosh of exhilaration went through her body. She could only imagine what a sip or a long drink would do to her.

"Wow," Zaria said.

The others chuckled and Fergus said, "Knocks your socks off, no?"

"It sure does." Zaria giggled. She felt much more relaxed now. "What does Slange—"

Zaria struggled with the word and Fergus finished for her. "It's pronounced slan-jee-var. It's the Scottish word for cheers. It means good health."

She was learning so much about this different wolf culture already.

Kenrick sniffed the whisky seriously, swirled it around, took some big sips, then said, "The 1963 cask?"

Fergus grinned from ear to ear. "That's my wolf. I felt it was worth breaking open the barrel for our special guest."

Did Kenrick's parents think they were already together? Had Kenrick told them that? Well, if she thought of her as a mate, she hadn't properly kissed her since they were on the plane.

Elspeth interrupted and said, "Heather? Zaria? Do you want to come and help me in the kitchen?"

Heather was straight off her seat to go. Kenrick took Zaria's hand and squeezed it. "Ma, maybe she doesn't want to go to the kitchen."

"Of course she does." Elspeth offered her arm. "Let's go and have some den talk away from these wolves."

Elspeth's smile defeated Zaria's nerves. She took her arm and said, "I'd love to."

Fergus, Kenrick, Rhuri, and Callum were sitting on the couch enjoying small glasses of whisky, while Milo sat on the floor showing Glen some of her witch skills, making their toy cars float in the air.

"So how was Wolfgang County? Are Dante and Eden well?"

Kenrick nodded. "They're doing well. Especially now that Leroux has been dealt with."

Callum sat forward in his seat. "Rhuri said you helped capture and kill Leroux."

"Aye, I was happy to help. The Lupas have no honour. Can you imagine a dominant attacking a pregnant submissive like Eden?"

"The thought makes me sick," Rhuri said.

"And your Zaria, she is a Lupa?" Fergus asked.

"*Was* a Lupa, and I don't know if she is my Zaria yet. She ran with her sister when she was sixteen. Her sister died giving birth to Leroux's child. Leroux had beaten her sister so badly that she couldn't shift."

Kenrick took a swig of whisky and enjoyed the burn running down her throat.

"What happened to the cub, Ricky?" Callum asked.

"He survived. He's called Marco. Zaria took the baby into Wolfgang County and left him on the doorstep of Dante's house. She knew he would be safe there. You know Flash of the Wolfgang pack?"

"Aye, Flash. I know of his family," Fergus said.

"Well, Flash and his partner Vance adopted him. Zaria always kept close to watch over him but was always on the run. The Lupa Second, Ovid, claimed Zaria as her own. She'd groomed her since she was a young girl, and once Zaria got away she was terrified of being captured by her again." Kenrick slammed down her glass on the coffee table. "When I think what she had to go through alone."

"You love her?" Fergus asked.

Kenrick nodded. "I loved her from the moment we found her on the road and I looked into her eyes."

"And what does she feel?" Fergus asked.

Kenrick ran her hand over her hair. "She's guarded because of her background, and she only agreed to come with me at the last minute."

Rhuri piped in, "But she did come, Ricky. To come to another country, another pack, another culture, is a huge decision. It's a decision that must be based on love."

Kenrick sighed. "I hope so. I told her she could go back whenever she wanted. She needs that freedom after what the Lupas did to her."

Callum asked Fergus for a top up to his whisky and said, "She's a beautiful wolf, Kenrick, and I saw the way she looked at you."

"But to be with me now means becoming Mater, with all that entails," Kenrick said.

Fergus leaned forward and said, "Do you think she will make a good Mater?"

Kenrick looked up at her pater and said without hesitation, "Aye, the best. She's had to take care of herself in a way no submissive wolf should have to. She's strong, intelligent, and a survivor. She would be an inspiration as our Mater."

"Then win her heart, wolf," Fergus said.

Zaria sat at the island in the middle of Elspeth's large kitchen with Heather, while Elspeth busied herself around the oven and steaming pots on the cooker.

"Are you sure I can't help?" Zaria asked.

"No, we're just about done." Elspeth took a bottle of sparking apple juice from the fridge and poured them all out a glass.

Zaria's nerves were back, just like back in Wolfgang County. She hadn't been around groups of submissives since she was at school, and you had to find your way in the hierarchy.

Heather was clearly prominent in the hierarchy by virtue of the fact that the Mater invited her this evening.

"I can't wait to introduce you to the rest of the younger gang of submissives," Heather said.

Elspeth smiled. "We thought it would be a bit overwhelming to invite more wolves tonight. So, how was Eden when you were with the Wolfgangs? Has she recovered from her attack?"

Anytime anyone mentioned Eden's attack, it made Zaria feel guilty by association. She was a Lupa, after all. Elspeth must be thinking the same and wondering why on earth Kenrick has brought her home.

"Yes, she was well when I was there. Very welcoming, they all were."

Elspeth leaned over and stroked Zaria's face. "You seem tense, lassie. I hope we're not making you feel that way."

The gentle caring of a Mater was something that she had missed out on all her life. Her sister never had the confidence or chance to be the Mater she should be.

"No, no. Not you. You've both been kind. I—I need to talk about the elephant in the room. I'm a Lupa. My pack attacked your cousins in the Wolfgang pack. How can you accept me?"

Heather stayed quiet and left the response to her Mater.

"You are you. We don't judge you by your pack or where you come from but by your deeds. From what I've seen and what my Ricky has told me about you, you have had to be stronger and more mature in your years than you should have been. You have survived on your own for a long time and put yourself in danger to keep both the Wolfgangs and your nephew safe. I need no higher recommendation than that."

Zaria let her head drop. It was hard for her to believe kind sentiments. She felt Heather's hand rubbing her back soothingly.

"Ricky says you've been a lone wolf for a long time. We can give you a loving pack if you want it."

"How could I ever be a good mate for your daughter?" Zaria said to Elspeth.

Elspeth sat down on the stool beside her. "I've prayed that Kenrick would find a loving mate all her life. When she didn't find one in the pack, I knew the Great Mother had someone special in mind for her. Someone to help lead the pack with care and gentleness. When she went to stay and work with Dante, I thought she might meet someone in the Wolfgang pack."

"And she found a stray instead," Zaria said.

Elspeth took her hand. "No, the Great Mother had you, a strong independent wolf, drop into her lap. When Ricky called home and told us about you, I knew my prayers had been answered. I could hear the love and adoration in her voice."

"This is all new to me," Zaria said. "Until I met Ricky and stayed with the Wolfgangs, I thought mating was just the subjugation of submissives. In the Lupa pack we were second-class citizens, and all I saw was abuse. I saw violence, hurt, and pain in all those mated pairs around me."

Elspeth shook her head. "I promise you that never happens in the Wulver pack. Any dominant who used their strength against their mate would be disgraced and driven from the pack."

Heather made the smallest of growls and nudged Zaria with her arm. "Callum wouldn't ever dare to think of hurting me. A dominant's strength is to provide meat for our table from the hunt, and to protect us."

Zaria gave a small smile. "It's just hard to let go of all my fears, and Ricky's not exactly a normal wolf with a simple life. She's going to be Alpha. She deserves someone like—"

"A strong, submissive wolf who has overcome adversity and will serve as an inspiration to the pack." Elspeth finished her sentence for her. "But I know it's not just a new life but a new role to fulfil, one that lasts a lifetime, so be sure it's what you want. But know this—no wolf will love you as much as my Ricky."

After a wonderful brunch full of laughter and tales of Kenrick's youth, they walked hand in hand down to the marketplace. As they walked down that wooden walkway and past the shops, with people going in and out, it was amazing to think that the humans who visited didn't know this existed beyond the treeline.

Lots of wolves came up to say hello and introduce themselves. All were warm and welcoming. As Zaria experienced how packs like the Wolfgangs and the Wulvers were run, it made her anger grow towards her own. The Lupa pack dynamics were so warped, they was bound to fail, and now with Leroux dead, she hoped the Lupas would be no more.

They got more smiles and waves from two women pushing prams down the walkway. Zaria turned to Kenrick and said, "Do all your wolves know I'm a Lupa?"

Kenrick shrugged. "Most probably. Den talk has likely spread news of you. You can't keep secrets in a pack."

"I don't know what it's like to be in a pack, a normal one, anyway," Zaria said.

Kenrick lifted her hand and kissed it. "I want to show you that you can be. That's what our first stop is about."

They walked into one of the small shops and Zaria smelled leather everywhere.

"This is our tanner. We get all our leather wristbands made here. Come on." Kenrick led her up to the counter, and a short stocky man with white hair came out from the back.

He saluted her and said, "Ricky you're back, and you've brought a pretty wolf with you, I see."

"Zaria, this is Larc—Larc, this is my friend Zaria," Kenrick said.

Larc bowed his head. "Pleased to meet you, miss."

Zaria couldn't help but smile at the warm-hearted man. "You too, Larc."

"Have you finished it?" Kenrick asked him.

"Aye, just give me a minute," he replied.

He went in the back and Zaria said, "What is he making for you?" Kenrick smiled. "You'll see."

Larc came back with a wooden presentation box and handed it to Kenrick. "Thank you for making it so quickly, Larc. I'll drop off that bottle of malt to you soon."

"You're very welcome, and no rush for the whisky. It's worth waiting for that special reserve."

Kenrick opened the box and inside Zaria saw the most beautiful woven wristband, similar to Kenrick's, only a bit slimmer.

"This is for you." Kenrick took it out and wrapped it around her wrist. At the front of the strap was a gold rectangle engraved with the Celtic wolf symbol that Kenrick and the other younger wolves had shaved into her hair.

"Ricky, it's beautiful," Zaria said.

Kenrick fastened it and held Zaria's wrist reverently. "It has a chip in it to let you in and out of the marketplace barrier. I want you to know—whether you stay here with me or leave and go back to America—that you have a pack here that you will always be part of."

That sentiment brought tears to Zaria's eyes. When she contemplated leaving Kenrick, she physically hurt inside, but it wasn't just about falling in love, though she was sure she *had*. But loving Kenrick came with a job, a role to fulfil, and she didn't know if she was strong enough for that...yet.

Zaria clasped her wrist. "This means so much to me."

Kenrick's face was beaming with happiness. "I'm glad. Now we've got two more places to visit."

"The distillery?" Zaria asked. She'd been looking forward to being shown around that.

"No, I thought we'd go there tomorrow. These two places have more meaning," Kenrick said seriously.

"Then let's go."

❖

Kenrick led Zaria out of the forest and out the guarded barrier. Zaria stopped and looked out over the loch.

"It's so...the landscape is breathtaking," Zaria said.

Kenrick was so happy Zaria could see what *she* saw. The majesty of the Scottish Highlands was almost ethereal in its beauty. It was no wonder the humans created so many myths and monsters like the Kelpie. The nature around them almost demanded myth and magic.

"I'm glad you like it," Kenrick said.

She led them past the distillery and they passed groups of tourists milling around. "Is it always this busy?" Zaria asked.

"It's much busier in the height of summer. We don't get a lot of good weather, but when we do, Wulver Loch can match anywhere in the world."

Zaria smiled. "I'm sure. Still, the weather's held since the rain when we landed."

"Aye, I think we'll be due a downpour now that you've said that," Kenrick joked. "How did you get on with Heather and my ma?"

"They were really nice. Made me feel wanted here," Zaria said.

Kenrick turned her head to look in her eyes. "Well you are, very wanted."

Even walking along the road, surrounded by humans, Kenrick felt the electricity between them. It was building and building with each passing hour. She needed to touch Zaria and be touched by her in return. Heat started to spread through her body at the very thought, but she didn't want to push Zaria. She wouldn't be what Ovid was.

No, not now. Luckily Zaria distracted her with conversation.

"Milo and Glen are great cubs—especially Milo, she's such a cutie," Zaria said.

"She is," Kenrick said. "I love all the cubs, but I've got a special bond with Milo. She's going to be very powerful when she grows up and will need a lot of guidance. She's not just half witch, half wolf. She's half *dominant* wolf."

Zaria sighed. "I can see that. Being a dominant wolf and going through the rush with all those hormones and drives is hard enough, without having magical powers."

"Aye. Rhuri has done a great job with her, but it's hard for a dominant to be both mum and pater. My ma, Heather, and lots of her friends help out a lot with Milo."

"She's a great kid. Do Rhuri's parents not help out?"

"They live with the English Ranwulf pack. They didn't take Rhuri's sister's death very well—when people die, some things get said that shouldn't. Anyway, Rhuri fell out with her parents, and they left to live with family in England," Kenrick said.

"That's really sad. Milo must miss having grandparents. I suppose that's why she calls your mom Granny. Has Rhuri never met a mate?" Zaria said.

"She's like me, never met anyone in our pack, and she's just put her life on the back burner for Milo's sake."

Zaria squeezed Kenrick's hand and smiled. "I hope she does meet someone. She's a great wolf. Big and scary at first glance, but you see gentleness in her eyes, just like you."

Kenrick screwed up her face. "Don't tell anyone that. I'm going to be an Alpha by the end of the week. That's just for you to know."

Zaria chuckled. "Okay, tough wolf."

They turned down a stone path, away from the tourist area, and at the end was a well-kept shrine of some sort. There were stones piled one on top of the other and fresh flowers all around.

"What is this?"

"It's called a cairn. It's an ancient Scottish way of marking sacred or important places in the landscape."

Zaria crouched down and touched the stones. There did seem to be a change of atmosphere here like sadness and reverence were hanging in the air. Then a thought hit Zaria. "Is this where your brother was killed?"

Kenrick nodded solemnly. "We had been warned there was a rogue Vampire in the area. He was on the run from his clan. Anyway, my pater put a curfew on all the cubs and restricted the area in which we could run during the day."

"Did your brother not keep to the rules?" Zaria asked.

"No, Donell never did like rules. We were twins but very different in personality. I always had to look after him and get him out of trouble. He sneaked out of the den to run, and when I realized he was gone, I went after him."

Zaria stood and took Kenrick's hand. "What happened?"

Kenrick stared at the stones. It looked like she was recalling her thoughts, like watching a movie in her mind.

"I heard him in distress. He was scared and trapped. I shifted and ran as fast as my wolf would let me. When I found him—" Kenrick's voice cracked with emotion. "He was already dead, the life sucked out of him by a bloodthirsty Vampire. We never caught the Vampire."

Zaria rested her head on Kenrick's heart. "I'm so sorry, Ricky."

Kenrick wrapped her arms around her. "From that day on I've carried the guilt of not finding him in time. I should have been his champion like I always was."

"You couldn't have known, Ricky. He broke the rules, but as soon as you found out he was gone, you went after him. This was not your fault."

Kenrick sighed and squeezed her tighter. "Maybe not, but it

doesn't stop the guilt. This is where he died, but his ashes were spread in the forest, so he could always be with us."

"That's a perfect place for him. Do you have any photos of him?"

Kenrick pulled her phone from her jeans pocket and flicked through her photos. "Here I am with him. That's me, Donell, Callum, and Rhuri when we were about seven or eight."

Zaria smiled. "You were all so cute. Donell looks just like you, except you're a bit bigger. Rhuri looks so different without her red hair."

"Yeah, she got that done when she was about sixteen. Her ma wasn't too pleased."

"Thank you for showing me this, and I'm so sorry you lost your brother, but I know he's in the Great Eternal Forest, watching and so proud of you," Zaria said.

"I hope so." Kenrick walked up to the stones, touched and then kissed the top stone. "Rest easy, Donell. You're always in our thoughts."

CHAPTER EIGHTEEN

After leaving the cairn, Kenrick led them deep into the forest. Zaria used Kenrick's phone to take pictures of the forest and interesting places they passed. They passed the Devil's Cave again so she could get pictures.

"Marco is going to love these photos. I'll email him tonight," Zaria said. "How much further are we going?"

"Not long. I'm going to show you the pack's most sacred spot. It's where I'll be made Alpha on Saturday."

"Oh, okay." Zaria felt nervous anytime mentioned Kenrick becoming Alpha. It reminded her how much she didn't feel good enough to stand by her side as Mater.

"I also promised to tell you the story of our pack's origins, and this place is a huge part of the story," Kenrick said.

They walked into a clearing and found a large ancient-looking standing stone circle. The way the trees surrounded the circle made the sunlight channel like a beam into the circle. It was beautiful. She immediately took a picture for Marco. "This is your pack's sacred place?" Zaria asked.

"Aye." Kenrick took her hand and gently pulled her into the centre of the circle. "This is where all our rituals take place—mating ceremonies, funerals, crowning the new Alpha."

"The stones look really heavy. How long have they been here?" Zaria asked.

"As long as our pack has. I think it's time I told you our origin story."

Zaria smiled. "Tell me."

Kenrick sat cross-legged in the middle of the circle and beckoned Zaria to join her. She sat across from Kenrick. Kenrick took her hand and held it tenderly while she began her story. "Did you ever hear the myth that the Celtic peoples of Britain and Ireland were descended from the pharaohs of Egypt?"

Zaria's eyes went wide with surprise. "Egypt? Are you kidding?"

Kenrick laughed. "Aye, people usually react like that. It's a myth in human history, but the wolf packs know the truth of the story."

"I can't wait to hear," Zaria said.

"Long ago, there was an Egyptian princess called Scota."

"Scota? As in Scotland?"

Kenrick winked. "Aye, you got it." She continued, "Princess Scota, unlike most women of her time and social standing, was a warrior. She fought in the pharaoh's battles and was greatly admired and celebrated as a hero. When she was younger she had read in her father's library about a powerful Goddess called the Great Mother who taught that male and female were equal and deserving of the same respect. Scota took that goddess as her own, and in return she was blessed with strength and skill in battle. As she grew older and led her father's armies like a seasoned general, the pharaoh agreed to make the Great Mother a main God of the Egyptian pantheon.

"His priests and advisors were horrified at this new Goddess—not to mention, that Scota had a female lover—and a civil war erupted. The pharaoh was killed and Princess Scota was told to take her followers and leave Egypt. She had five ships and some of the Egyptian treasury. During their journey she had a vision where she spoke to the Great Mother. She promised that Scota and her people would never be hunted again, but they would become the hunters.

"The Great Mother gave them the ability to transform into powerful wolves at will and asked that Scota found communities in the north, based on the rules of the wolf pack, where individuals would no longer be judged by sex but by their natural abilities and were free to love as they wished, like Scota loved her mate Gia. Scota saw this as a chance to create a utopia, a new world away from human constructs. She wanted to head north but some of her followers wanted to head east, so two ships left them, and Scota headed north."

Something clicked in Zaria's mind. "Wait, do you think those wolves that left Scota were the ancestors of the Lupas and other Eastern packs? The Lupas say that we were descended from the Goddess herself, but not where we came from."

"Could well be. That makes sense," Kenrick said.

"So what happened after she headed North?" Zaria asked.

"Well, the Goddess asked her to found packs in every corner of the country where they first made landfall."

"Here in Scotland?" Zaria asked.

Kenrick chuckled. "Well, we say she landed on the Scottish coast and founded the first pack in this stone circle, and then went to England, Wales, and Ireland. The Irish Filtiaran pack say she landed in Ireland then came here. It's always a good-natured argument between us and our Irish cousins, but there's one thing we do agree on."

"What's that?" Zaria asked.

"She died and was buried with her mate in Ireland. Princess Scota was revered by the human Celtic population too, and she and her army came to their aid many times when invaders attacked them. They have a sign that marks her grave, but no one but the Filtiaran pack know where her real burial place is. It's said that when the packs need her the most, she will be reborn to lead them."

"Wow," Zaria said. "What an amazing story. Something to have pride in."

"She and her followers built this stone circle with blocks of sacred stone they brought from the Great Mother's temple in Egypt. I'll be crowned Alpha on the Stone of Destiny. It was part of the alter in the temple."

Zaria furrowed her eyebrows. "Wait, I think I've heard of the Stone of Destiny. Didn't the humans crown their kings of Scotland on it?"

Kenrick laughed. "Yeah, and it was taken from the Scots, and the kings and queens of Britain were crowned on until it was given back to the Scots, not too long ago, but what *they* have is just a piece of stone. We have the real stone, always have."

"You have such a strong tradition here. The Lupas don't have anything like that," Zaria said.

Kenrick kissed her hand. "You don't need to be a Lupa, if you stay." Zaria thought silently for a few seconds. Kenrick took her hesitation as a brush-off. She stood up quickly and said, "I'm sorry. I don't mean to be pressuring you."

Zaria joined her up on her feet. "You're not, Ricky. I just have a lot to think about."

"It's the Alpha thing, isn't it?" Kenrick said.

Zaria put her hand on Kenrick's chest. "Just give me some more time to find my feet. I've been a lone wolf for a long time."

Kenrick nodded. "I know."

"Thank you for telling me your story. Princess Scota sounds like an amazing warrior woman."

"She's always been my inspiration. We better head back," Kenrick said with a hint of hurt in her voice.

When they got home to Kenrick's den, Kenrick headed off to a meeting of the elite wolves, ahead of her ceremony on Saturday. Zaria felt tired, so she took a nap. But she must have slept for a while because it was dark when she woke up.

She left the bedroom in search of Kenrick, dressed only in the shirt Kenrick gave her. It made her feel more content to be surrounded by Kenrick's scent. She didn't see Kenrick around, so she must still be with her elite wolves.

Kenrick had explained that in the run up to her ceremony on Saturday, she had to take part in many rituals—combat, spiritual, and purification—to prepare for her role.

It occurred to Zaria that the packs who maintained a bond to their rich cultural heritage, like the Wolfgangs and the Wulvers, were more stable and successful communities. If she was right about her ancestors being the ones who'd left Princess Scota to head out on their own, they'd made a huge mistake.

It was well past light-up time, so she went out to the balcony to see the lights and the stars. She stood leaning against the balcony and gazed out at the wonderful sight of all the lights that lit up the dens and trees between them. She looked up at the clear sky with the stars twinkling in the sky.

Zaria sighed. It was just impossibly peaceful and beautiful here.

She knew she was beginning to fall in love with Wulver Forest, just as she was with Kenrick.

Marco would love to come and visit me here.

She stopped in her tracks. Was she starting to think of this place as her home? If she closed her eyes and blocked out her insecurities and worries, she could see herself making her home here as Kenrick's mate, living the calm, quiet, loving life she'd never thought possible.

Marco could come and stay in the holidays and play with Milo and the other kids. It could be bliss. It could be, if she was brave enough to take it.

Zaria opened her eyes and took a huge breath, taking in the scent of the forest. It was different this time. This time she could scent fire, smoke, burning wood, and if she listened carefully, she could hear chanting and shouts. Maybe that was from Kenrick's ritual.

A minute later she knew she was right when she heard Kenrick's unmistakable howl cut through the dark night. It was a howl of victory, of dominance, of need, of sex.

Zaria gasped as her body reacted. Her nipples grew hard. Her sex throbbed with want for her wolf. Her teeth erupted, and she found herself howling in return. Fire and need spread across her skin and she just had to be touched. She unbuttoned the shirt to expose her breasts and lightly stroked her fingers over her nipples. Something had changed. Zaria's wolf had enough waiting. She wanted her mate, and she howled in desperate need for Kenrick to return.

Zaria could feel Kenrick howl in response and run through the trees to come to her.

The need in her sex was so overwhelming that she had to touch herself. She slipped her hand into her panties and one finger dipped into her wetness to stroke her clit.

"I need you, Ricky," she groaned.

A few minutes later she heard footsteps running up the walkway to the den and heard deep heavy breathing across the room. When Kenrick's low growl made her skin erupt in goosebumps, she took her hand from her panties and turned around.

The sight she saw made her want to drop to the floor and give herself to Kenrick. Kenrick was dressed only in jeans, no shoes or T-shirt. Her skin glistened with a sheen of sweat, her eyes were deep yellow, and her teeth were elongated.

She had white and blue war paint smeared in patterns across her chest and face, and her dreadlocks were hanging loose. She looked wild and dangerous, a Celtic wolf warrior, exactly as she imagined Kenrick's ancestor, Princess Scota.

"You called me," Kenrick said in a deep wanting voice.

Zaria walked over to Kenrick's bed and held out her hands. "I did."

But instead of coming to her, Kenrick looked down to the floor and balled her hands tightly. "Not like this, not after combat when my hunger is so desperate." Kenrick's breathing was harsh and rapid.

"Why?" Zaria said.

Kenrick looked up quickly. "Because I love you, and I don't want to ever look at you and hurt you like Ovid did."

She really loves me. Ovid was why Kenrick had been holding back since they arrived in Scotland. She hurried over to Kenrick and cupped her cheek. "You could never look at me or treat me like Ovid. She wanted my body, my status in the pack, but you have done nothing but care for me. I'm a wolf, I won't break." Zaria stroked her fingers all across Kenrick's painted chest. "You're a warrior, Ricky. I want my warrior to touch me, to make me come."

Kenrick squeezed her eyes shut tightly as if she was trying to restrain herself. Zaria used her instincts and pushed the finger she had touched herself with past Kenrick's lips. Kenrick groaned and sucked her finger deep into her mouth. She felt Kenrick's sharp canines graze her finger, and she longed to feel those teeth on her breasts and nipples.

"Please, Ricky. Don't hold back," Zaria groaned.

Kenrick still held herself taut, so Zaria scrapped her nails deeply over her chest.

Kenrick roared and grasped Zaria's hand.

Gasping, Kenrick looked down at the drops of blood mixing with the blue paint on her chest. Zaria bobbed her head down and ran her tongue over the gashes and tasted Kenrick's blood. The taste exploded on her tongue, and at that moment she knew no other wolf would ever fill her heart.

She could feel her features shifting, and her urge to mate, to bite was overwhelming. "Fuck me, Ricky. Make me yours."

Kenrick's restraint broke. All her good intentions about going slow couldn't withstand Zaria's call, especially after proving herself in the combat ritual. She wanted to fuck, to come, prove she was strong for her lover, and a worthy mate.

She lifted Zaria and carried her over to the bed. She put Zaria down on the bed and used her teeth to rip open her shirt. Zaria was looking up at her with yellow eyes, dazed and wanting.

Zaria lay naked in front of her. She opened her legs and laid her head to the side in submission. She was totally wet, seeing her Celtic wolf warrior standing over her. "Ricky, I'm yours."

Kenrick growled and ripped her jeans off. She climbed on Zaria and rubbed her face over Zaria's breasts. "Mine."

"Yours." Zaria surprised herself by wrapping her legs around Kenrick's waist and pulling her into mating position.

No foreplay, no taking it slow, Zaria just wanted Kenrick now. Kenrick still hadn't moved her hips. Even in her need, her lust, Kenrick was still making it Zaria's choice.

Zaria pulled Kenrick's lips down to hers. "Fuck me, wolf. Fill me up."

Kenrick closed her eyes and moaned in pleasure at her mate's words. She kissed Zaria hard and started to thrust softly at first. Zaria moaned into the kiss and dug her nails into Kenrick's shoulders.

Kenrick took that as a challenge and held Zaria's wrists above her head. Every thrust of her hips felt so right, like taking a step into the Great Eternal Forest. She felt Zaria tighten her legs, drawing Kenrick's sex further in. "Zari. I love you. I need you so much."

"Come over me, in me," Zaria pleaded.

Kenrick's thrust harder and faster. Her hips were unstoppable now. She could feel her essence building and about to spill over and into her lover's sex.

Zaria's moans were growing louder. "Ricky…"

She leaned over, inches from Zaria's face, and gazed into her deep yellow eyes. "Turn over on your belly and look at the stars."

Zaria looked confused at first but she turned over and Kenrick pulled her hips up. Zaria got on all fours and gasped. Now she knew what Kenrick meant—she wanted Zaria to come while looking out the wall of glass. You could see the stars, the fairy lights, and the expanse of darkness over Wulver Loch.

Kenrick pushed back into mating position and started to thrust, picking up her speed every few seconds. She had always dreamed of doing this, and now she was, with the love of her life.

"Great Mother. It's too much, too beautiful, feels too good," Zaria said. Then she turned back and looked right at Kenrick. "Make me come, warrior."

Kenrick couldn't hold out any longer. Her hips thrust uncontrollably. She wanted nothing more than to mate-bite Zaria right there, but she would never do it without being asked.

So as she felt Zaria tighten around her clit, she raised her head and roared as she came and exploded into her mate in pure bliss.

CHAPTER NINETEEN

Zaria's eyes flickered open and she became aware of where she was. Kenrick was wrapped around her, loving her, protecting. She could hear the heavy pitter-patter of rain, the sound of birdsong, and the cold breeze coming from the open balcony doors.

What a way to wake up. It might not be hot here in Scotland, but Zaria thought this must be like the Great Eternal Forest in the afterlife. The rain made everything smell so fresh, so new, and that matched how Zaria felt this morning. She had been reborn after making love with Kenrick. The old frightened Zaria, always on the run, was replaced by a contented wolf, living and loving as she should have been her whole life.

She turned around in Kenrick's arms and felt the satisfying pain of her scratches and bites and smiled when she saw the matching ones on Kenrick. Zaria chuckled when she saw the blue paint from Kenrick's body all over the white sheets.

Kenrick didn't open her eyes but said, "What do you find so funny, lassie?"

She kissed Kenrick on the nose. "Good morning. I was thinking maybe white bed covers aren't a good idea."

Kenrick stretched her long powerful body and then rolled on top of Zaria. "It was worth it. We'll buy new ones."

Zaria chuckled. "I think you're right."

"Aye, of course I am. I'm going to be the Alpha," Kenrick joked and started to kiss her.

"There's that arrogant Alpha I knew was inside of you," Zaria said.

Kenrick stroked the hair away from her face. "To think that I was frightened of telling you I was going to be Alpha."

"To think when I woke up in the Wolfgang hospital I was frightened of you because you were dominant."

"You were never taught what an honourable dominant wolf should be like," Kenrick said.

Zaria ran her fingers up and down Kenrick's strong shoulders and arms. "Oh? What should one look like?"

Kenrick growled softly and nuzzled her neck. "Your wolf should be strong enough to protect you, be devoted to their mate's and family's happiness. Put their submissive mate first in all things, provide meat for their mate's table, and most of all do as they are told in the den."

Zaria raised an eyebrow. "Really? Do as they are told by their submissive mate?"

"Have you never heard the heard the expression *Mate's den, mate's rules*? Or in my ma's case, *Mater's den, Mater's rules*?"

Zaria sighed. "The Lupas think mates should be seen and not heard, so no."

"Zari…" Kenrick rolled over and pulled Zaria on top. Kenrick wanted to make sure Zaria was clear she would always be safe if she consented to be her mate. Even though they'd made love last night, Kenrick didn't try to mate-bite Zaria. She wasn't going to mess up this chance at happiness, not now that she and Zaria had come so far.

"What?" Zaria said.

"You know if you decide to stay with me, with the pack, you would always be safe. You've seen my ma and pater, and Heather and Callum. We are nothing like the Lupas."

Zaria cupped Kenrick's cheeks. "I know that. You are the kindest, gentlest wolf I know. It's taken some time to trust, but I can't ever imagine any circumstance that you would hurt me."

"I would die first," Kenrick said solemnly.

Zaria's eyes shone yellow, her wolf close to the surface. She pounced on Kenrick's lips with such passion it took Kenrick by surprise. She deepened the kiss by grasping Kenrick's dreads and pulling them close.

Kenrick snarled. She was hard, wet, and ached to thrust into her mate. They hadn't said it yet, but as far as Kenrick was concerned they were mated. She was just going to let Zaria have the time to make sure she was ready for what being her mate meant.

She dragged her wolf teeth down Zaria's neck. Zaria opened her legs for Kenrick and she dug her nails into Kenrick's shoulders.

"Yes, Ricky."

Just as they were getting lost in lust, Kenrick's phone on the side table started to play a loud alarm. Kenrick jumped and grabbed the phone. "Fuck!"

"What is it?" Zaria said.

Kenrick sat up quickly. "There's an important meeting at the distillery this morning. It's my pater's last one as CEO, and he's handing over to me, and I'm late. Some Alpha." She growled in panic.

Zaria reached up and took her hand. "Hey, it's okay. How long do you have?"

"I've got twenty minutes to get there. I haven't had my morning run, I'm covered in blue and white, I need a shower, and I need to fuck you so badly or I am going to explode."

Zaria smiled and sat up. "Well then, we'll need to combine a few of those. Come on, wolf."

Zaria pulled Kenrick by the hand in the direction of the outside shower, and Kenrick's look of panic turned into a ravenous smile.

"Good thinking, lassie." Kenrick pressed on the shower and they stepped underneath.

The hot water hit Zaria's body and she leaned back to wet her hair. She put a large dollop of shower gel in each of their hands and they began to wash each other.

Kenrick pulled her close and, while they kissed, rubbed her hands up and down her back, soaping her up. Zaria pushed her hips further into Kenrick's sex as Kenrick rubbed the soap and her hands all over Zaria's back.

Zaria pulled away from the kiss and said, "The first time I saw you under this shower, I wanted to come in with you and beg you to fuck me."

Kenrick groaned and spun her around so Kenrick's sex was pressing into her buttocks.

Oh, Great Mother. My fantasy is coming true, Zaria thought.

Kenrick put some more shower gel on her hands and lathered it all over Zaria's breasts. Zaria pushed her backside into Kenrick, presenting herself for her mate. Her wolf had been telling her from the beginning that's who Kenrick was, and now she believed it. This wolf, this pack was her future. She couldn't turn her back on this.

Zaria leaned her head to the side to give Kenrick access to her neck and grasped Kenrick's hair. She heard a low growl. Kenrick seemed to like it when she pulled on her mane of hair.

Kenrick kissed and teased her with little nips. Then she said, "I need to fill you up, Zari." Kenrick groaned.

"Yes." Zaria covered Kenrick's hands on her breasts and encouraged her to squeeze.

Kenrick moved them a few paces forward so Zaria could brace herself against the shower wall.

Zaria bent over, giving Kenrick access to her from behind. Zaria shouted in pleasure when Kenrick's claws scratched from her neck down to the bottom of her spine.

"Mine?" Kenrick questioned.

Zaria turned her head to look back at Kenrick. She was partially shifted and looked wild. "Yours," Zaria replied.

Kenrick parted her buttocks and her clit slipped into mating position. Kenrick groaned in bliss.

Zaria pushed back with every thrust Kenrick made. Her sex was throbbing and readying to come as soon as Kenrick filled her with her essence.

Kenrick thrust faster and faster, every thrust bringing pleasure to Zaria. She looked to the side at the rain battering down from the skies above just a few feet away from them, while the shower thundered down on them. It was as if they were making love out in the open forest, with the refreshing rain falling on their hot bodies, with the fresh scents of the forest surrounding them.

This was what wolf love was meant to be like. This was real, and Zaria knew this was it. She belonged here with this wolf.

Kenrick's groans became deeper and her breath shorter. "I'm going to fill you up, Zaria."

Zaria leaned back and said, "Bite me."

Kenrick didn't seem to understand at first because she just nipped the skin of her neck.

"No," Zaria said seriously, "mate-bite me when you come."

Kenrick's thrusts slowed. "What? Are you sure?"

Zaria reached back and caressed the side of Kenrick's face. "Yes. I want to stay. I love you, Ricky. Make me your mate."

Kenrick's voice became emotional when she said, "You love me?"

"Yes. I'm yours. Fill me up and make me yours." Kenrick's thrusts hastened and become harder. "Yes, Ricky."

"I love you." Kenrick was breathing hard and about to come and Zaria would just be seconds after her.

It happened so quickly. Kenrick roared in pleasure, then sank her teeth into Zaria's shoulder.

The chemicals from Kenrick's bite swarmed through her body. Her orgasm exploded and her body felt so light, and she experienced an intense high, both physically and mentally. She could feel Kenrick in every cell of her body.

They both fell to the shower floor, gasping for air.

Kenrick held her tight, safe and cocooned in her arms. "Thank you, thank you, my darlin' lassie."

"Ricky, I need to look at you." Zaria turned in her arms and kissed Kenrick softly. The Kenrick she saw when she turned around was not the fierce Alpha who protected her from Leroux and Ovid. She was intensely emotional as she gazed at Zaria, and her eyes were filled with such love.

Kenrick caressed her cheek. "Did you really mean it? You love me and want to stay?"

"I wouldn't have asked you to mate-bite me if I didn't. I love you, Highlander, and I want to be a Wulver."

"I know I bit you, but before you seal our bond, are you really sure? You know what being my mate means."

Zaria wiped a strand of wet hair from Kenrick's face. "Yes, I know what it means. I don't know if I'll ever be good at the job. I've never lived in a normal pack. My sister was a Mater, but it didn't mean the same under Leroux's vicious rule. But I'm going to try my best to be the best mate to you, and pack mate to your wolves."

"You don't need to try. You're kind, caring, and the strongest wolf I've ever met. You survived, lassie—the Lupas couldn't keep you down—and now it's time to enjoy life with me."

Zaria was overcome with love for Kenrick. Her wolf had enough waiting and she sank her teeth deep into Kenrick's neck. Zaria could feel them becoming one now they had both bitten and joined.

She pulled back and saw the fresh blood dripping from Kenrick's mate bite. She leaned over and licked the blood from her wound. She loved the taste and knowing she had caused it.

Zaria heard in her mind, *Can you hear me, bonnie lassie?*

I can hear every word. We're joined. She threw her arms around Kenrick. *I love you.*

You're not a Lupa any more, lassie. You're a Wulver and you're safe at last.

CHAPTER TWENTY

Love and the bliss of afterglow for the newly mated pair soon turned to panic when Kenrick remembered she was late for her meeting. She tied back her damp hair with her leather band, while Zaria quickly got Kenrick's suit out of the wardrobe.

"The black suit?" Zaria asked.

"Aye, black's my colour." She pulled on the trousers as quickly as she could, then looked down at the clock. "Shit. I'm supposed to be there now. Great start to the new era of the Wulver pack. The new CEO is late."

Zaria handed her the black shirt. "Your pater will understand."

"Can you text him from my phone? Just say I'm coming in five minutes and I've got good news."

Zaria typed quickly on Kenrick's phone. "Wait, what good news?"

"I've found our new Mater." Kenrick winked. "That should soften his wrath."

Zaria giggled and touched her mate bite. "Oh yeah, that."

Kenrick pulled on her shirt and fumbled over the buttons because she was going so fast. "I hate this thing."

Zaria stopped her and said, "Take a breath. I'll do it. What do you think your parents will say?"

"My pater will be over the moon. He always told me I'd find my Mater, even when I despaired that I wouldn't. You know, I felt so guilty in the lead-up to becoming Alpha that I couldn't give my pack a Mater. It was like I was failing them before I began, because the Mater is the heart of the pack."

Kenrick saw a look of worry pass over Zaria's face. She held

Zaria's hands as they reached for her top button. "Hey, listen—you'll be fine. We've both got a lot to learn about our new life," Kenrick said.

Zaria pursed her lips and gave her a quick nod. Kenrick knew that Zaria was going to need to gain a lot of confidence, but she was certain with her mother and the other submissives' support, she would find her place.

"What will your mom say?"

Kenrick let out a long breath. "She'll be overjoyed, suffocate you with love and affection, but bite my arse from one end of the forest to the other."

Zaria looked surprised. "Why?"

Kenrick pointed to Zaria's mate bite. "Mate bite before mating ceremony? My ma is really traditional, and she's always given me the lecture about respect and waiting."

"But it was my idea. It wasn't your fault, Ricky."

Kenrick snorted. "You think my ma will believe that? I'll get the blame, but she'll be so happy at the same time."

Kenrick tucked in her shirt and took her jacket from Zaria. "Right, I think I'm ready. Remember, I'm going to show you around the distillery today. Will you be okay this morning?"

Zaria nodded. "Yeah, I thought I'd do some grocery shopping— you don't have any food. Heather said she'd go with me down to the marketplace. If that's okay with you?"

Zaria looked down and grimaced slightly and Kenrick felt worry and tension through their physic connection. It was a strange reaction to what she had just said. Kenrick didn't have time to investigate it just now but she would later.

"Aye, nae bother, here." Kenrick took out her wallet and handed Zaria her credit card. "Get whatever you need. Food or things for you, the den. I'll write down the PIN on my way out, but I've got to run."

Zaria clasped the card tightly. "Thanks."

Kenrick rushed to the kitchen counter and scribbled a note with the code. Then she ran to the door but was stopped when Zaria said mentally, *Stop right there, wolf.*

Zaria walked to the door and grasped Kenrick by the shirt. "Don't walk out of here without giving me a kiss."

Kenrick grinned. "Sorry." Then she pulled Zaria into a kiss.

The kiss deepened. Zaria growled and pushed Kenrick up against the wall. The very cells in her body were screaming to be close to Kenrick, loving her, caring for her. Then she pulled back. "You better get to work."

"Aye, cheers, kiss me like that and send me off to work." Kenrick snorted.

❖

Kenrick took the congratulations of the board members as they left the boardroom. The news of her new mate had turned the serious handover of business power from her pater to a joyous occasion. Once the last wolf left, Kenrick looked up to the other end of the table and saw her pater silently smiling at her.

"You know your mother is going to kill you," Fergus said.

Kenrick smirked. "She'll forgive me."

"You've chosen well, wolf. You make a bonnie couple."

"Thanks for making her so welcome, Da. She's had such a hard life so far, but now I want to make the rest of it special," Kenrick said.

"We will surround Zaria with the love of the pack, don't worry about that." Fergus stood up and walked over to the window that looked out over the loch. "This is all yours now. Look after her well."

"Course I will, Da." Kenrick joined her dad at the window.

"If you're lucky, one day you'll be handing over the reins to your own cub, and I can tell you nothing makes you prouder." Fergus kissed Kenrick's brow.

❖

Heather came to meet Zaria at their den and engulfed her with hugs when she saw her mate bite. They walked down to the marketplace.

"Are you going to postpone the Alpha ceremony, so you can have your mating ceremony first?" Heather said.

"I don't know. I hadn't really thought about that." And she hadn't. Last night and this morning all she thought about was how much she loved Kenrick and the urge to mark her as her own. She never thought she would succumb to that urge, and here she had with a wolf who was going to be Alpha, just like her sister.

A small knot of worry started to form in her gut. Then she

remembered her apprehension this morning when she'd hinted that she would need money for food.

Just like Marta.

How many times had she watched her sister be controlled by money. Leroux didn't give her access to any of their money, so she would have to go crawling to Leroux every time she needed something for the den.

Zaria remembered Marta putting it off until she absolutely had to and the fear in her eyes when she did—then Leroux's cruel smile as Marta begged.

But that wasn't Kenrick, her more logical mind told her. It was hard to fight against what she had learned as a child. She had come such a long way in a short time, and Kenrick was the reason for that, but it would unrealistic to think that she wouldn't have fears and concerns.

Heather stopped and put her hand on her shoulder. "Are you all right, Zaria?"

Zaria smiled. "I'm fine. There's just a lot to think about. Ricky and I need to talk about it all. It's all happened so fast."

"I know. But you'll have lots of help. Come on."

Heather led her down to the marketplace and each wolf bowed their head as they passed. The few dominants in the marketplace saluted her too.

"Why are they doing that? They don't know me, and Ricky isn't even Alpha yet."

"They don't need to know you. What they know is Ricky chose you to be their Mater, and they trust her that you will be a great Mater."

Zaria felt that knot of worry again. "Can we sit down for a minute?"

"Sure." Heather led her over to a bench by the side of the walkway. "What's up?" Heather asked. "I can scent your worry."

Zaria sighed. "I was brought up in a pack that didn't follow normal wolf pack rules. I have no experience as to how I should behave, how I should interact with other wolves as Mater. I watched how effortlessly Eden embodies the role in the Wolfgang pack, and Elspeth here. How could I ever compete with that? I'm good at two things, running and hiding. I was never equipped for a life like this."

Heather took her hand. "It's not a matter of competing, Zaria. It's about learning and making the role your own. Ricky will have to do the same as you. I'm sure you know her insecurities about becoming

Alpha. She's carried the guilt of her brother's death all these years, and wondered if she is the rightful Alpha, but I can see since meeting you that she's gained a new confidence. Let her and us do the same thing for you."

Zaria smiled and squeezed Heather's hand. "It's just a lot to take in."

"Ricky said your sister was Mater in the Lupa pack," Heather said.

"Yeah, but it wasn't the same thing. No submissive, not even the Mater, had any role in the pack. The dominants kept us on a tight leash."

"Do you think if your sister had been born in a pack like ours or the Wolfgangs she would have made a good Mater?"

Zaria nodded and smiled enthusiastically. "Oh yes. Marta was the kindest, gentlest person I know. Always thought of others before herself, that's why she got…" Zaria hesitated. "That's how she got killed. Thinking of everyone else before herself."

Heather looked right into her eyes and said, "Then think of this as an opportunity to live the life she couldn't. You can take the chance at life Marta couldn't, and I'm sure she'll be watching you with pride by the side of the Great Mother."

Zaria grasped the necklace around her neck, the one that connected her to her mother and Marta, and that knot of worry shrank ever so slightly. Could this be her chance to live the kind of life Marta should have had?

One thing she did know for certain was that Marta would rest easy in the Great Eternal Forest knowing that both Marco and she were safe and Leroux was dead.

"You're right. I need to try because I love Ricky and this is my chance for happiness," Zaria said.

"We haven't known each other long, Zaria, but I've known Ricky my whole life, and me, Callum, and all our other friends are going to support you all the way. No matter what."

Heather was a lovely, caring, gentle woman. Zaria knew they were going to be the best of friends. Then Zaria heard her name called from across the marketplace. She looked up and saw Milo running to her with a big smile on her face.

"Hiya, Zaria. I heard you were going to be the new Mater," Milo said excitedly.

Heather chuckled and Zaria said, "I suppose I am. Aren't you supposed to be in school?"

"Aye, my class is over there." Milo pointed to a small group of kids on the other side of the marketplace, standing with an elderly woman. "We're having art class down by the loch. I'm going to paint the Kelpie, but none of my other friends believe I saw it."

Heather nudged Zaria and said, "Well, you've got to keep an open mind. We are wolves, after all."

Zaria opened her arms and invited Milo in for a hug. She empathized with Milo. They were both outsiders to the pack, and trying to find their way.

"I believe in you, and I believe in magic, so anything is possible, Milo," Zaria said.

"Will you come with me to look for the Kelpie sometime, Zaria?"

"Sure, I will. Why don't you introduce me to your friends and teacher?"

It was time to start making friends and bond with the pack.

Kenrick sat at her pater's desk, now her own, in their office on the top floor of the distillery. Her pater had gone to meet with some of the elders of the pack to try to make arrangements for a mating ceremony. It was going to be a rush, but Fergus felt it was important that Zaria took her place by Kenrick's side in the Alpha ceremony, and to so that they had to be officially mated.

She just hoped Zaria didn't feel too rushed or pressured by it all. Earlier in the afternoon she had felt Zaria's stress through their new mate bond, but it soon calmed.

Kenrick was on the computer making inquiries about the new equipment she wanted installed all over the business. She had learned a lot from Dante and wanted to make Wulver Whisky and Spring Water a truly streamlined, modern company.

Kenrick's research progress had been slow. Everything she looked at seemed to remind her of Zaria, and her whole body screamed for her to go home and spend the day wrapped around her in bed. Normally a newly mated pair would stay close to each other for at least a week or two after mating, but circumstances dictated that wouldn't be possible.

She could hear her mother's I-told-you-sos loud in her mind. That was one of the practical reasons wolves historically avoided the mate bite till after a mating ceremony, so they could enjoy their honeymoon and give their partner all their attention.

Kenrick leaned back in her chair and shut her eyes. Her mouth started to water as she remembered sucking Zaria's nipple and rolling it around her tongue.

"Drunk on love, Rickster?"

The new voice made her jump violently out of her skin. "Bloody hell!"

Wolves were usually never taken by surprise. Another creature's scent always gave them away, unless the wolf's mind was too caught up on their mate.

"You nearly gave me a heart attack, Rhuri," Kenrick said.

Rhuri had the biggest smile on her face and opened her arms wide. Kenrick went to her and they hugged like the old friends they were.

Rhuri smacked her on the back. "Well done, pal. You've finally found your teeth."

Kenrick touched the mate bite on her neck with pride. "Hey, you can talk."

Rhuri sat down on the other side of the desk and snorted. "Please, with looking after Milo, I don't have time to sneeze, far less meet lassies. The Great Mother hasn't found Mrs. Rhuri in Wulver Forest and I don't have time to look around."

Kenrick took her seat again. "Well, I had to go all the way to America, but I found my lassie."

"You did." Rhuri grinned. "She's a beauty and I know she'll make a great Mater. Milo hasn't stopped talking about how cool it is to have an American wolf in the pack."

"I can't believe how lucky I am. It's taken a lot to get her to trust me," Kenrick said. "She's been through so much in her life, and I want to give her the family, the pack, she's never had."

"We'll look after her and make sure she feels part of the Wulvers, don't you worry about that. Anyway, looks like I've got a stag party to plan, and I've got just the whisky barrel in mind for the party," Rhuri said with an even bigger grin.

"Aye, I bet you have. I don't know how we're going to fit it in before Saturday's Alpha ceremony. I've still got the purification ritual on Friday," Kenrick said.

Rhuri laughed. "Purification comes after whisky and lots of it."

"I'll talk to Zaria later. My pater had a few ideas about how to plan the mating around my ceremony," Kenrick said.

"Aye, just let me know and I'll sort it. So, how did the board meeting go?"

Kenrick pulled at her shirt collar. "Apart from me being late, it went well. My pater's talked about this day since I was a cub, but it always seemed so far in the future."

Rhuri leaned. "I know how hard it'll be to give up your job out in the forest, working downstairs with all the wolves."

"When I left to go and work with Dante, I was dreading it, but so much has changed." Kenrick got up and walked to the window that looked out over Wulver Loch. "Dante showed me that I can put my own stamp on the business and drive it forward. Pater was right to send me to work at Venator. I'm so full of ideas and I need you to help me."

"You know I'm your right paw. Whatever you need, I'll be there," Rhuri said.

Kenrick sat on the edge of the desk. "We need to upgrade our IT systems, build a social media presence."

Rhuri tapped her fingers on the desk. "I think we'll need some outside human help on that."

"We will, and I know it's a risk to let human eyes into our business, but the Wolfgangs make it work. Wulver is a well respected brand name all over the world, but I think there's more we can do. I'd like to attract a younger market to our whisky, maybe make some new drinks?"

Rhuri raised her eyebrows and smiled. "I like it. You do really want to shake things up."

"What's the point of new leadership if we don't try new things, eh?" Kenrick said. "Now I've got Zari by my side, I feel like I can do anything."

"Aye, you're right there." Rhuri stood up and said, "Right, I better go and check on the boys in the malting room."

"Oh, one more thing. Four of the older elite wolves have decided to step down with my pater. So I need you to draw up a list of some new candidates for me."

"No problem." Rhuri thumped her chest and left, leaving Kenrick counting down the hours till she saw her mate again.

❖

Zaria couldn't ever remember laughing so hard as she listened to Heather and her friends recount stories of Kenrick and their childhood together.

After meeting Milo in the marketplace, Heather took her to a tea shop to meet her old school friends.

The tea shop was nothing like the diners she had worked in all of her adult life. It was everything she imagined a traditional British tea shop to be. Polite serving staff, wearing black and white with crisp white aprons. Immaculate tablecloths and napkins, cakes and tiny sandwiches on a tiered cake stand, and real china cups and saucers. She imagined the tea shop by the loch for the human tourists was similar.

Zaria felt out of place at first in the genteel little place, but Heather's friends made her so welcome and at her ease. As a submissive wolf coming into the pack, she knew how important it was to be accepted with the higher ranking Wulver submissives.

There was Donny, an angelic-looking male submissive wolf, with the most gorgeous shoulder-length blond hair. Then Florrie, a short female with elfin features and a pixie style hairstyle. And finally Moira, an elegant woman with jet black hair and the most gorgeous Irish accent.

Donny was the most talkative of the group and a lot of fun. Zaria was trying to keep up with the new names and places in the story, and take it all in.

"Judah, Ricky, Marcus, Lukas, and Rhuri put the bucket of fish guts over the door, sure that Callum was going to come through the door—"

"So," Zaria interrupted, "Judah is your mate, Donny, Marcus is yours, Florrie, and Lukas is Moira's?"

"And you've already met my Callum, Zaria," Heather finished for her.

"Got it," Zaria said. "What happened next?"

Donny continued, "They held their breath, kept as quiet as wee mice. The door opened..."

Zaria chuckled as Donny mimed the door opening dramatically.

"Then in walked the Mater, who got a bucket of fish guts on her head," Donny said.

Zaria gasped then smiled. "She did not."

"Oh, she most certainly did," Florrie said smiling.

Moira poured more tea into Zaria's cup and said, "I've never heard the Mater growl as loud and fiercely as she did that day."

Heather leaned in and said, "The whole pack of cubs shifted and ran deep into the forest. They were so frightened to come back that some of the adult wolves had to be sent out to gather them up."

"What did Elspeth do to them?" Zaria asked. She could just imagine the look on a much younger Kenrick's face when she realized what she had done.

Donny lifted a dainty salmon sandwich from the cake stand and held it aloft. "The Mater said if they loved fish so much, they could work in the fish packaging facility at the other end of the loch and gut fish every day after school for a month."

"It's not the most pleasant building, as you can imagine," Heather said, "but surprisingly Moira's mate Lukas grew up to manage the fish side of the Wulver business."

Moira took a sip of her tea and smiled. "Yes, I think the fish got into his blood then."

"So what do you think of our wee marketplace and pack lands, Zaria?" Florrie asked.

"It's absolutely beautiful. Very cold compared to back home, though," Zaria joked.

"Cold and rainy," Donny added. "That's Scotland, but you couldn't find a prettier place to live."

There was one thing she had wondered. "How do you keep it so private and hidden from the human tourists who come to visit?"

"We have had a few interlopers over the years," Heather said, "but they are on our private land so we shut off roads and pathways, and we keep the treeline high at the back of the tourist buildings. It's not perfect, but we lead a private life here."

Zaria suddenly felt intense sensation in her mate bite. She gasped and touched her neck. Kenrick was feeling something intensely. She closed her eyes for a few seconds and analysed the sensation. It was deep need, want, for sex, for Zaria. Zaria became aroused instantly. Her nipples hardened and her sex was wet and aching.

"Drunk on love, ladies," Donny said loudly.

Zaria snapped her eyes open and felt heat come to her cheeks. She shouldn't be thinking deeply sexual thoughts in this traditional tea shop.

The women laughed at Donny's words, and Heather said, "Don't worry. You're newly mated. It's natural."

"Talking of newly mated," Florrie said, "when are you having the mating ceremony?"

"And the hen night?" Donny said with excitement.

Zaria raised an eyebrow. "Hen night?"

Heather patted her hand. "Scottish for bachelorette party."

"Then there's the purification ritual to organize," Moira told Heather.

The women and Donny started to talk and make plans for all those things and that little knot of worry started to grow again. Zaria's new friends didn't mean to pressure her, they were trying to be kind and welcome her into the pack, but it felt like she was being rushed towards a role she wasn't confidant she could perform. She had to talk to Kenrick about it.

Chapter Twenty-one

Kenrick paced impatiently outside the distillery building, waiting for Zaria to arrive. The longer the day went on, the hungrier and more desperate Kenrick became for Zaria's company.

The need her body felt inside was so hard to control. She wanted more than anything to shift and run, to track down her mate, but she knew Zaria was with Heather and meeting some of the other submissives. So it was important to let her mate find her way.

Finally Kenrick saw Zaria walking from the barrier that separated their world from the human one, up the slight incline to the distillery.

She strode over to meet Zaria and immediately took her into her arms. "I missed you so much."

Zaria stroked a teasing finger down Kenrick's cheek. "I could feel you, Ricky."

Kenrick sniffed all around her mate bite and neck, spreading her scent over her mate.

Zaria kissed her softly and just as she was about to deepen the kiss she heard voices beside them. Zaria looked around and saw a group of human tourists, who were about to go in and take the public tour, staring at them. She whispered, "I think humans are still a bit shocked at two women kissing."

"Let's get back to this later then, without an audience." Kenrick took her hand and led her around to the back of the distillery. "Are you ready for your tour?"

Zaria smiled. "Isn't that what's happening at the entrance round there?"

"Nah. This a special tour only given by me. I want to show you all about Wulver whisky."

Zaria kissed her cheek. "Show me then, wolf."

Kenrick opened up one door and they entered a huge shed. To get fully into the room you had to get past a thick glass security door, locked by a code. Kenrick punched in the number and opened the door.

The first thing that hit Zaria was the strong smell of cereal, and the second thing was the size of the room. "Wow, it's so big," Zaria said.

"It needs to be. We produce a lot of whisky," Kenrick said proudly.

The floor was covered in a carpet of grain and five men and woman in overalls walked up and down the floor with what looked like snow shovels, lifting and tossing the grain. When the wolves saw it was Kenrick who had came in, they stopped what they were doing and saluted before getting back to their jobs.

"What is this grain and what are they doing?" Zaria asked.

"I'll show you." Kenrick took her hand and led her further into the room. She kneeled down and scooped up a handful of grain. "This is barley. The barley contains starch and we need to convert the starch into soluble sugars to create alcohol."

Zaria took some grain from Kenrick's hand. "Where do you get this from?"

"We have a good relationship with a few human farmers in the area. They keep us well supplied. When we get it from the farmer it's soaked in water for two to three days, then spread out on this malting room floor to germinate." Kenrick pointed to one of the seeds. "You see the green shoot there?"

"Yeah, what do those guys with the shovels do?" Zaria asked.

"The barley needs to be a certain depth and temperature, so they turn it over to make sure all the barley is germinating evenly."

"What happens next?" Zaria asked.

Kenrick had never felt prouder than showing Zaria the Wulver pack's pride and joy. The interest and enthusiasm she was showing excited her, giving her a rush.

"When the green shoots appear, we have to stop germination by drying it in a peat fuelled kiln. The type of peat and how long it's dried gives every whisky it's distinct flavour."

Zaria smiled and said. "I can see how proud you are of this place."

"I am. We're a family, a pack, and this whisky flows in our veins." Zaria kissed her cheek. "Show me more, mate."

❖

Zaria was loving every second of her tour. She never knew the whisky making process was so clever and intense. From the malting house, Kenrick led her through to what she called the mashing machines, where Kenrick explained they mixed the milled grain with the fresh Wulver Loch water to extract the sugars.

There was a lot of the process and terminology Zaria didn't understand, but she loved listening to the passionate way Kenrick described it. She then led her through to the distillation room where huge copper kettles, bowl shaped at the bottom and thin at the top, held the liquid.

This area was noisy, filled with busy workers. She even spotted Rhuri at the other side of the room. Higher up on the wall there was a platform that led along the side of the room. The human tourists were being shown along by another member of staff.

"What goes on here?" Zaria asked.

"These stills hold the liquid called the wash and distil the alcohol from it twice, to take away the impurities. All these people are called still workers. They are highly skilled and do the tricky part of removing the alcohol from the heart of the distillation. Not too weak and not too strong."

"Just right, as Goldilocks would say," Zaria joked.

Kenrick chuckled. "Aye, lassie. Quite right."

Zaria loved the look of happiness in Kenrick's eyes. She could scent the confidence and strength and literally feel it in her body. Kenrick truly had the strength of an Alpha, and it made her want Kenrick really badly, but that wasn't going to be possible for a while.

As they watched the activity in the room, Rhuri walked over to join them with a big bear of a man. He had long black hair twisted into a braid that hung down the back, undercut like the other younger wolves with the Celtic wolf symbol, and a goatee ending in a braid with silver ring fastenings.

These wolves were very different to their American counterparts,

Zaria realized again. They still kept that ancient Celtic tribe vibe with their traditions and appearance.

Both wolves saluted and bowed their heads to Zaria.

"Hi, Mater, let be introduce you to our master distiller, Judah," Rhuri said.

Zaria was struck silent for a second. It was the first time anyone had addressed her as Mater. It felt so strange. Kenrick squeezed her hand.

"I'm not quite Mater yet," Zaria said.

Kenrick leaned closer and said, "As good as. You're my mate and the wolves want to show their respect."

Zaria nodded, then the wolf's name clicked in her head. "Judah? You're Donny's mate?"

Judah smiled. "Aye, that's me, Mater. Nice to meet you."

"I just had tea with Donny, Heather, Florrie, and Moira," Zaria said.

Judah rolled his eyes. "I hope he didn't tell too many embarrassing stories."

Zaria pursed her lips and nodded. "There were one or two. One about a bucket of fish guts."

Rhuri, Judah, and Kenrick looked at each other, clearly embarrassed. Kenrick cleared her throat. "Aye, not one of our better ideas. Anyway, Judah does a brilliant job here, and Rhuri helps me oversee the distillery, the forestry, the fishery, and the bottling plant."

"You're all kept really busy then," Zaria said.

"Sure are," Rhuri said.

Judah smiled and nodded, "I better get on. Great meeting you, Mater."

"You too." Zaria was really heartened by the welcome she was getting from all the Wulvers. She thought they might resent a foreigner coming into their pack and mating with the most eligible wolf, but the opposite was the case.

"Are you enjoying the tour?" Rhuri asked.

"It's so interesting. Oh, I saw Milo this morning. Her class was going to do their art lesson down at the shore."

Rhuri smacked her forehead. "Shit...eh, sorry for the language. The cubs have a short day today. There's a teacher's meeting or something. She needs to be picked up from school in a couple of hours."

Kenrick said, "Don't panic. Go and get her or I'll ask my ma to get her."

Rhuri shook her head. "Your ma's got to help take care of Ms. Norah today."

"One of our elderly wolves," Kenrick explained. "Just go early and take Milo home."

Rhuri growled softly. "I can't, Marcus had a problem over at the bottling plant. I said I'd go over there next, and I hate always asking Heather, Florrie, and Moira. They have their own cubs to deal with."

Zaria felt so bad for Rhuri—she looked really conflicted. Zaria had an idea. "Why don't you go get Milo, and I'll be finished my tour by then. I can take her. Milo wanted to show me the loch anyway."

Rhuri screwed up her eyes. "Are you sure? You've just arrived and I'm dumping my problems on you already."

"Don't be silly, you're not. I'm glad to help. Besides that's what Maters are there for."

She felt Kenrick stand straighter, heard her almost growl, and felt her arousal through their connection. Zaria wasn't quite sure why.

"Thank you, Mater. I really, really appreciate it. I'll get back to work just now and go and pick Milo up when it's time."

When Rhuri walked away, Kenrick said, "Thank you for that, lassie. I know she finds it difficult asking for help all the time. She's a proud wolf and she does the best she can, but a dominant can't be everything to a cub. She has so many responsibilities to the pack, especially now as she's going to be Second."

Zaria turned around and put her hands around Kenrick's waist. "Rhuri needs a mate to help her."

"I know, but it's hard for her. Look how far I had to go to find mine." Kenrick leaned in and kissed her softly on the lips.

Kenrick's hunger was growing and Zaria was responding. It had been too long since they had last touched properly, but they were being watched by humans passing through the room and the other wolf workers.

"Where next?" Zaria asked.

Kenrick grinned like a Cheshire cat and whispered sexily, "The cellars below this room. Come with me."

❖

Zaria followed Kenrick down two sets of stairs to an underground cellar, much bigger than the first room they visited. The light was dim and it was much cooler down here. Rows and rows of dark oak casks, one on top of the other, lined the walls and the centre of the room.

Kenrick stayed by the stairs and Zaria walked ahead. "It's surprisingly big down here. You'd never think there was a place like this under the distillery building."

Kenrick walked up behind her and traced her fingers down Zaria's bare arm. Zaria shivered. Kenrick's arousal that started upstairs only got stronger as they descended. She could feel it in her blood, and her wolf dared her to respond, but not yet.

"Where are the people though? The tourists?" Zaria asked.

"They don't get to come down here. This is private. There are a few other places next to this building that they visit, but this is just for Wulvers. We call this warehouse number one. Let me show you."

As they walked Kenrick kept her hand on the small of Zaria's back, making her shiver.

"Officially this is called the maturation room. Once the whisky is distilled, the spirit is put in these casks. In Scotland the spirit has to mature in these casks for three years before it can be legally called whisky."

Zaria looked to Kenrick. "Really? That's a long time."

Kenrick shook her head. "Not for a good single malt. They take a lot longer. During the maturation process the spirit reacts to the outside air that seeps through the wood, and about two per cent escapes through the wood. In Scotland the humans call it the angels' share, but I prefer to think the Great Mother enjoys the fruits of our labour."

"It's amazing. I never knew so much went into it. You're so knowledgeable."

"It's in—"

"Your blood. I remember."

They still hadn't gotten halfway down the cellar. "Where are we going?"

Kenrick smiled. "Wait and see."

They finally came to the end aisle of the room and turned left. There was one cask sitting alone on a table with a gold tap on it and above it a coat of arms. Above that was a large ancient looking sword with a gold handle.

"What is this? Zaria asked.

"This coat of arms represents the descendants of Princess Scota and the weapons she left us with. To each pack she gave a weapon that was part of our ancient heritage. The Wulvers got the sword."

Kenrick laid her hand on the barrel with reverence. "This is the first ever cask of whisky we produced on our land. When Princess Scota left us to found the other packs, we had to learn from the human locals to live in this environment. It was quite different from Egypt, as you can imagine. One of the things they taught us was how to make a spirit called whisky."

"What a cool story. We had nothing like this. Clearly my descendants took the wrong option when they left Princess Scota's voyage," Zaria said.

"At my Alpha ceremony, I and the elite wolves will drink some of this cask, and the sword will be presented to me as a symbol of power," Kenrick said.

When Kenrick said power, Zaria growled without even thinking. She could feel Kenrick's power and her wolf demanded to feel it.

You're calling me, Kenrick said telepathically.

Zaria turned away and walked over to the rows of barrels on the wall, purposely ignoring and challenging Kenrick.

Kenrick walked over slowly, a low growl escaping her mouth. Zaria turned around and backed up against the barrels.

"What are you growling about?" Zaria asked.

"You. I want you." Kenrick's eyes and teeth shifted as she bore down on her.

Zaria's heart started to flutter. "What if someone comes down here?"

"They won't." Kenrick popped open the button on Zaria's jeans and sucked on the mate bite on her neck.

Zaria gasped when Kenrick thrust her fingers deep inside her. She moaned, "Ricky, that's so deep."

"You like that?" Kenrick dragged her teeth over the mate bite she made.

"Yeah...more." Zaria's hips were gyrating backward and forward, faster with each thrust.

Kenrick slipped in a third finger and stilled her hand. "Is that okay?"

"Uh-huh," Zaria groaned, almost in pain.

Kenrick pushed her fingers in and out, taking her pace from Zaria. When her hips thrust faster, so did she, until Zaria shouted desperately, "Bite me now."

Kenrick sank her teeth into Zaria's neck, and Zaria did the same to her. The bite on Kenrick's neck was gloriously painful.

She just had to come. Kenrick turned Zaria around and pulled down her jeans to expose her mate's buttocks, opened her own jeans, and thrust against Zaria hard and fast.

"Yes, come Ricky," Zaria moaned.

Kenrick was going to come all over her mate in seconds. Then Zaria pushed her buttocks hard into Kenrick's sex and it was all over. She cried into the crook of her mate's neck, emptying her essence all over Zaria's cheeks.

When Kenrick got her breath back, Zaria giggled and said, "Big bad wolf."

CHAPTER TWENTY-TWO

Zaria walked outside the distillery and saw Rhuri pull up in her Land Rover. Milo jumped out and ran to hug her.

"Hi, Mater. Rhuri said we were to call you that now."

Zaria ruffled Milo's curly hair. "When we're together you call me Zaria."

Rhuri lowered her window and said, "Thank you so much for this, Mater. I'll try not to be too long."

"Don't worry about. Do what you have to do." Zaria smiled and they both waved her off.

She took Milo's hand and said, "Okay, let's go and see if you can show me the Kelpie."

They walked down to a part of the shore that was quieter. It was later in the day and the tourists were heading home.

"Why don't we sit on those rocks." Zaria led them over to a collection of stone boulders sitting by the water's edge.

They sat down and Milo said, "Alpha Fergus told me giants put these huge rocks here."

"This place is just full of cool legends," Zaria said with a smile. "So, when did you see this Kelpie?"

Milo picked up some small rocks and threw them into the water. "A few weeks after I came to the Wulvers, after my mum died."

Milo looked down at her feet and Zaria put her arm around her. She could feel her pain so deeply. Milo's situation was so similar to Marco's.

"You know, I have a nephew back in Wolfgang County called

Marco. He lost his mom too, and I lost my sister, but you know what helped? Talking about it with Ricky. Do you talk to Rhuri?"

Milo shook her head. "No, it makes Aunt Rhuri sad and made my grandpa and grandma leave Wulver Forest."

Tears rolled down Mio's cheeks. Zaria remembered Kenrick telling her about Rhuri's parents. She couldn't imagine turning her back on a child. Zaria had lived a life on the run and in poverty just so she didn't lose contact with Marco. "You mustn't feel bad about them leaving. People do strange things when they're sad and their heart is broken."

Milo hugged her tightly. "I'm really glad you're here, Zaria. You're different, like me."

Zaria kissed her head. "Different is a good thing. We all have different strengths. Look how awesome you are. You're going to have the strength of a wolf and the powers of a witch."

"I guess so, but sometimes I feel too different from the other cubs," Milo said.

"We're both in the same boat. I'm an American walking straight into the Wulver pack to become Mater. Maybe because were different we can help each other out. You know more about the Wulvers than me, and you can talk to me about anything. Your mum, school, witch stuff, what do you think?"

Milo wiped away her tears and smiled. "I'd like that. Here, let me show you something cool my tutor taught me."

Milo picked up a stone and held her palms one above another. She whispered an incantation and levitated the stone, then pushed her hands towards the water, and the stone flew across the loch until they lost sight of it in the distance.

"Wow! That was fantastic, Milo. Who's your tutor?" Zaria asked.

"Madam Hilda. She comes once a month to teach me about my magic," Milo explained.

"Is Madam Hilda a witch?"

"She lives much further north in an old castle with her clan. They're called the BaoBhan Sith." Milo struggled over the words.

"I've never heard of them," Zaria said. It appeared as if there was a whole new world of paranormal and mythical creatures for her to learn about in Britain.

"Aunt Rhuri says they are like fae and Vampires mixed together. It's confusing but they know about magic, and Ms. Hilda is really cool and nice," Zaria said.

"I'm glad. So, teach me about this Kelpie. You saw it just after you arrived here?"

"Yeah." A big smile and excitement came back to Milo's face. "I was here myself and it was quiet everywhere. Then I heard this noise, water rushing. I looked up and it like a wave, but the rest of the water was still."

"Did it just look like a wave?" Zaria asked.

Milo shook her head. "As it got closer I saw it looked like a horse's head. Then it stopped in the middle of the water and just stared at me."

"A horse? Strange in water, isn't it?" Zaria said.

Milo nodded. "Aunt Rhuri says it's a water spirit, but because the ancient Celtic people around here sacrificed horses to it, it took on the appearance of a horse in water. But it's a shapeshifter. Stories say it's appeared as women, men, and all sorts of creatures."

"So what happened then, when it stopped?"

"I heard a noise and looked away, and when I turned back it was gone, but I know what I saw. Do you believe me?"

Zaria stroked Milo's back. It was very important to Milo that she was believed, and Zaria did believe she saw something. "Sure, I do. With these paranormal creatures around, there's no telling what might be out there. Do the humans know about this myth?"

Milo laughed. "Yeah, they come with binoculars and fancy boats with radar to try to find it. They sell Kelpie souvenirs in the gift shop too, but she won't show herself to lots of people like that."

"You think it's a she?" Zaria asked.

"Yeah, I can feel it in here." Milo pointed to her chest.

Zaria shivered as the breeze picked up. She looked around and realized it was getting late. The evening gloom was settling over the landscape. When she looked around, Zaria got the feeling someone or something was watching them. She felt like she had when she was at the airport arriving in Glasgow. She sniffed the air but couldn't discern anything other than the natural scents around them. The hairs on the back of her neck stood up, but she shook it off. It was all the talk of mythical creatures.

"It's getting late. We better get you back. Thanks for telling me about the Kelpie." Zaria hugged Milo but couldn't shake her bad feeling. "Let's go."

❖

Kenrick had never been so eager to get back to her den in her life. Normally after work she'd spend time at her mum and dad's or with Rhuri and Milo, since the rest of her friends were mated and went home to be with their mates.

It was crazy to think that was the position she was in now. Mated to Zaria, the wolf that the Great Mother dropped into her lap. Now she understood why her friends were all so eager to get home after work.

Every inch of her being needed, hungered, demanded she be with her mate. As she got closer to her den, her mate bite started to throb and her skin began to tingle. When she got to the bottom of the stairway, Kenrick scented meat cooking and heard the laughter of her mate and her mother.

Kenrick got a warm glow inside and ran up to her door. She walked through and found the happiest sight she'd seen in her den— Zaria and her mother making food together and getting on so well. She was so glad the two women in her life had hit it off. Not only for her, but Zaria needed family and the mother figure she hadn't had since her sister died.

"There's my big bairn." Elspeth walked over and gave her a hug.

"Ma, I'm going to be Alpha in a few days. Do you have to call me a bairn?" Kenrick said.

Elspeth kissed her on the cheek and said, "You'll always be my bairn, Ricky. Even when you have grey hair like me."

Kenrick rolled her eyes and kissed her mother. When she got closer, her mother whispered, "Thank you for bringing us Zaria. She's perfect for us, and we are perfect for her, but you better have your mating ceremony soon, or I'll bite your tail. Don't think you're too old for that."

"Thanks, ma, and I promise it'll be soon."

Elspeth went back over to Zaria and hugged her. "I'll leave you to it, Zari, and thanks again for helping with Milo."

"Anytime," Zaria replied.

As soon as Elspeth left Zaria ran and jumped into Kenrick's arms. "I missed you so much." Zaria growled and rubbed her scent all over Kenrick's neck.

"I missed you too." Kenrick kissed her and carried her over to the kitchen island. While they kissed, Kenrick ran her hands underneath Zaria's top and scratched her belly.

I want you, Kenrick thought while they kissed.

"Nu-uh." Zaria pushed her away and Kenrick didn't resist. She was always careful to show Zaria that she could stop anytime she wanted, and nothing had changed now they were mated and never would. The way Ovid abused Zaria's innocence and control would never happen again.

Mating and making love were a gift to Kenrick, but it was Zaria's right to bestow that on her.

"I've got it all planned," Zaria said. "We'll have our first dinner together, then lie in the hammock at light-up time, watch the stars, and talk."

Kenrick nuzzled her cheek. "Sounds perfect. You know how good it feels to have you here in my den, cooking for me?"

Zaria smiled. "Yeah, I think I do, Highlander, but remember, I learned to cook in diners, so it might not be up to your mom's standards."

Kenrick playfully growled into her neck. "It'll be amazing."

Zaria giggled. "Your mom did tell me your favourite foods, so hopefully I'll do okay at this domestic thing. Go and get changed out of that suit. I know how much you don't like it."

Kenrick walked away towards their bedroom then turned around and said, "Zari? You've made me the happiest wolf in the world. Thank you for trusting me."

"I love you," Zaria replied.

Zaria didn't think she had ever felt more content in her life, or—thinking about it more deeply—she had never had the security to feel any contentment. But lying here in the hammock on the balcony, in the arms of her new mate, was bliss. After dinner they came out to watch light-up time, which Zaria thought was magical, and then she lay with Kenrick and, wrapped around her, looked up at the stars on a crisp, cold night.

Zaria sighed as Kenrick stroked her hair. "I hope that was a happy sigh," Kenrick said.

"Oh yes. I've never experienced this…safety, I suppose. I've always had to keep moving, always on the run looking over my shoulder, and this is the first time I can stand still and appreciate life around me."

Kenrick kissed her head. "I'll always keep you safe, Zari. You're mine now, and I'm yours. No one can ever change that. I'm so happy you like Wulver Forest. I worried it might be a big change for you."

Zaria laughed softly. "The weather is. It's colder and rains a lot, but I don't think there's anywhere more beautiful. Making your dens high in the trees makes you feel you're a part of the living forest."

"The forest, the animals we hunt and take care of, it's in our blood," Kenrick replied.

Zaria reached up and caressed Kenrick's cheek. "As well as the whisky?"

"That too. We have strong blood," Kenrick joked.

"Oh, I know."

"How did you get on with Heather and her friends?" Kenrick asked. She wanted to bring up the ceremony, but she had to know if Zaria had settled in with the pack and if she would be ready.

"They were so nice and welcoming. Even the wolves in the marketplace were nice. They kept calling me Mater, which I found strange at first. I thought they might take a while to warm up to the stray American wolf, but they didn't," Zaria said.

Kenrick squeezed her. "Of course they accepted you. You're my mate, my Mater, and in any case we all grew up together. They are good wolves."

"I haven't been in a group of submissives since I was sixteen. I'm going to have to learn to open up. I'm so used to hiding," Zaria said. "What was your mom whispering to you before she left?"

This was as good a chance as any to bring up the ceremony subject. "Just reminding me that a ceremony comes with mating."

Zaria looked up at her. "Did you ask your pater about it?"

Kenrick was nervous about Zaria's reaction but it had to be

discussed. "Uh…yeah. He left the distillery and went to speak to all the pack elders about it."

"What did they say?" Zaria asked.

"That's the thing. I don't want you to feel pressured or anything, and I know it's taken a lot for you to give up your life in America and come to another country to be with me. It's so much for you to take in and—"

Zaria frowned and tried to push herself up in the hammock, making it swing. "They don't want me as your mate, as your Mater?"

Kenrick pulled her back down. "No, no, it's not that. The complete opposite in fact. The elders and the elite wolves think it would be better for the pack if we were mated before my Alpha ceremony."

"Do they want you to postpone your ceremony?" Zaria said.

This was the part that was making her nervous. "No they'd like to do both, our mating ceremony first, before becoming Alpha and Mater officially."

"Oh," Zaria said quietly.

Kenrick knew this was going to be too much, too soon. "Look, I can speak to them. I understand you think it's too soon."

"No, don't do that. I want us to be officially mated as soon as we can. I want to feel I have a home at last. I just didn't think that I'd be part of the Alpha ceremony."

"You're my Mater. We lead together," Kenrick said.

Zaria got a faraway look in her eyes and Kenrick could sense hurt. "If my sister could see me now. When Leroux killed her pater, my sister had nothing to do with her coronation, as Leroux called it."

"Like I said," Kenrick replied, "I think she'll be watching from the Great Eternal Forest, proud that you are going to be able to do all the things she couldn't or wasn't allowed to."

Zaria nodded but didn't say anything.

Kenrick still had a thought from earlier that was nagging her. "Zari, can I ask you something?"

Zaria threaded her fingers through Kenrick's. "Anything."

"When I was rushing to get dressed this morning and you asked about buying some food, I could feel you were frightened. Did I do something?"

"You never do anything to frighten me, Highlander. It was just a flashback memory that made me freeze for a minute."

Kenrick moved their clasped hands just under Zaria's T-shirt and stroked her soft stomach, trying to make her feel as safe as possible.

"It's amazing how your brain takes in memories you don't even know you have, then hits you with them one day out of the blue," Zaria said.

"Tell me and I'll chase it away," Kenrick said. She could feel how tense Zaria was as she relived what was in her mind. "You're okay, you're safe."

Zaria took a breath and said, "It was the money thing. Leroux didn't let Marta have access to their bank account, their money, so everything she needed, food, clothes, anything for the den, she had to ask for. It was about Leroux's control. I remember being a little cub and watching the glee on Leroux's face as Marta begged her for money. It turned my blood cold, remembering that. Marta would put it off for as long as she could—she was always tense and nervous about Leroux's reaction. If she caught her at the wrong moment, it would sometimes not be glee, but fury or anger. She always paid for what she got, physically or mentally."

Now Kenrick understood everything and she supposed a lot of these traumatic memories would come up often in their life together.

"Lassie, I think you know in your heart that I would never, ever do that to you. We are and will always be a team, but I also know that fears and memories like that can be irrational and play on your mind no matter how much you try to fight them. Let me tell you something that you don't know."

Zaria shifted in her arms. "What?"

"Before we left Wolfgang County and I didn't think you were coming with me, I did something that probably would have made you mad but—"

Zaria gave her a sly smile. "What did you do, Highlander?"

Kenrick traced soothing circles on Zaria bare stomach while she spoke. "My wolf knew that you were my chosen mate, even though you didn't."

"I did," Zaria interrupted. "I was just scared to admit it."

"Okay, aye, but every fibre of my wolf being is programmed to take care of my mate. I couldn't leave you with no means of taking care of yourself. So I opened a back account in town and gave Eden the details to give you after I was gone. I was going to keep it topped up with money so I could take care of you even when I couldn't do that in person."

Zaria looked at her silently at first, and then her eyes started to glow yellow and Kenrick could sense and scent her arousal.

"You're right. I would have been pissed off at the time, but not now," Zaria said in a low voice.

"I promise you, Zari. My den, my business, my pack, everything I own is yours—"

Before she could finish her sentence Zaria grasped her dreadlocks roughly and pulled her down into a deep kiss.

Kenrick's wolf responded and started to partially shift and her mate bite throbbed. She nipped Zaria's tongue with her teeth while she ripped the T-shit she was wearing to shreds. Now Zaria's breasts were exposed to the cold air and her arousal made her nipples rock hard.

Zaria took one of Kenrick's hands and placed it on her breast while she pushed the other down to the button of her jeans.

Telepathically, Zaria said, *Here. Make me come right here.*

Kenrick softened and slowed their kiss. She wanted to show Zaria how much she loved her and that it didn't always have to be fast and rough as Were sex could be. She opened the button on Zaria's jeans and pushed her hand into her underwear. She moaned when she was met by Zaria's sex saturated with wetness.

You're soaking wet, mate.

That's because I'm yours. Touch me, Zaria said.

Kenrick split her fingers around Zaria's clit but kept them still. Zaria moved her hips, trying to get some relief and growled, *Touch me, Ricky.*

Kenrick pulled back from the kiss and said, "Are you mine?"

"Yours, always yours, Ricky."

"Look up at the stars, lassie, and don't stop looking," Kenrick said.

Zaria did with a moan of frustration. It was cold, crisp night, not a cloud in the sky, and when she looked up, it appeared as if she was gazing across the universe. It was beautiful.

Kenrick started to move her fingers slowly and rhythmically grasped Zaria's breast and pinched her nipple. Zaria's body was on fire, a contrast to the cold night. She thrust her hips in time with Kenrick's strokes.

As her orgasm built higher, she felt lighter, almost like her body was rising higher and higher to the stars she was gazing at.

Kenrick whispered in her ear, "I used to lie out here on my own, lonely and hungering to find my mate somewhere in the world. I prayed to the Great Mother to find me someone to love."

Zaria groaned as Kenrick quickened the pace and every few strokes thrust her fingers inside Zaria's opening.

"And she sent me the wolf of my dreams," Kenrick said softly.

"Yes, I'm yours. I need to come, Ricky."

"Keep looking at those stars and know that you've found your place, found your pack, found your home, and found the mate who will protect you and love you forever."

Kenrick gave her deeper strokes inside and Zaria met them with her thrusting hips. Zaria's orgasm was building from somewhere low and deep, but as deep as it felt, her body flew higher with every one Kenrick's strokes.

It appeared as if the stars were surrounding her body, and she was floating somewhere up there in the vastness of space. She moaned low as if she was in pain when the deep orgasm passed the point of no return and she lost control.

Zaria grabbed Kenrick's hair as her powerful orgasm rushed from the base of her spine and took over her body. The stars that had been surrounding her now exploded in front on her eyes and turned to pure whiteness as she closed her eyes tightly. Then she felt it—a connection to the trees, the land, the loch. Everything that made Wulver Forest, she now was part of it. Zaria was home. The thing she'd never thought possible.

"Ricky," Zaria shouted.

As the rush of orgasm calmed, she became aware of the crisp, cold air cooling her hot body.

"I love you, lassie."

"I love you."

Zaria was home.

Chapter Twenty-three

The next couple of days, the pack worked hard to prepare and organize everything they would need to add a mating ceremony to Kenrick's Alpha ritual. All the shops by the shore side of the loch posted closed notices for the weekend, and the barriers at the entrance to the loch were to be closed to limit the number of humans around.

Everyone was working tirelessly to make this day one to remember, and Kenrick couldn't have been prouder of the way her pack had opened its arms to Zaria.

Tomorrow they would go through purification rituals separately, before the ceremonies the next day, but today were their respective stag and hen parties.

Kenrick was packing her rucksack with her fishing equipment and a change of clothes. Rhuri had arranged a fishing and camping night, over on the other side of the loch where there was less chance of bumping into humans, and then who knew what Rhuri had planned. Most likely it would involve the finest of Wulver malt whisky.

She looked over from the bedroom to where Zaria was sitting at the island in the kitchen. Zaria was video-calling Marco with their good news and they'd been talking for nearly an hour. It was wonderful to see her mate building a relationship with the nephew she had sacrificed so much for.

Zaria turned around and beckoned her over.

She walked over and placed her hands on Zaria's shoulders. Kenrick could see Vance behind Marco, smiling and relaxed. Vance and Flash were encouraging Marco to get to know Zaria. It could have been so very different and awkward. "Hi, Marco, how are you?"

"Great, Ricky. Look, I haven't taken it off." Marco lifted his wrist to show the leather wristband she had given him.

"Cool."

From behind him Vance said, "Congratulations, Ricky. Mated at last?"

Kenrick chuckled. "Well, on Saturday officially."

Zaria reached for Kenrick's hand on her shoulder. "Vance says that Marco can come visit us in the next school holidays. Isn't that exciting?"

Kenrick knew how much that meant to Zaria and how much trust Vance and Flash placed in them, to let him come. "That'll be so much fun. There's lots of cubs for you to play with, and I'll take you on some cool runs."

"I can't wait, Ricky," Marco said excitedly.

"Well, I better let you go, Marco," Zaria said. "Good luck with your game on Sunday."

"Thanks, Aunt Zari. Send me lots of pictures of your mating ceremony."

"We will. Thanks, Vance. Speak soon."

They waved goodbye and hung up. Zaria sighed.

"Was that a good sigh?" Kenrick asked.

"Yeah, and a relieved one," Zaria said. "I don't have to worry about him any more. He's safe and sound and I can be the aunty I always wanted to be." Zaria stood up and went into Kenrick's arms.

Kenrick said, "You are both safe. Leroux is dead and the pack's dispersed. You just have to concentrate on making your life and Marco's life the happiest they can be."

Zaria snuggled her cheek into Kenrick's neck. "I hope our cubs are like Marco. Good, kind wolves."

Kenrick grinned from ear to ear. This was the first time Zaria had mentioned cubs, so she must be feeling at home. "How could they not be? Look at their parents," Kenrick joked.

Zaria laughed and stepped back from her mate. "So are you ready to go, Highlander?"

"Just about. I've got all my fishing gear and a change of clothes. Rhuri and the others are bringing the camping gear."

"Don't drink too much." Zaria jabbed her finger into Kenrick's chest playfully.

"Don't worry, lassie. I know my limits. Besides, the purification ritual tomorrow will help with that."

Zari narrowed her eyes and folded her arms. "I don't know if I like that answer. Just make sure you're in good condition for Saturday."

"I will. I hope you'll have fun with my mum and the other submissives. There'll be lots more wolves for you to meet at your hen party," Kenrick said.

Zaria put the flat of her hand on Kenrick's chest. "It'll be great, but I'm going to miss you."

After they parted tonight, they wouldn't see each other until their mating day. That was a long time for two newly mated wolves.

Kenrick put her nose in the crook of Zaria's neck and inhaled her scent. "After this we'll never be apart again."

Zaria grasped Kenrick's dreadlocks, as she liked to do, while her mate rubbed her scent all over her face and neck.

"So you don't forget you're mine," Kenrick said.

"I'd never forget." Zaria slipped her hands down the back of Kenrick's jeans and dug her nails in her buttocks while she kissed her neck.

Kenrick growled. Her body was starting to hunger. "Don't do this when I have to go, lassie."

Zaria grinned and lowered herself to her knees.

"What are you doing?" Kenrick asked.

Zaria gave her a saucy smile and started to unbuckle her belt. "Giving you something to remember me by."

"Zari—"

Zaria didn't listen. She pulled down Kenrick's jeans and jockey shorts. She snuffled her nose into Kenrick's sex and felt how turned on she was. Her clit was already engorged and protruding. She wasted no time and sucked Kenrick's clit into her mouth. Kenrick moaned and threaded her fingers through her hair. While sucking Kenrick's clit, Zaria rolled her tongue all around the base, which seemed to be driving Kenrick wild.

Never would she have believed that she would be on her knees in front of a dominant, and enjoying giving her pleasure. But she trusted Kenrick, and it gave Zaria pleasure to give this to the love of her life.

"Fuck, yes, Zari. Just like that," Kenrick said as her hips undulated.

Zaria increased her pace and pulled Kenrick closer by holding her buttocks.

"Going to come," Kenrick growled.

Zaria looked up for a second and saw Kenrick with her head back, eyes closed, enjoying every second that Zaria was giving her. She could tell Kenrick was moments from coming, so her fingers shifted to claws and she dug them into her mate's buttocks.

She gently bit Kenrick's clit and then sucked furiously. Kenrick howled in pleasure while she held Zaria's head in place.

"Fuck," Kenrick said as her breathing calmed. "You're a bad influence on me, Zari."

Zaria gave one last kiss to her sex and got up. She smiled at how relaxed and blissed out Kenrick looked. She gave her mate a kiss and whispered, "Have a good stag party, but remember who you belong to, Ricky."

Kenrick took Zaria's hand and placed it on her chest. "Your paw is imprinted on my heart."

Zaria had never run with so many wolves before. The current Mater, Elspeth, led the pack of about twenty male and female submissives through the forest. Elspeth and Heather thought it would be good to start the hen night with a run together, because nothing bonded wolves like running.

Zaria's wolf was behind Elspeth's grey wolf, while Heather's reddish wolf brought up the rear with all the rest of the friends. They were nearing the end of the run. She had splashed through streams, jumped over fallen tree branches, and followed some interesting scents.

Elspeth's wolf slowed up and the rest followed until they came to a stop and gathered around the Mater.

What a great run everyone, Elspeth said. *My stamina isn't as good as you younger wolves'. Let's head back, get changed, and meet at my den in an hour to toast our new Mater, with a wee dram.*

A chorus of howls rose to Elspeth in return and the pack started to break up. Elspeth's and Heather's dens were close by Zaria and Kenrick's, and so they padded back together.

When they got back to her den, Zaria said, *Thanks, that was a great. What do you think the dominants are doing?*

Heather's wolf snorted. *Playing at being cave wolves. Roasting fish over the fire, drinking too much whisky, and telling dirty jokes. We'll have much more fun, believe me.*

Elspeth added, *There will always be a part of the Celtic warrior in the dominant Wulver. We must let them play sometimes. Fergus will look after them. Go and get changed, Zaria, and I'll see you at my den in an hour.*

I'll call for you, Heather said.

Okay, see you soon.

Once they left, Zaria's wolf ran up the walkway to the den. She shifted back to skin, opened the door, and stepped inside. All at once, Zaria felt hands around her mouth and throat. She couldn't see them but she knew that scent anywhere. Ovid. She was so high from her run and the safety she felt, that she hadn't taken notice of the scent that haunted her dreams until it was too late. She had let her guard down.

She struggled as much as she could but then felt something stabbing into her arm. As she started to lose consciousness, she heard Ovid say, "I told you I would always find you. You're mine."

Then the blackness enveloped her.

CHAPTER TWENTY-FOUR

It had been a good evening's fishing, in good company. Kenrick caught a fair few fish and enjoyed the camaraderie, and now they were sitting around the campfire they had built on the beach, roasting fish and some steaks they had brought with them over the fire.

The atmosphere around the fire was lively. A bottle of whisky bottled the year Kenrick was born was being passed around the elite wolves and Kenrick's other friends, who all sat on logs around the perimeter.

Kenrick was sitting with her pater, Rhuri, and Callum, eating some fish and meat off her plate. She was enjoying herself but just couldn't keep her mind off Zaria.

"You're quiet, Ricky," Fergus said.

"Aye, you should be enjoying every last moment of freedom," Callum said. "As soon as you're mated, you won't get a say in life again."

Kenrick looked up at him and smiled. "But you wouldn't change being mated to Heather for one minute, would you."

Callum grinned back. "Not for a moment. Heather can boss me about as much as she wants. She and the bairn are my world."

"So why are you quiet? Is there something wrong?" Fergus asked.

"No, I just can't stop thing about Zari. When I'm apart from her it hurts deep inside." Kenrick put her plate down and took a sip of whisky.

Her pater patted her on the back. "That's only natural. You always will feel that, but it gets easier to deal with."

Judah, who was sitting next to Fergus said, "Sometimes I find myself going crazy during the day, wondering if Donny and the cubs are safe, our bond is so strong, but you just have to trust they are okay."

Kenrick nodded. She was sure their bond would only grow stronger after their mating ceremony.

"You've found a good wolf to be our next Mater, Ricky," Fergus said. "I'm proud of you. Zaria has a unique experience of the world to bring to her role, and it's always good to bring new blood into the pack."

Rhuri sighed and poured herself a large drink. "You're a lucky bastard, Rickster. You're all lucky bastards. I think the Great Mother forgot about me."

Kenrick gave Rhuri a soft punch in the arm. "I thought that too, and look what happened."

"My situation's different though. Not every wolf will want a mate who was a cub."

Fergus leaned over and patted her knee. "The right one will, Rhuri. You have to keep your eyes open, though. Don't make her come up and slap you in the face."

Rhuri smiled. "I'll try to keep that in mind, Alpha. So? Have ye thought about where ye might take Zaria on honeymoon?"

"Aye, I thought it would be great to take her to Egypt, Princess Scota's homeland. Retrace the steps of the pack. There're some beautiful places to visit. Let me show you—"

Suddenly Judah stood up and looked into the darkness. "I can feel Donny—he's running here. Something's wrong."

Kenrick and the others stood up quickly.

"Get a torch," Fergus said.

Lukas, Moira's mate, ran over to one of the tents, brought back a torch, and gave it to Judah, while the other wolves looked for more torches. Kenrick, Fergus, and Callum followed Judah into the darkness. In seconds they saw a pair of yellow eyes catch the torchlight.

"Donny!" Judah called. Donny's wolf ran straight Judah and shifted to skin He was panting with the exertion of the run. Judah put his arms around him. "What's wrong, mate? Are you okay?"

"Aye, the Mater sent me because I'm the fastest runner. No one answered their phones."

Kenrick pulled out her phone and saw a dozen missed calls. "It was too noisy. We couldn't hear them."

"Alpha, Ricky, it's Zaria. She's gone."

Kenrick felt a rush of panic and fear just like she'd experienced in Wolfgang County. "What do you mean, gone?"

"We all went a run together, then back to our dens to get changed. We agreed to meet at the Mater's den in an hour. Zaria never turned up."

"Did you check our den?" Kenrick shouted.

Judah grasped his mate more tightly and growled a low warning.

Kenrick shook herself. "I'm sorry for shouting, Judah, Donny. Tell us what you know."

"We checked your den. Zaria wasn't there, but there was sign of a struggle and a wolf scent we didn't recognize."

Kenrick had a sick feeling in the pit of her stomach. For the first time every wolf looked to her instead of her pater. They knew instinctively she was the strongest wolf among them now, but she hated to circumvent her pater's authority.

She looked at Fergus and he put his hand on her shoulder. "You are Alpha in all but name—we both know that. Lead us, and we will find your mate."

A new confidence came over Kenrick. This was her pack to lead, and she would lead them to hell if it meant getting Zaria back.

"Wolves, get prepared to shift. We are going on a hunt. A wolf has taken one of our own, your future Mater, and we are going to take her back."

The wolves shouted, "Yes, Alpha."

Kenrick tore her clothes off so she could shift, as did the rest. Kenrick had the worst feeling. There was one wolf still alive who wanted Zaria and obsessed enough to try to take what was hers.

Ovid.

Zaria was abruptly awakened by water being splashed in her face. She gasped and opened her eyes.

"You're finally awake," a voice said.

Zaria's vision came back slowly, and she saw the person who fuelled her nightmares. "Ovid."

Ovid was crouched down in front of her. Her face was scarred down one side and she appeared to have lost an eye in her fight with the Wolfgangs and Kenrick. She had obviously been too injured to shift in time to completely heal her injuries.

Zaria took stock of her injuries and surroundings. She was naked, something was making her woozy and sleepy, and looking down she saw she had silver manacles on. Beside her she saw the memorial to Kenrick's brother, on the edge of the forest only a few hundred yards from the loch. This was where he died. Why had Ovid brought her here?

"Hello, Zaria."

That voice along with the woozy feeling made her turn to the side and vomit. Ovid held a bottle of water to her lips.

"Drink this. You've got silver in your system."

Zaria smelled that it was indeed plain water so she took a drink and cleared the bitter taste from her mouth. "Why are you doing this?" Zaria asked.

Ovid reached out and cupped her cheek. "Many reasons, one being that you're mine, and I don't like people taking what is mine."

Zaria felt fury like she hadn't ever had the chance to express before. "I belong to Kenrick Wulver. Look at my mate bite."

Ovid's hand shot out and grabbed her throat while her shifted claws tore through her mate bite.

Zaria howled in pain, both physical and mental. Her mate bite had been desecrated.

"You belong to me," Ovid shouted. "You always have and always will. I made you mine that day in the forest, remember?"

Zaria struggled against her restraints, but it was useless. The silver just drained the energy right out of her. "Remember? I've remembered it in my nightmares every night since it happened. You groomed me ever since I started going through the rush, you sick freak."

Ovid pulled her to her feet and slammed her up against the tree behind her. "You don't seem to remember the Lupa rules. A submissive should be seen and not heard."

"I've found my voice since I left the Lupas." Zaria summoned enough strength to thrust her head forward and headbutted Ovid in the face.

Ovid squealed in pain and grasped her nose. "You bitch."

Zaria received a blow to the face and a punch to the stomach.

"Did you really think you could have your happy ever after with your Scottish barbarian? You were promised to me and helped that bitch Marta get away from her mate."

"Don't you dare talk about Marta—Leroux beat her to a pulp," Zaria said.

Ovid grabbed her hair painfully. "She was Leroux's mate. She could do what the hell she liked with her mate. Just as I can with mine, but you don't stop with running. You lure Leroux and me out and help destroy us. You're a traitor to your own kind."

"I'm not a Lupa, I'm a Wulver," Zaria spat.

"Not for long." Ovid licked the bloody mess she had made of Zaria's mate bite. "You're mine and you will be no one else's."

"Kenrick will find me." Zaria only prayed it was in time.

"Your barbarian destroyed everything." Ovid walked away and let rip on a neighbouring tree with her claws. Blood dripped from Ovid's injured claws, and Zaria's blood dripped from the teeth that had ripped her mate bite apart. Ovid's eye and face were shifted, and she looked terrifying and out of control.

Ovid stalked towards her slowly. "If your barbarian hadn't intervened, then the Lupas would now have the Wolfgangs' pack lands and wealth. We planned everything perfectly. The attack, the ring to drain Dante's power—now our Alpha is dead, most of our strongest wolves are dead, and the pack that's left has dispersed and broken apart. The Lupa pack is dead because you couldn't be a good little submissive and brought your barbarian into our relationship."

"We have no relationship. You assaulted a sixteen-year-old. Did that make you feel like a big powerful wolf, rather than the pathetic mutt you really are?"

Ovid swung her arm and her claws ripped across Zaria's face. "I waited long enough on you. Leroux said you were mine," Ovid screamed.

Zaria spat blood from her mouth. She felt like she was going to lose consciousness but used every ounce of her strength to stay alert. If she wasn't alert, she might never wake up again, and she had to see Ricky again.

"Why did you bring me here?" Zaria said in a raspy voice.

"I've done a little digging and I thought, what better way to destroy Kenrick than to find her beloved's body at the site where she found her brother's."

Zaria knew it would destroy Kenrick. She already felt terrible guilt about not finding her brother in time. "Don't, please," Zaria pleaded.

Ovid stepped so close she could feel her breath on her face. "You like begging? Why don't we relive our first time together."

❖

Kenrick howled to signal her wolves to stop. They had been following a trail from her den for twenty minutes but it kept branching off. She turned to her pater and friends around her.

Pater, Ovid's laid some false trails. We need to split up.

Fergus said, *Are you sure it's this Ovid? Didn't you say the Lupas were destroyed?*

Not all, Pater. Ovid and some of the others ran. But I know in my heart it's her. She's never given up on finding Zari, and now she has nothing to lose. I've felt Zaria's pain since we entered the forest.

We will find her, Rhuri said.

Kenrick growled and got her wolves' attention. *Rhuri, Judah, Marcus, and Lukas, you're with me. Pater, split the rest of our wolves into smaller groups.*

Fergus snuffled and licked her snout. *We will find your mate. I promise you.*

Kenrick nodded. She just prayed that Zaria was still in one piece. *Let's go. We'll follow the scent straight ahead.*

Kenrick and her closest friends set off at a run. She felt Zaria and her pain with every stride she took. She felt sadness, hurt, and fear.

Rhuri ran beside her. *The scent is strong, they must be near. We will get her, Ricky.*

Kenrick growled, *I can feel Zari. She's scared. She's been frightened of Ovid since she was a cub. I'm going to make sure my mate's safe, and then I'm going to rip Ovid's fucking head off.*

Don't worry, Alpha, you'll get the first and last bites, Rhuri replied.

After another few miles, Kenrick gave her wolves the signal to slow. The scent was leading them in the direction of her brother's memorial.

Ovid wouldn't dare take Zaria there, would she?

❖

Zaria could barely keep her eyes open. Between her injuries and the silver sloshing round her veins, it was hard to fight her body's instinct to shut down and fall into the blackness. She slumped against the tree while Ovid paced in front of her, talking on her mobile phone.

Ovid was different from the confident cruel wolf Zaria remembered, and not just physically. Mentally she appeared broken, and that made her all the more dangerous. She hung up the phone and walked back over to Zaria.

"On your feet."

When Zaria didn't respond, Ovid dragged her to her feet. "It's time for me to go, and that means we get to finish what we started all those years ago."

Zaria tried to touch the mate bite on her shoulder.

Through the fog of pain Zaria could hear Kenrick say, *I'm coming—hold on, lassie.*

But there was no time. It was over. Somehow she always knew she would never be free of the wolf who groomed her. Being on the run and always looking over her shoulder had meant Zaria had contemplated death a lot.

She didn't feel bad for herself, but she felt deep pain in her heart for Kenrick. Losing a mate was like losing part of yourself. A mate was a wolf's whole reason for being, and many didn't survive, if they were widowed young.

Ovid ran her razor sharp claws up and down Zaria's naked body, hard enough to leave bloody gashes.

Ovid wanted to ruin the body she wouldn't give her, Zaria thought, acknowledging it was a pretty weird time to be psychologizing someone.

"You and your sister have nearly destroyed the Lupas, but I won't allow us to die. I will rebuild, and I will kill everyone you love, including your precious Marco."

Fear and panic gripped Zaria. Not Marco, not Marco.

"He's next and guess what? You and your fucking sister get ringside seats from the Eternal Forest."

Fury exploded from Zaria. She used every inch of her remaining energy to fight Ovid. "No! Don't you ever go near Marco. The Wolfgangs will kill you first."

Ovid slammed her back against the tree so hard, she heard her ribs cracking. The pain was overwhelming, but it would be over soon. Ovid placed her claws on Zaria's neck.

"Any last words, bitch?"

Zaria had no strength. Pain lived in every inch of her body, so she did the last defiant thing she could do and spat in Ovid's face.

Ovid growled and dug her nails into her throat. "All because you couldn't do what you were told, pretty girl. Goodbye."

Zaria closed her eyes and waited for the pain, but instead she heard a huge thud and Ovid was knocked away from her. She opened her eyes and saw Ovid rolling on the ground, holding her ribs and stomach, but Kenrick wasn't there.

Over at the edge of the treeline she saw Milo standing there quietly. Then she looked at the spot where Ovid was standing and saw a pool of water. What the hell had just happened?

Whatever it was bought her enough time, because she could scent Kenrick approaching. She signalled to Milo to hide in amongst the trees. Milo did and Kenrick leapt out into the clearing, and onto Ovid.

Rhuri, Callum, Judah, Marcus, and Lukas also appeared from the trees, snarling and fierce. Ovid was pinned down and Kenrick looked up at Zaria. She roared when she saw her injuries, but instead of ripping out Ovid's throat then and there, she stepped back and said, *Get on your paws, you pathetic mutt.*

Ovid shifted, and a ragged black and grey furred wolf emerged.

The two wolves circled each other and Rhuri took position beside Zaria, guarding her.

Ovid said, *Four against one? Is that what your barbaric pack think is fair?*

No one will be fighting you but me, mutt. My pack lives by honour and fairness, things that Lupas just don't seem to understand.

Kenrick padded closer and Ovid snapped and growled a warning. Kenrick said, *Any dominant wolf that raises a paw in anger to a submissive is a pathetic coward, not worthy of the name wolf.*

Ovid growled. *You are weak-toothed dogs who let submissives walk all over them.*

Kenrick's wolf stopped pacing. *We'll see how strong toothed you are when you fight a wolf of your own size.*

Ovid sneered. *You'll never be able to change that she's mine. I had her first, and now she wears my mate bite, and she'll die with it. I ripped yours out.*

Kenrick leapt through the air and landed on Ovid's back. Ovid swiped and missed many times, as if Kenrick was playing with her. Zaria was frightened. Ovid was not as strong or as big as Kenrick, but she was cunning and had nothing to lose.

Kenrick taunted, *Come on, big wolf. Swipe me, rip my throat, like you do to the submissives in your life. Come on, hit me.*

Ovid was enraged and launched a succession of blows and snaps of her teeth, but Kenrick was so agile and fast, and kept dodging everyone. She jumped over Ovid and landed a deep bite on her flank, making Ovid whine.

Zari is my mate. She's my mate because she chooses to be, and not out of fear. You will never take her, Kenrick said.

Ovid's wolf was breathing heavily and struggling with her deep bleeding injury. She made another launch for Kenrick, but Kenrick easily swiped Ovid across the face, causing a horrifically deep gouge.

Zaria could see Ovid trying to stand but failing. *Please let this be over.*

Kenrick stood over Ovid, growling. *Get up. I thought you liked beating up wolves? No, just wolves weaker and smaller, because you are a pathetic mutt. Get up and fight me.*

Ovid didn't move, so Kenrick looked over at Zaria. *You see? You never need to be frightened of this mutt ever again.*

Zaria saw it in slow motion. Out of nowhere Ovid jumped at Kenrick. Zaria shouted the warning. "Ricky, look!"

Just in time Kenrick dodged. Ovid fell to the ground, and in seconds Kenrick was over her and ripped her throat out, ending it at last.

Kenrick shifted to skin and said to her wolves, "Watch her."

She then hurried over to Zaria and pulled her bloody naked body into her arms. "You're safe, lassie. I have you. She can't hurt you now."

"Milo's here," Zaria said.

Kenrick looked up and said, "I see her. Don't worry, she's safe. Rhuri has her."

"Love you, Ricky."

Kenrick kissed her head. "I love you, and no one was ever going to take you away from me."

Zaria felt the blackness begin to envelop her. "She injected me with silver. I'm cold."

She saw panic in Kenrick's eyes and she barked, "Callum, run to the hospital. Tell them Zaria has silver poising and I'm bringing her in."

Yes, Alpha.

Zaria couldn't stop her eyelids from closing, and the last thing she heard was, "Don't close your eyes. Stay with me. I need you, lassie."

Zaria drifted into the blackness. *At least I died in my mate's arms, and Ovid is dead forever.*

CHAPTER TWENTY-FIVE

Kenrick checked her appearance in the mirror while Rhuri strapped the last bracer on her arm. She was wearing tartan trousers, a leather belt, leather bracers on her arms, and nothing else. Her chest and feet needed to be bare for the ceremony.

Callum popped his head in the door of her den. "They're ready for you."

Kenrick let out a breath.

"Are you ready for this?" Rhuri asked.

Nerves, fear, and responsibility churned inside her, but she wasn't going to let anyone see that. The only one she ever felt comfortable enough to show her emotions to was Zaria, and she wasn't here.

"We've put it off long enough. It's time we started afresh. Are you ready, Rhuri? After today you are Second."

Rhuri, often the joker in the pack, looked at her seriously. "I'm ready and I'll always be there for you."

Elspeth and Donny braided a few strands of Zaria's hair in the traditional Celtic way.

"Thank you for helping me prepare for this, Elspeth," Zaria said.

Zaria had only been out of hospital for three weeks. It had taken a lot of care to heal her of the silver poisoning. The doctor had said she could have quite easily died from the amount of silver in her system. But Zaria had fight left in her, and she wasn't going to let Ovid win.

The mating and Alpha ceremonies had to be postponed, but after a week of being out of the hospital, Zaria insisted the ceremonies go ahead. Kenrick agreed only if they had the ceremonies one week apart, to give Zaria time to recover. She still had her weak moments and needed a lot of rest, but the doctor said that would pass eventually.

Zaria looked down at the gold Celtic wedding band on her finger. It had only been a week, but Zaria couldn't remember a happier one. She finally had her mate and her pack. The postponement did give Marco a chance to fly over for her ceremony. Flash and Vance had only been too happy to bring him. It would have really made her sister Marta so proud to see him there.

She briefly touched the hematite stone pendent that linked her to her family. *I know you're watching, Marta.*

Elspeth kissed her on the cheek. "It's Mum, remember. You're our family now, and I'm overjoyed. I'm lucky to have such a brave daughter."

"Well, I appreciate how you've looked after me." She turned to her new friends, Heather, Donny, Florrie, and Moira. "And I mean all of you. I wouldn't have gotten back to health so quickly without you all."

Heather put an arm around her shoulders. "You are pack and a Wulver now."

Donny kissed her cheek. "And Wulvers always take care of each other."

"I think that's your hair all done. What do you think?" Elspeth said.

Zaria was worried when she saw the traditional Mater ceremonial outfit, concerned that her body wouldn't do the barest of leather strapped bras and short tartan skirt justice. Elspeth had explained that the outfit had to leave you bare as possible, so that the traditional Celtic woad war paint could be easily applied to her during the ceremony. The same would be the case for Kenrick.

Elspeth and the others were wearing similar outfits, but much more modest, and Elspeth, as Mater, wore a tartan shawl thrown over her shoulder and pinned with a Celtic brooch.

Zaria's darker hair and skin marked her out from most of the pack, but dressed in this traditional outfit, and with her hair braided like this, she felt connected to the Wulver past, to their ancestors. She only hoped they approved.

"Yeah, I think the braids are perfect," Zaria said.

Elspeth smiled. "Then we are nearly ready, but before we go, all of you gather round." She waved the women and Donny over and encouraged everyone to hold hands. "Today is a momentous day. Fergus and I will step down as Alpha and Mater and walk into retirement to enjoy our older years together, to look after the pack in different ways, and hopefully to enjoy our grandcubs when they come along." Elspeth winked at Zaria.

Zaria never thought she would have a mate. So now the prospect of bring cubs into the world, into the safety and security of this pack, was exciting.

Elspeth continued, "We will have a new Alpha and Mater, a new pack Second, and new senior wolves. Heather, Donny, Florrie, Moira, since your mates have taken the place of the older wolves who've retired from the elite wolves, you are now the senior submissives of the Wulvers."

Zaria felt a bond of deep friendship growing with these wolves and knew they would always be there for her.

Elspeth said, "We will always have a stronger bond than anyone else in the pack. It is our responsibility to support Zaria in her new role. This is all new to her, so we need to make sure she always feels she can do her new job safe in the knowledge that we are behind her every step of the way. You also have to be leaders. A change in pack leadership always creates some uncertainty, so you have to show them the confidence you have in Ricky and Zari."

Heather squeezed Zaria's hand. "We always will."

"Let us pledge an oath," Elspeth said. "Repeat after me. We pledge our friendship, service, and loyalty to Zaria Wulver, the new Mater of the Wulver pack."

They all repeated Elspeth's words and the sentiment of it made tears well up in Zaria's eyes. All her friends hugged her in turn. Zaria truly was home.

Chapter Twenty-six

Kenrick stood amongst the trees, on the edge of the forest. A few hundred yards away, the ceremonial stone circle, built by Princess Scota and her people, waited for her. The beat of drums echoed through the forest, along with rhythmic chants and the occasional howl. All the pack was gathered outside the circle, with the higher ranking wolves circling the stones along with the drummers.

Smoke from the ceremonial fires filled the air, the rowan wood being burned crackled, and autumn leaves and twigs lay under her feet, connecting her to the Mother Earth and giving the space an ancient atmosphere.

Kenrick could feel the beat of the drums in her bones. After her mating ceremony, this was the most important day of her life, and she could feel the expectation in the air around her.

She ran her hands over her dreadlocked hair nervously. She had always dreaded this day coming because she didn't feel good enough. She had failed her brother, so how could she protect her pack? But so much had changed. Kenrick's visit to Wolfgang County had shown her that she could lead and do it in her own way, but what changed everything was meeting Zaria.

She looked down at the gold Celtic band on her finger. Zaria's love had given her confidence, someone to protect and love. Now she could offer her pack a Mater, and one who she knew in her heart would be as loving as her mother was to the pack but who would do things in new ways.

After Ovid's attack. Zaria told her about her experience with Milo and what she thought was the Kelpie helping her in her hour of need, and Kenrick felt in her heart the Great Mother had destined her to find Zaria. She was always sceptical about the Kelpie stories, but Zaria might not be alive today if whatever Milo brought with her hadn't pushed Ovid from Zaria.

She wished Zaria was beside her, but she was standing on the other side of the stone circle waiting for her part in the ceremony. She heard footsteps and turned to see Hilda, leader of the BaoBhan Sith, the all-female clan of mystical Scottish vampires.

They lived at the very tip of Scotland in the old Debrek castle. No one knew much about the BaoBhan Sith, but they had been great friends to the Wulvers over the centuries, and they shared similar beliefs about the Great Mother Earth. Only last week Hilda had been here to preside over her mating ceremony.

"You are nervous about your destiny, Kenrick?" Hilda asked.

Madam Hilda had a serene energy that calmed others around her.

"Aye, destiny puts a lot of pressure on your shoulders," Kenrick said.

Hilda knew not to touch a mated werewolf, but she placed her hand inches from Kenrick's chest, and Kenrick felt a warm, serene energy flow into her. "Princess Scota would be so proud of you and will bless your reign over the Wulvers."

"Thank you." Kenrick felt calmer. "Have you spoken to Zaria?"

Hilda smiled. "Yes, she's fine. Don't worry."

Just then the beat of the drums changed, and Hilda said, "It's time to meet your destiny."

Kenrick took a deep breath and followed Hilda as she led her to the circle. As she approached the circle she saw her elite wolves standing directly in front of the standing stones forming a guard of honour. Behind them were the drummers, and the rest of the pack stood in a large crowd beyond.

As she walked into the circle, her elite wolves banged their short swords on the round shields they were holding, in time to the drummers' beat, while chanting her name. If an outsider saw this ceremony, they would think they had stepped back in time to prehistory.

Kenrick's pater Fergus stood on a small stone platform at the top of the circle with his outgoing Second standing beside him. She followed Hilda up to the platform and Hilda stepped in behind Fergus.

The drums fell silent and Fergus remained silent but gave her a wink. This was her moment to claim. She held out her arms wide and said the words that had been laid down for millennia.

"Alpha you have led the pack with strength and led them to many victories in battle, and as the seasons have passed you have gained wisdom but lost strength along the way. Strength must always lead, and I stand before you as the strongest wolf in the Wulver pack. I claim your leadership as my own and respectfully request that you step aside and allow me to claim my right as your heir."

Fergus smiled at her and she let out a sigh of relief. She was convinced she was going to forget the words to the traditional claim.

Madam Hilda said, "Wolves of the Wulver pack. Kenrick daughter of Fergus has come before us to claim her right to lead the pack. Do you accept her as your one true Alpha?"

All the wolves shouted *Aye!* in unison while the elite wolves banged their shields.

❖

Zaria watched Kenrick from the edge of the forest. They had run through this ceremony a few times over the week, but doing it for real in front of the pack was a different thing altogether.

She felt her hand start to shake when Kenrick gave her claim, then felt Elspeth's hand slip into hers.

"You'll be okay. I'm with you," Elspeth said.

It was only the two of them over on this side, and she was so glad she had the Mater with her. Then it hit her—she was only minutes away from being the Mater herself. It was an awe-inspiring thought. Would she be here in Elspeth's spot someday, being a support to her own cub's mate?

It gave her a warm glow inside, knowing any cub of hers would be brought up in this safe, supportive environment, so unlike her own childhood. She listened to the drums' and shields' beat and heard the wolves call out Kenrick's name. Zaria admired the way the Wulvers kept their traditions and history alive. She was sure it gave the pack a secure feeling of continuity stretching back in time and forward into a bright future.

The drums stopped and she heard Fergus saying to Kenrick, "Do you have a mate to stand beside you as Mater?"

Kenrick replied in a strong, proud voice, "Aye, Zaria of the Wulver pack."

Zaria's heart started to thud in her chest and her mouth went dry. *This is it.*

"Zaria of the Wulver pack, come forward," Fergus called.

Elspeth squeezed her hand and said, "It's time."

She took a breath and followed behind Elspeth. The throng of the crowd around the standing stones made way for them. They walked into the circle and the crowd closed again. Zaria was so nervous that she clenched her hands into fists so they wouldn't shake.

Zaria stopped beside Kenrick, and Elspeth continued on and stood on the stone platform beside Fergus.

Kenrick took her hand and whispered, "I love you, lassie."

Kenrick's words started to calm her heart.

Fergus turned to Hilda and said, "Kenrick has consented."

Hilda walked down from the platform and stood in front of them, and Milo walked out from the crowd to be Hilda's helper. Milo had been delighted to be chosen by Zaria for this role. They had grown extremely close. Milo was special, she had a bright future, and Zaria wanted to help her any way she could.

"Kenrick, Zaria, kneel," Hilda said.

Hilda was an impressive sight in her long green dress. She was a beautiful woman and Zaria had a hard time believing that she was centuries old. Zaria hadn't mixed with Vampires before.

"Kenrick, when I took part in your birthing ceremony, I had a vision that your life would be an extraordinary one. A life filled with honour, family, and protecting your pack against all foes. It is my honour to perform this ceremony for you," Hilda said.

Hilda turned to Milo and nodded. She lifted the bunch of rowan wood she held, then held her other hand over it and whispered an incantation. The ends of the wood ignited in flame, and Milo looked so pleased with herself when she handed it to her mentor. Hilda appeared so proud of her.

"Thank you, little wolf," Hilda said.

She waved the bunch of burning twigs around both Kenrick and Zaria whilst she said, "May our Goddess, the Great Mother, give you the strength to lead and protect your pack."

Hilda looked to the other side where Heather, Donny, Florrie, and Moira stood, holding bowls of blue woad paint, and nodded.

They came forward, the drums began to beat again, and they started to paint Celtic symbols over Kenrick's and Zaria's torsos, arms, and face. Zaria truly felt she had travelled back in time a thousand years. While they painted the intricate symbols, Hilda chanted blessings in ancient Gaelic.

Once the painting was finished, Hilda stepped back, and Fergus asked Milo to bring forth a wooden bowl with the sacred whisky from the first cask made on their territory.

Hilda held it aloft and said, "Kenrick Wulver, do you swear to protect your pack with your life and keep the Great Mother's traditions on our land?"

"Aye, I swear," Kenrick replied in a loud voice.

Zaria gulped when Fergus turned to her. "Zaria Wulver do you swear to care and protect your pack as a mother wolf would do her cubs?"

"Yes, I swear," Zaria said in a croaky voice. Fergus gave her a wink and went back to Kenrick.

He dipped his finger into the whisky and drew the Wulver pack symbol on her forehead. "Kenrick, you are the embodiment of Princess Scota, who was the first Alpha of our kind, the woman who founded our pack and our lands, and who herself anointed her first successor in this very stone circle, before founding the Irish, English, and Welsh packs." Fergus then handed the bowl to Kenrick to take a sip. "In Princess Scota's words, when you drink this whisky, you are embodying the blood of your pack and all your sister packs. Always remember they share your blood, your history, and be ready to stand beside them if they are ever in need."

Kenrick passed the whisky to Zaria. Since she was intolerant to whisky, she could only touch her lips to it and hand it back. Even the little on her lips started a pleasant burn that travelled through her body, and suddenly she felt more confident.

Fergus instructed them to stand and Elspeth and his Second, Angus, came down off the podium to join him.

"Do you have a Second, Kenrick?" Fergus asked.

"Aye, Rhuri is my chosen Second."

Rhuri walked from the side dressed in tartan trousers, a lace-up white tunic, a short sword on her hip. Like Kenrick and her, she was barefoot.

Angus bowed his head to Fergus and then took off her fur cape, then handed it to Rhuri. Rhuri bowed, took the cape, and placed it on Kenrick. It clipped at the front with a gold chain. Then Angus lifted off the cross shoulder leather scabbard with the ancient sword Zaria had seen in the whisky cellar. Rhuri took the sword and placed it over Kenrick's shoulders.

Fergus said, "Princess Scota gave this sword to her successor as a symbol of authority for all the Wulver Alphas to come. It is now yours."

Hilda helped Elspeth off with her cloak and put it around Zaria's shoulders. Elspeth said, "Take care of your pack as if they were your own cubs."

Zaria felt a deep responsibility in that moment, and she promised herself to dedicate her life, long or short, to these people who took in a stray and made her Mater.

Kenrick turned and kissed her softly. "Nearly there, lassie."

Fergus then addressed Rhuri. "Rhuri, do you pledge your loyalty, life, and body to your Alpha and Mater?"

"Aye, with all my heart," Rhuri replied confidently.

"All three of you are now the heart of the Wulver pack." Fergus took Elspeth's hand and grinned with pride. "With a heart like this, the Wulver pack will go on from strength to strength. Wolves, I give you your new Alpha and Mater, Kenrick and Zaria."

Every wolf there, including Fergus and Elspeth, dropped to one knee and punched the air chanting their names.

Kenrick took both Zaria's hands. "We did it, Mater."

Zaria could feel Kenrick's new power coursing through her body. Her dominance was thrillingly exciting, and she couldn't wait to get back to their den, to bite and claim her. What a long way she had come since Kenrick first found her by the side of the road outside Wolfgang County.

She had been terrified of dominant wolves, so much so that Kenrick felt she had to hide who she was, but when she looked at Kenrick now, it should have seemed so simple. Kenrick was born to be Alpha and Zaria as born to be the one by her side. She had been running her whole life, but little had she known that she was running to her new home.

"We sure did, Alpha," Zaria said, beaming.

Kenrick turned back to the ensemble of wolves and lifted her fist. "Good hunting, wolves."

"Good hunting, Alpha," they replied.

Zaria sensed the love from all the wolves there to them both. She truly was home—at last.

About the Author

Jenny Frame is from the small town of Motherwell in Scotland, where she lives with her partner, Lou, and their well-loved and very spoiled dog.

She has a diverse range of qualifications, including a BA in public management and a diploma in acting and performance. Nowadays, she likes to put her creative energies into writing rather than treading the boards.

When not writing or reading, Jenny loves cheering on her local football team, cooking, and spending time with her family.

Jenny can be contacted at www.jennyframe.com.

Books Available From Bold Strokes Books

Blood of the Pack by Jenny Frame. When Alpha of the Scottish pack Kenrick Wulver visits the Wolfgangs, she falls for Zaria Lupa, a wolf on the run. (978-1-63555-431-1)

Cause of Death by Sheri Lewis Wohl. Medical student Vi Akiak and K9 Search and Rescue officer Kate Renard must work together to find a killer before they end up the next targets. In the race for survival, they discover that love may be the biggest risk of all. (978-1-63555-441-0)

Chasing Sunset by Missouri Vaun. Hijinks and mishaps ensue as Iris and Finn set off on a road trip adventure, chasing the sunset, and falling in love along the way. (978-1-63555-454-0)

Double Down by MB Austin. When an unlikely friendship with Spanish pop star Erlea turns deeper, Celeste, in-house physician for the hotel hosting Erlea's show, has a choice to make—run or double down on love. (978-1-63555-423-6)

Party of Three by Sandy Lowe. Three friends are in for a wild night at billionaire heiress Eleanor McGregor's twenty-fifth birthday party. Love, lust, and doing the right thing, even when it hurts, turn the evening into one that will change their lives forever. (978-1-63555-246-1)

Sit. Stay. Love. by Karis Walsh. City girl Alana Brendt and country vet Tegan Evans both know they don't belong together. Only problem is, they're falling in love. (978-1-63555-439-7)

Where the Lies Hide by Renee Roman. As P.I. Camdyn Stark gets closer to solving the case, will her dark secrets and the lies she's buried jeopardize her future with the quietly beautiful Sarah Peters? (978-1-63555-371-0)

Beautiful Dreamer by Melissa Brayden. With love on the line, can Devyn Winters find it in her heart to stay in the small town of Dreamer's Bay, the one place she swore she'd never remain? (978-1-63555-305-5)

Create a Life to Love by Erin Zak. When sixteen-year-old Beth shows up at her birth mother's door, three lives will change forever. (978-1-63555-425-0)

Deadeye by Meredith Doench. Stranded while hunting the serial predator Deadeye, Special Agent Luce Hansen fights for survival while her lover, forensic pathologist Harper Bennett, hunts for clues to Hansen's disappearance along the killer's trail. (978-1-63555-253-9)

Endangered by Michelle Larkin. Shapeshifters Officer Aspen Wolfe and Dr. Tora Madigan fight their growing attraction as they work together to destroy a secret government agency that exterminates their kind. (978-1-63555-377-2)

Incognito by VK Powell. The only thing Evan Spears is focused on is capturing a fleeing murder suspect until wild card Frankie Strong is added to her team and causes chaos on and off the job. (978-1-63555-389-5)

Insult to Injury by Gun Brooke. After losing everything, Gail Owen withdraws to her old farmhouse and finds a destitute young woman, Romi Shepherd, living in a secret room. (978-1-63555-323-9)

Just One Moment by Dena Blake. If you were given the chance to have the love of your life back, could you ignore everything that went wrong and start over again? (978-1-63555-387-1)

Scene of the Crime by MJ Williamz. Cullen Mathew finds herself caught between the woman she thinks she loves but can no longer trust and a beautiful detective she can't stop thinking about who will stop at nothing to find the truth. (978-1-63555-405-2)

Fear of Falling by Georgia Beers. Singer Sophie James is ready to shake up her career, but her new manager, the gorgeous Dana Landon, has other ideas. (978-1-63555-443-4)

Daughter of No One by Sam Ledel. When their worlds are threatened, a princess and a village outcast must overcome their differences and embrace a budding attraction if they want to survive. (978-1-63555-427-4)

Playing with Fire by Lesley Davis. When Takira Lathan and Dante Groves meet at Takira's restaurant, love may find its way onto the menu. (978-1-63555-433-5)

Practice Makes Perfect by Carsen Taite. Meet law school friends Campbell, Abby, and Grace, law partners at Austin's premier boutique legal firm for young, hip entrepreneurs. Legal Affairs: one law firm, three best friends, three chances to fall in love. (978-1-63555-357-4)

The Last Seduction by Ronica Black. When you allow true love to elude you once and you desperately regret it, are you brave enough to grab it when it comes around again? (978-1-63555-211-9)

Wavering Convictions by Erin Dutton. After a traumatic event, Maggie has vowed to regain her strength and independence. So how can Ally be both the woman who makes her feel safe and a constant reminder of the person who took her security away? (978-1-63555-403-8)

A Bird of Sorrow by Shea Godfrey. As Darrius and her lover, Princess Jessa, gather their strength for the coming war, a mysterious spell will reveal the truth of an ancient love. (978-1-63555-009-2)

All the Worlds Between Us by Morgan Lee Miller. High school senior Quinn Hughes discovers that a broken friendship is actually a door propped open for an unexpected romance. (978-1-63555-457-1)

Falling by Kris Bryant. Falling in love isn't part of the plan, but will Shaylie Beck put her heart first and stick around, or tell the damaging truth? (978-1-63555-373-4)

An Intimate Deception by CJ Birch. Flynn County Sheriff Elle Ashley has spent her adult life atoning for her wild youth, but when she finds her ex, Jessie, murdered two weeks before the small town's biggest social event, she comes face-to-face with her past and all her well-kept secrets. (978-1-63555-417-5)

Cash and the Sorority Girl by Ashley Bartlett. Cash Braddock doesn't want to deal with morality, drugs, or people. Unfortunately, she's going to have to. (978-1-63555-310-9)

Secrets in a Small Town by Nicole Stiling. Deputy Chief Mackenzie Blake has one mission: find the person harassing Savannah Castillo and her daughter before they cause real harm. (978-1-63555-436-6)

Stormy Seas by Ali Vali. The high-octane follow-up to the best-selling action-romance *Blue Skies*. (978-1-63555-299-7)

The Road to Madison by Elle Spencer. Can two women who fell in love as girls overcome the hurt caused by the father who tore them apart? (978-1-63555-421-2)

Dangerous Curves by Larkin Rose. When love waits at the finish line, dangerous curves are a risk worth taking. (978-1-63555-353-6)

Love to the Rescue by Radclyffe. Can two people who share a past really be strangers? (978-1-62639-973-0)

Love's Portrait by Anna Larner. When museum curator Molly Goode and benefactor Georgina Wright uncover a portrait's secret, public and private truths are exposed, and their deepening love hangs in the balance. (978-1-63555-057-3)

Model Behavior by MJ Williamz. Can one woman's instability shatter a new couple's dreams of happiness? (978-1-63555-379-6)

Pretending in Paradise by M. Ullrich. When travelwisdom.com assigns PR specialist Caroline Beckett and travel blogger Emma Morgan to cover a hot new couples retreat, they're forced to fake a relationship to secure a reservation. (978-1-63555-399-4)

Recipe for Love by Aurora Rey. Hannah Little doesn't have much use for fancy chefs or fancy restaurants, but when New York City chef Drew Davis comes to town, their attraction just might be a recipe for love. (978-1-63555-367-3)

The House by Eden Darry. After a vicious assault, Sadie, Fin, and their family retreat to a house they think is the perfect place to start over, until they realize not all is as it seems. (978-1-63555-395-6)

Uninvited by Jane C. Esther. When Aerin McLeary's body becomes host for an alien intent on invading Earth, she must work with researcher Olivia Ando to uncover the truth and save humankind. (978-1-63555-282-9)